'This is stylish and extraordinary writing. It's puzzling and perplexing but so damn good. There is something quite mesmerising about this story that defies genre and quite frankly, logic. Stunning ... this will linger in my mind forever' Random Things through My Letterbox

'One of the most f*****up yet brilliantly insightful, cleverly emotional, pitch perfectly plotted novels I've read in YEARS' Liz Loves Books

'It's darkly twisted and deliciously distorted, shocking and completely mind-warping!' Book Obsessed

'It's beautifully written. The writing is staccato – fast-paced and compelling' Off-the-Shelf Books

'Wow, just WOW! Dark, absolutely genius, addictive and deliciously disturbing' Made Up Book Reviews

'The very distinctive Will Carver style that I so adore is here in spades. The noirest noir. Highly recommended!' From Belgium with Book Love

'*Good Samaritans* showed Carver as an author to watch. *Nothing Important Happened Today* cements him as an author to watch very, very carefully. He's one of a kind, and part of me is kind of glad. I'm not sure I could handle more than one of him' Espresso Coco

'Carver pulls this work together with a deft hand and provides a conclusion that is as twisted as his premise, and along the way he has stunned, frazzled the brain and made this reader think hard about how she sees the world' Live & Deadly

'The writing is fast-paced and snappy ... clever, devilish, disturbing and stylish with a vein of black humour coursing through the pages ... a book that raises its middle finger to conformity, to genre, walks its own path and it is brilliant' The Tattooed Book Geek

'It's an utterly compelling and gripping read. It's addictive, luring us in with its sharp, witty prose, its brief chapters, its concise snapshots into people's lives, its delving into the mind of a killer, its scrutiny of the daily, hourly difficulty of many lives. I was engrossed from the very first unusual and dramatic page' For Winter Nights

'Deliciously twisted and wickedly fascinating' Chocolate 'N' Waffles

'A dark and utterly riveting book that will shock and surprise you in equal measure. I will definitely be reading more from Will Carver!' On-the-Shelf Reviews

'An amazingly original and extremely shocking story of manipulation' Novel Deelights

PRAISE FOR WILL CARVER

'Totally addictive. Like *Fight Club*, only darker' S.J. Watson

'So dark, so cool' *Heat*

'Will Carver's invigoratingly nasty novel ... is a bleak vision of life: not the whole truth of it, thank God, but true enough to impart to the reader the thrill of genuine discomfort, presented with the chilly conviction of Simenon's most unflinching *romans durs* and just as horribly addictive' Jake Kerridge, *The Telegraph*

'Carver weaves these strands together for an unsettling but compelling mixture of the banal, the horrific and, at times, the near-comic, wrong-footing the reader at every turn' Laura Wilson, *Guardian*

'In this frantic read in sheer overdrive, Carver appeals to the worst voyeur in all of us and delivers the goods with a punch and a fiendish sense of pace and dark humour ... my type of noir' Maxim Jakubowski, *Crime Time*

'Must Read!' *Daily Express*

'*Good Samaritans* is his best to date – dark, slick, gripping, and impossible to put down. You'll be sucked in from the first page' Luca Veste

'Oh My God, *Good Samaritans* is amazing. I'm a little in love with your writing, Will Carver' Helen FitzGerald, Author of *The Cry*

'Sick ... in the best possible way. Will Carver delivers a delicious slice of noir that will have you reeling' Michael J. Malone

'If you're looking for a genuinely creepy thriller, check out *Good Samaritans* ... completely enthralled' Margaret B Madden

'A twisted, devious thriller' Nick Quantrill

'A dark and addictive novel that felt deliciously sexy to read, like I should read it where no one could see' Louise Beech

'A pitch-dark, highly original, thrilling novel. If you're a fan of *Fight Club*, you'll love this' Tom Wood

'A provocative, heady, unique, challenging read and it is absolutely blimmin' wonderful!' LoveReading

ABOUT THE AUTHOR

Will Carver is the international bestselling author of the January David series. He spent his early years in Germany, but returned to the UK at age eleven, when his sporting career took off. He turned down a professional rugby contract to study theatre and television at King Alfred's, Winchester, where he set up a successful theatre company. He currently runs his own fitness and nutrition company, and lives in Reading with his two children. *Good Samaritans* was book of the year in the *Guardian*, *Telegraph* and *Daily Express*, and hit number one on the ebook charts.

Follow Will on Twitter: @will_carver.

NOTHING IMPORTANT HAPPENED TODAY

WILL CARVER

**ORENDA
BOOKS**

Orenda Books
16 Carson Road
West Dulwich
London SE21 8HU
www.orendabooks.co.uk

First published by Orenda Books 2019
Copyright © Will Carver 2019

ISBN 978-1-912374-83-0
eISBN 978-1-912374-84-7

Typeset in Garamond by typesetter.org.uk
Printed and bound by CPI Group (UK) Ltd, Croydon CR0 4YY

For sales and distribution, please contact info@orendabooks.co.uk

For nobody

'Nobody joins a cult. Nobody joins something they think is going to hurt them. You join a religious organisation, you join a political movement, and you join with people that you really like.'

Deborah Layton – Peoples Temple member.

We are The People of Choice
The ones now with courage
And we choose not to fear
This is one solution
It is not the end
Nor is it the beginning
There are always more who choose to live
There is but one certainty

PROLOGUE

Nobody cares anymore.

By the time they get to him, nearly a year has passed.

The public have lost interest, moved on to something new.

Some old schizo takes himself to the woods to commit suicide. So what? How is that a loss? How is that news? Schedule it as an afterthought.

You put a gun to your head and squeeze the trigger, there's no time for second-guessing. You jump off the roof of a multi-storey car park, it's difficult to back out when you're twenty feet from hitting the concrete.

There's a strip of duct tape on the ground that he ripped off his face when he changed his mind and tried to call for help. Nobody came. There are scratch marks on his wrists where he tried to escape and some abrasions on the tree from the handcuffs. The key that was thrown out of reach is somewhere beneath the leaves.

Who gives a fuck? Some stupid, old fool wanders into the forest, tapes his mouth shut and handcuffs himself to a tree. He throws the key away so he can't get out. And he waits to die in a long, drawn-out and painful way. So what?

It was his choice, right?

His decision.

Here's the kicker: the idiot strapped himself to the trunk with his hands above a branch. He couldn't get the cuffs lower than three feet from the ground. So there was no way to lie down on the floor when he needed to sleep.

When he is found, his wrists are bearing the full weight of his body. His left shoulder against the tree trunk, his head lolling forwards, the fronts of his legs dragging across the floor, his back unnaturally arched. There are marks on his body from animals who only found him because he shit his pants repeatedly in those first four agonising days.

The silly fool with a note in his pocket saying that he is the *last one*. A person of choice. That it needed to be done in this way because he had to not want to die.

Otherwise it wouldn't count.

But nobody cares. It's over.

Nobody will know who he was.

Nobody will remember his name.

The guy is a goddamned Nobody.

PART ONE
CULT

1

We don't have to say *go*.

Or *jump*.

Or count down from three.

We just know.

For we are The People of Choice, the ones now with courage. And we choose not to fear.

You know us. We've stocked your supermarket shelves. We've poured you coffee. We water your plants and feed your cat while you are on holiday.

We couldn't possibly be in that group. That crazy cult. No way. Our boys play football together. We are your neighbour. We are your nephew. We are your daughter. We recommended that film you liked so much.

We are everywhere.

And we leave our homes and workplaces from the various dots across the capital and congregate on Chelsea Bridge as arranged, none of us offering a formal introduction, nobody speaking at all. Our paths have crossed on numerous occasions – nothing worth noting; nothing to dwell on.

We are just nine lives.

Nine personalities.

Nine problems.

Nine decisions.

We each received our calling this morning, the verification of our membership. A letter that confirmed our importance, our place in history; the continuation of this legacy. We all read that it was our time and knew immediately where we should meet and when. We knew what to bring and how we should use it.

We are one solution.

This is not the beginning.

We are but nine more.

Four of us approach the self-anchored suspension bridge from the south, Battersea and beyond. Five from north of the river come via Chelsea and Pimlico. For some, this is not the closest bridge to their house, but this was the agreement.

It must be here.

We know what to do.

Those from the south arrive at intervals, each wearing the same expression, each with a choice, each passing a bearded man with a video camera aimed in the wrong direction, ready to capture nothing important to the west. Missing an opportunity.

One becomes two and two become four until all nine of us are sitting, motionless, gazing to the east, waiting for the moment. We don't count down; we don't speak.

We don't have to.

We just know.

And we stay seated for a while, perched on the great steel box that runs the length of the bridge on both sides of the road, overlooking the path ahead and the river beyond. This is our time for final contemplation.

This is our moment of selection.

We sat behind you in class. We washed your car while you went shopping. We employed you. We are your father. We gave you that recipe for shortbread. We stitched your daughter back together when she came off her bike.

And we open our rucksacks at the same time, still seated on

the cold metal, still looking out across the blackening water; the bulbs that illuminate the elongated M-shaped suspension create a matching W in the pool beneath. And we put on our black jumpers.

Each of us pulls our head through first, leaving the hood up.

The Lovers.

The Ungrateful.

The Poet.

We all slide our arms in. Left, then right.

The Doctor.

The Nobodies.

And Young Levant.

Our decision has been made.

We don't have to say *go*.

Or *jump*.

Or count down from three.

We just know.

2

OTHER PEOPLE

The trick to running a cult is to get other people involved. Not new members or followers. Not more subscribers or a greater mailing list. It doesn't matter if there are six people who think someone is Jesus or there are a million admirers hoping for a seat on the spaceship that will fly them away as Earth implodes with greed and apathy.

It's not the apostles that make the cult.

It's everybody else.

What is needed are the other people. Because other people always fuck things up.

Take the small town of Antelope, Oregon. A smudge on a map. Fifty people looking for quiet. They need a post office, a general store, a school and a church to exist. Not to survive. They haven't moved here for that. Everybody knows everybody and everybody wants to be alone. Because they've come here to see out their years in peace. Then die.

Drop in four thousand disciples adhering to the philosophies of Bhagwan Shree Rajneesh. Watch as they are welcomed as a peaceful people, renouncing a world of materialism in favour of a spiritual life. Embrace their desire to establish their own community.

Now get other people involved.

See how the word 'community' transforms into the word 'commune'. Now wait as tensions rise and hostility grows. Wait a little longer. Because here come the other people. And it's easy to take other people and make them fear something. Soon, a school teacher or postal worker or bar owner or dairy farmer has used the word 'cult'.

Sit back and bask in your success as civilians are weaponised and cafes are poisoned and phone lines are tapped.

This is other people.

Take a student pastor at the Somerset Southside Methodist Church, Indiana. Tell him that he can't integrate black people into his congregation. Piss him off. Give him a crusade.

Watch as he moves on and gives people hope. See his drive for racial equality. You don't call the healings fake. Not yet. You call them Baptists. You say they are a church. He calls them the Wings of Deliverance.

Now let him open a soup kitchen for the poor, then watch

as other people become involved. Because other people have an innate ability to take something good and turn it straight to shit.

Migrate that church to Guyana. Call it a compound. Call it Paradise. Call it Jonestown. Say that members did not travel there of their own free will. Get other people to interfere. Intervene. Get shot at. Wait a moment while everything is ruined. While nine hundred men and women take cyanide to kill themselves. Let them poison their children.

Now you can call it a cult. And feel safe that you're not one of them.

You.

Other people.

Take David Koresh. Take Waco. Tell the world he has several wives and fucks his kids. Set fire to buildings. Smoke him out. Kill twenty of those kids while you're there.

Get involved.

Take the Manson Family. Take Scientology. Take any passage from any holy book out of context.

Take the unknown and drop in some fear and insecurity.

What have you done?

You.

The other people club.

You. At arm's length. Outside looking in. With your judgement and your free choice and your safety. You don't understand.

Not one of these people thought that they were part of a cult.

And you, you're no different. You could be part of a cult right now and you don't even realise. You think you have a choice.

So, put that rope around your neck.
Now wait.
Here come the other people.

THAT MORNING

3

225–226 – LOVERS

For the last week, they've been telling each other one thing they like about the other person, every day. And it seems to have been working.

They're fucking when the first child walks in. It's the same morning sex they used to love before kids came along. When he would lie on top of her and they'd look at each other, pretending that they didn't care about his sweaty, clammy skin and her stale breath.

But it's passionless now. Forced. And they don't look at one another. And they don't bother with foreplay or kissing or talking.

Or tenderness.

Or feeling.

They're still spooning when that first kid walks in.

The little shit says, 'Mummy' in a half excited-by-a-new-day, half still-rubbing-his-eyes way. He toddles over to the bed and starts tugging at the covers that disguise his parents' activity. They tell him that he has to stop. That they're just having a cuddle. That he needs to go downstairs and put the television on.

But the little brat decides that he doesn't want to go downstairs without mum and dad. That he wants to perch on the edge of the mattress, swinging his legs, until they get up with him.

They are trying.

Desperately trying to love each other.

Again, they push, telling him that they'll only be a minute or so, smiling like everything is normal, ruining the moment even further. In their heads they tell themselves that it's not the kids' fault. It's theirs.

And they are still linked together when another child dodders around the doorframe.

The one they stupidly thought could save them.

Make them a real family.

They don't want to shout at the kids or tell them off. Because neither wants to be the bad parent. Because they only truly love *them* now. And it doesn't do those boys any good. They're moments away from abandoning everything and letting the little pests get their way again.

This is how every day starts. Though not always with pitiful intercourse.

Then the letterbox slams shut downstairs and the mail crashes to the doormat. Two utility bills they won't worry about, a pizza delivery leaflet, a free catalogue that arrives every month from a website that was only ever visited once, a card from the local estate agents showing which houses have been selling in the area, requesting to give them a valuation on their property, and one final letter addressed to both lovers.

It uses their names. Not their numbers. Not their job. Not their archetype. Not their clearest personality trait.

It's their time.

Congratulations. You have been chosen. Your membership request has been accepted.

And they are still just hard and wet enough to continue when both children innocently race out of the door to collect the benign bills and junk mail and death sentence. The bed squeaks ferociously for another twenty seconds or so to mark the last moments of their frigid ceremony, their attempted intimacy.

They are both empty and unfulfilled when the two boys come skidding back into their lie with a plastic-wrapped furniture brochure and innocuous white envelope. They're sitting up now. The boys make paper aeroplanes from unwanted flyers.

The lovers are shocked at the size of the bills they won't have to pay. They don't yet realise that gas usage and interest accrued means nothing to those who are chosen.

In the final envelope are two pages. Reading a few words ignites them into action. Both of them slipping out from under the sheets, both throwing on something to cover their modesty, both exiting the bedroom, descending the stairs with two contented children in tow, the furniture publication left resting on the quilt, both walking barefoot on the cold kitchen tiles and both standing in front of the stove, ignoring the children who are pulling at them from behind.

He holds down the button to produce a string of sparks and turns the dial that releases the gas they won't have to pay for. Once the hob is fired up, she places the letter and envelope into the flames and they both wait, staring until it is flaking, brittle carbon, incinerating the evidence.

As they discussed.

As was agreed.

As the others will be doing right now.

What a team.

And they crouch down to be at the same level as the boys – it's easier to think that they'll be better off without them. And they kiss their children. And they tell them that they love them.

And they make breakfast.

This may be their last day, but it should be no different from any other.

4

231 – UNGRATEFUL

Still hungover at noon, she opens the bank statement first, skipping all the outgoing figures next to items like shoes and bags and bar tabs and restaurants and other things she knows she doesn't need but at the time believed were imperative to her happiness.

It's not happiness.

And it's never enough.

Five tattoos only felt better than four tattoos for a moment. The joy of ten thousand social-media followers was as fleeting as the climax she faked with that reality TV contestant. The drug doesn't work.

Her mother had told her that fulfilment can only be achieved when you choose to give something back. She's only been gone two years but her daughter has forgotten this lesson.

The ungrateful young woman skims over the evidence of the mistakes she hasn't learned from and heads straight to the reality of the figure written in red ink at the bottom of the final page. The expression on her face doesn't alter, it does not convey what she feels inside, but the tears offer a clue.

There's a second letter from the bank confirming an increase to her overdraft limit. And a wave of relief washes the tears away, diluting another headache. And the severity of real life dissipates for a few seconds.

But her credit-card bill reintroduces panic. She's been saving it for days.

She throws up into her mouth and swallows it back down.

There are four other credit cards.

Her father only knows about one.

Her sister has one card that she clears each month. And she remembers their mother.

The bathroom door is locked, as it always is. Just in case. She sits on the closed toilet lid, the tiles are cold beneath her bare feet, reminding her that she, at least, has some capacity to feel. She stands up, takes a swig of water from the tap at the sink and splashes water against her sad-clown face. Looking at herself in the mirror, she takes a picture with her phone. Not for social media. For her. And she drops back to her position of self-pity.

There's more.

She tells herself that she can't open another bill. That it will kill her. That she will have to confess to her father and he will have to bail her out again. And everyone will know.

But one of the letters in her growing pile of debt and guilt will get her out of this mess.

One white envelope contains her exit strategy.

It gives her the choice.

She tears a strip of toilet roll to wipe those drugged panda eyes, lifts the toilet slightly from her seated position and pushes the mascara-blotted paper through the gap between her legs before sitting down again to work through the last few letters.

Her store card has £2,668.48 outstanding. Her allowance will easily cover the minimum monthly payment, but paying a similar amount on the rest of her cards leaves her feeling crippled. *And it's only four months until Christmas.* And the only way she knows to cope with the stress is to buy herself something nice. Something she doesn't really need. Something else she can't afford.

That momentary high to break up the misery.

It's a relief that the final letter has no transparent window detailing her name and address.

Save the best until last.

Ease the hurt.

Reward yourself.

She throws all the other letters into the bathtub to her right. She can't deal with them now. And she makes a small incision at the corner of the flap, inserts her finger and runs it along the length of the envelope.

There are two pages inside. The first piece of paper contains only four words.

Nothing
Important
Happened
Today

And she is grateful to read mail that, for once, is not covered in red ink.

5

232 – POET

There's a patch of blue ink connecting his torso to the bed sheets where his ballpoint pen exploded and leaked during the night. The notepad came to no harm. He finds it lying neatly atop a screwed-up T-shirt crumpled on the floor. He reaches down with his right hand, brings the pad up to his chest, finds the last page he wrote on and holds it above his face.

There isn't the erratic scrawling he's used to seeing when trying to get an idea onto the page quickly. It's free-flowing. Nothing has been crossed out. No blue smudges or fingerprints or torn corners. Some of his best work, he thinks.

Then his arm starts to ache, his feeble bicep burning, but he reads it through again, smiling to himself at the words he massaged together, the verse he created from nothing.

He drops his arm down to the mattress and stares at the yellowing swirls of his ceiling. An effect as outdated as his parents' values.

The skin covering his ribs feels tight where the ink has dried. He reaches his left hand around, instinctively touching the area, and it dyes his fingertips, pre-empting his crime.

He sits up, swivelling around so his feet touch the floor. He reads his words again; it's rare to still feel enthusiasm the day after writing something. And he scratches between his legs, leaving three blue fingerprints behind. His mother would call it 'evidence of perversion'.

Leaning across to his bedside cabinet, the poet rummages around the drawer, looking for another pen to add a couple of lines that will punctuate his latest creation. He finds folded papers and tissues and remote controls and the tools used to assemble his bedframe and elastic bands and a broken action figure he thought he'd lost years ago, but no pen. He slams the drawer shut, masking his mother's initial ascent of the stairs; the sound of that first creaking step is muffled by his impatience.

Then he's frantically scouring the room for anything he can write with, a pencil, a crayon, eyeliner. He spots a ballpoint pen next to his computer keyboard. It's from the same pack of three that the exploding one came from. He bounds over to his desk, dodging items of clothing thrown across the floor yesterday.

The chair is stacked with shoe boxes and meaningless paraphernalia. He takes the pen and scribbles on one of the boxes to get the ink moving, turns to his unfinished poem and leans against the wall, ready to scribe the final couplet to his opus.

That's when his mother walks in. With all her established propriety. He would expect her to knock but, for some reason, this morning, she does not.

She's probably done it on purpose, trying to catch me in the act of something depraved so she can suitably punish me.

He turns to face her as the door swings into the room, the open notepad in his left hand, a biro in his right, cold blue tattoos splatted across his ribs, elbow and penis. She attempts to hide her shock but he hears her inhale.

Her eyes are fixed on him, flitting down briefly to his exposed, patterned dick, and he sees her soul physically tut. But she remains dignified, as is usual, takes two steps towards his desk, places his mail down without uttering a word, turns her back on her deviant offspring, taking one last look of disgust, and exits.

The poet is still. Shocked yet apathetic. Dumbfounded yet feeling as though he has disappointed her in some way.

And the couplet he had in mind dribbles out of his head for ever.

Nothing will ever be as good.

He slams himself back against the wall, the pen poised to trickle two lines of genius, but nothing comes out, only a dot of ink as the nib rests futile against the paper. He pushes harder, his anguish growing, then he pulls downwards sharply.

Now the page has a tear.

Now it is smudged.

Now it is ruined.

He thrusts the pen in the direction of the closed door his mother has just escaped through and the folded pad follows in a flurry of fluttering pages before the thwack of leather against wood. He's sweating. His chest lifts higher with each rage-fuelled inhalation.

What could be so important that she would interrupt me at such a crucial time?

He paces over to the envelope and tears it open. Inside are two pieces of paper. One is the suicide note that he'd hoped he would write himself; the other tells him that he should desist with his angst and prepare himself to enter a new plane of existence.

And he calms down immediately.

He is to continue as usual, as though nothing significant will occur today.

Like every impotent day.

Last night he dreamt about killing his mother.

But this is a day just like any other.

6

CONSTANT RECRUITMENT

Of course, in order to have *other* people, you must first have people. The drawback of a successful suicide cult is the constant recruitment.

Take the London Underground. Take the Indonesian police headquarters. Take the Boston Marathon. Take an election rally in Pakistan. Take an Australian nightclub. Drop in some guy who is lost or angry. Who has been convinced he's moving on to something better, that he's a soldier or a martyr or part of something important. Tell him there are virgins waiting on the other side to suck his dick.

Wash his brain. Clean it right up so he can do your dirty work.

Give him a vest.

Give him a trigger.

Give him a reason.

Now wait. Wait until the news confirms the death toll. See how his neighbours say he was *a quiet man*. Listen as they talk of his disillusionment and hatred of the world, how he disowned his family. Watch some psychologist spout that men have no outlet for their emotions, that it's a societal problem, that it's culture, that he was forgotten.

Listen out for the words 'insanity', 'crazy' and 'group mentality'.

It's predictable conjecture.

They don't know that he had second thoughts, that he shit his pants before pressing the button that released thousands of ball-bearings and nails in an explosion that tore his body apart in every direction. That even if he'd decided it was wrong or brutal, his choice to complete the task was taken away by that point.

And now, that political party or religious movement or government-funded operation has to go out and find another person to be labelled as an outsider.

The enrolment process can be exhausting.

But we need these people so we can have the *others*.

And these people are easy to find. They are everywhere.

The key to building a successful cult is to fill it with real people.

Take absolutely anybody. Find some common ground. Use it as your starting point. Listen. Don't do too much talking. Power comes from hearing what others have to say. Now tell them what they really need. Believe that what you are saying to them is true. Now you can manipulate them to do what you want.

Forget the rejected, the isolated, the solipsistic. None of that matters.

Get someone with an education. Give yourself some credibility.

Get taken seriously.

Because everybody wants to feel like they are a part of something. Something bigger than themselves. Give them something they can belong to. They can be a lawyer, an actor, a philanthropist, an artist, a physician. They don't have to be crazy. Let the other people call them that. They're not the ones you want.

Get a doctor or a teacher or a police officer.

Then fill in the gaps with some nobodies.

7

230 – DOCTOR

She got into it to help people. She'd considered the police, of course. And being the daughter of a parish priest could have sent her in an entirely different direction, but the more she heard about God, the more ridiculous it sounded, the more idiotic her father appeared, the dumber her mother looked for going along with it, the more gullible the loyally stagnant congregation seemed for buying into it.

She didn't like the way religion boasted contentment, loving thy neighbour, doing unto others as you would have them do unto you. Because she never saw that. Even the most God-loving were God-fearing. Love and fear can feel similar but they are not the same.

She could think of more direct ways to help those who were afraid.

And the police force seemed more reactive than preventative. How many people would she really help? Locating and prosecuting the person who stabbed and killed somebody's kid may be justice, but saving that child's life seemed more beneficial. For her soul, at least. The soul her father believed was damned if she didn't hold God in her heart.

Her heart was too busy pumping oxygen and nutrients around her body and removing metabolic waste; there was no space for anything else in there.

Becoming a doctor would be her devotion. And the medical degree had the added bonus of taking her away from her backward Buckinghamshire hamlet for seven years.

But, recently, it has been hard to keep up.

And it's getting worse.

The world is getting worse.

Obesity is very real. She sees it every day. People are fatter. They're unhealthy. They get everything they want at the simplest convenience. Music, films and books downloaded straight to an electronic device. There's nothing physical to hold on to.

People used to have the occasional lazy night and get a takeaway meal. They'd walk or drive and pick up a dinner that they didn't have to prepare themselves. Now, the same device that they listen to music on, read their books on, watch their films on, will order their food, and arrange for it to be delivered with one click. They can even get a taxi to bring them their food if the restaurant doesn't deliver.

Heart disease is on the rise. As is diabetes. And children are suffering, too. More people die in the world from obesity-related illnesses than die of starvation. And she sees adverts for fuller-figured women's clothing lines. And there are 'plus-sized' models. And she wonders whether that is the right message to be putting out there to the masses. Yes, love your body, own your figure, but not at the expense of your personal health.

And the drinking. Why is everyone drinking so much? Why are teenagers showing up at the hospital with half a bottle of vodka in their body? Why are they drinking so much beer that they think they can climb a tree or drainpipe? When did the end-of-the-night fight become so fashionable? She's stitching and gluing and stapling heads every Saturday evening.

And all the adults were drinking one or two glasses each night but now it's a bottle. And their liver can't keep up because they're also eating so much processed crap.

And it seems like everybody is depressed and everyone is in complete despair. And it's not surprising because the world is going to shit and one of the women who only wanted to help now shares that despair.

Because she can't keep up.

Because she's being forced into a reactive rather than preventative role.

Because she realises that her dad was right all along: the only way to get the best out of these people, to make them see that they aren't invincible, that they are killing themselves on the inside, that they are the worst our species have ever produced, is not through love and nurturing and education, it's through fear.

And she doesn't want to think like this.

She wants to help.

The doctor is asleep when her letter arrives. It was another arduous nightshift, which tested her knowledge, training, and faith in science and people. She's exhausted. She could sleep through the entire day until her next shift. But she won't. Her alarm is set for the afternoon. She plans on going to the gym, like she normally does. Her daily workout.

She wants to sleep.

She doesn't want to die.

That's her choice.

8

229 – NOBODY #1

You know him. He's that guy you notice out on the street or at the park or on the train but you've never spoken to. He's the one who apologised about your library fine but still took your money. He's the one who walked you to the exact location on aisle fourteen and pointed at the jar of tahini you couldn't find.

He's the person you see all the time but don't really re-member.

And he doesn't want to be here.

He thinks he's a nobody when, in fact, he is everybody.

Only one choice remains.

Choose death to live.

Choose life and die.

He chooses anonymity and fading into the background and a forgotten face or name.

But one choice is the same as no choice.

If nobody joins a cult, then he must be Nobody.

9

228 – NOBODY #2

It's probably best if she is skipped over too.

Just another nobody.

Not even worth separating her from the other Nobodies.

At least keep her away from the six who think they are Somebodies.

She doesn't feel that the intricacies of her career bear any light on her decision to jump. Neither does the relationship with her partner. You won't find her note, either; she shredded it and flushed it. Four separate flushes in all. One for every word.

As she was told.

We are all the same, really, she thinks. Coming from the same family or genus or kingdom, or whatever. She wasn't always listening and absorbing information at school.

They are all supposed to feel the same sense of privilege that comes with their time of calling.

It's what they are all working towards.

So, blah blah, she got a letter. Blah blah blah, she destroyed any evidence. Blah-de-blah, she is still going to work today even though she knows what she is facing later this evening.

Blah fucking blah.

They're the same.

A bunch of nobodies that don't really want to go.

They just don't know it yet.

10

227 – NOBODY #3

This one is filler on your favourite album.

One of three in a cluster of nine, swinging in the shadows, swathed in a darkness that protects an identity that means nothing anyway. He hopes they concentrate on the others. He hopes he can continue to be ignored.

This one lives and dies in hope.

His parents will miss him, so will his grandmother. For a while they'll wonder where they went wrong, then they'll realise it wasn't their fault or their problem to solve and repair.

And then they'll start to forget.

He hopes.

Eventually they will realise that he was part of something. Something significant. Something huge and memorable, maybe even historical. They will tell themselves that he has gone to a better place. But they will assume that, underneath, he was actually unhappy. And they'd be wrong about that. This one is perfectly content.

It's not pertinent to the case that he lives alone or that he visits his last surviving grandparent on a daily basis. This is not going to help anyone piece things together. This one was chosen and that is all there is to it. It was his time. It was his choice.

A solitary white envelope drops through his door in the morning. He is sitting on the sofa wearing an unwashed robe and scuffed moccasin slippers watching an old cartoon he remembers from childhood that he downloaded illegally from the Internet. He wouldn't normally bother getting up as he was only part-way through his bowl of cereal. The date on the milk was dubious at best. But he doesn't often receive mail unless his mum slips a cheque through the post without his dad knowing.

This nobody bends down to the mat and swipes at the letter. Turning it over he can see that it is his address and it is his name. It is not imperative that his name be known or postcode or borough or the last job he had. He is nobody; just skip all the details.

There is no sign of his mother's sloping handwriting; the label has been printed. He tears at the flap but ends up running a finger along the top edge inside, leaving a mangled perforation.

Two slips of white paper for Nobody.

The first page contains only a few words but he realises immediately what is going to happen. He has been chosen. This is his catalyst.

And all hope leaves him.

He is less than nobody now.

He is everybody.

And he is a number.

This nothing rolls the first message into a thin tube and pokes it through the guarding mesh of the gas fire until it touches the hot orange grille on the other side. He presses hard so that it concertinas and more of the surface is touched by the heat. He lets go, one end of the paper resting on the metal lattice that protects his hands from being burned, and repeats the process with the envelope. There were no specifics on how this act should be administered but he has been instructed to dispose of these elements.

Then he puts his pre-typed farewell note into the pocket of his rancid robe and returns to the Nobody-shaped indentation in his sofa cushion where he picks up his way-past-its-sell-by-date breakfast and sniggers at the animated French dog, dancing pixels across the screen.

He'll visit his grandmother a little later, as he always does. He loves her. He loves seeing her. No point changing anything. No reason to do anything different.

He knows it will break her heart but she can't come with him. She doesn't belong with The People of Choice. She is not like them. She'll be fine.

People always move on.

Forget about this one.

Please.

11

EVERYONE IS CRAZY

There was a time, and it wasn't that long ago, when being crazy, actually, meant something.

Now, everybody's fucking crazy.

Look at Manson and his *family* and Helter Skelter. Think about Sun Myung Moon and two-thousand couples being matched up and married off at Madison Square Garden. Consider Heaven's Gate and trying to catch up with a UFO being chased by a comet.

Where are these crazies?

Now, you have to be Harold Shipman just to get noticed among the lunatics and terrorists and school shootings.

You probably don't even know who David Miscavige is.

And you think it's easier to recruit the nobodies, that there's nothing to them, that they are the menial workers, the drop-outs. That they are somehow weaker.

You're wrong. Anybody can feel like a nobody. Like the thing they are doing doesn't matter. Like they wouldn't be missed by anyone if they were gone.

And it's not just the recent batch of entitled millennials, who want everything and want it now and for no effort. It's not just women looking at magazine covers and feeling overweight and ugly. It's their parents, too. Feeling inadequate as social-media personas illustrate the perfectly content lives of everyone around them. When they are seeing loving marriages and family get-togethers and time spent active or with grand-children or pets. When people have time to work and look after each other and take pictures of the cakes they have baked and iced with their delicately manicured and creative hands.

And their own parents, who can't keep up with the pace of technology and feel that the youth of today have no concept or respect for what they have lived through. And their diets are so poor that they have diabetes and pills that counteract the effects of the pills they already take every day.

Starting a cult is easier than ever.

Because people want a way out of their lives; they want it to be simple. A tablet that will melt all the fat so they don't have to work hard at the gym or quit bacon. Or some medication prescribed by a lazy doctor that will perk up your mood and mask your pain or aid your insulin production so that you can still scoff donuts.

There's cognitive behavioural therapy.

And neuro-linguistic programming.

And everyone's a whack job because they can be or because it's somehow cool.

They are crying out for their brains and their souls to be washed.

And it degrades the thoughts and feelings of those who are truly suffering.

It's the people who, actually, want to die that should be allowed to live.

Now, everybody is a little bit crazy, so to cut through all the depression and morbid obesity and cars ploughing through crowds of civilians, you have to put nine people on a bridge with ropes around their necks just to be heard.

12

233 – YOUNG LEVANT

'Maybe Sunday.' That's what he says.

Maybe we'll talk more openly on Sunday.

He hangs up the phone after failing to have a real conversation with his uncle. Again. His psychiatrist tells him that they have things to discuss; that it would be helpful to have his uncle come in on one of the sessions so that he can hear about Young Levant's father, his brother. His uncle will never agree to that.

Maybe the old man already knows these things.

Maybe he feels the same way.

Maybe. Maybe, Maybe.

The only definites that Young Levant feels he has in life are that he hates his father, he is a failure, and he will die. And he will be taking others with him.

He's in bed. He has been most of the morning. Fully dressed from the night before, perhaps even the one before that. He takes very little notice of time dwindling away. He chooses to immerse himself somewhere within the blur.

And he knows that it must smell in that room, but he'd have to get up, go outside and then come back to truly understand the extent of his wallowing.

The inside of his mouth feels like moss. His teeth are coated in something matte in texture. And his hair appears almost black due to grease. He deals with this by pulling the duvet over his head.

This isn't how he wants to look when he dies.

That would be pathetic.

Everything inside is telling him to get up and just how easy that will be, but he can't force himself. He can't tear himself away from the comfortable filth in which he resides. He understands that it seems stupid. That he knows how he feels and how it affects anyone he comes into contact with. That he gets it is wrong and he is doing it to himself. That he could stop feeling this way if he really wanted. He even knows when and why and how it started.

It's not chemical imbalance.

It's not hereditary.

It's technique.

That's what his psychiatrist tells him. He can teach Young Levant how to cope if that is what he truly desires.

It's Friday. It's his last day. He has to get up. He needs to clean himself up, wash his hair and body with something that smells like aloe vera or coconut, spray it, brush his teeth and swig some mouthwash. He has to look his best. He can't look pitiful or deplorable or worthless.

He's the one you can see in the picture.

He stands out from the rest.

The other eight that he takes with him.

He doesn't really want to die.

None of them do.

That's how it works.

That's why they have to go.

With his head under the covers, wrapped in his own stench, smothered in neglect, he thinks of his uncle and whether they'll ever have that much-needed conversation.

Of course, they won't. Unless somebody manages to stop him in time. That's what usually happens. His mother will turn off the gas or walk in while he is cutting himself or his uncle will get to the house before an ambulance, despite his age, and make him throw up or a friend he no longer has will pull him back from the edge or a girlfriend who never wanted *all this drama* will call his bluff and tell him to 'just fucking do it, then'.

Not this time.

Young Levant hears light footsteps and heavy breathing outside his cocoon and, eventually, is nudged in the side. Ergo is a cross between an Alsatian and a Collie. Entirely black hair. With a wonderfully composed temperament; it can't be easy for him having Young Levant as a companion. Ergo was a gift from his uncle, rescued from Battersea. He said something about it complementing his condition.

With the covers pulled back down to his waist, the dog looking at him, Young Levant believes he sees the dog smiling, trying to pick his owner up to take him outside, asking him kindly to provide food. Suddenly, he wonders who will take care of Ergo when he is gone. Surely his uncle; he wouldn't send him back to the dogs' home. Surely.

And it dawns on him that he is actually depended on.

That means something, right?

That means I shouldn't jump?

The message is still the same if there are only eight of them?

He strokes Ergo's head tenderly and smiles back at him. Of course, he knows that he has to go through with it; he started this.

'Come on, then,' he resigns, sitting up, and Ergo turns and trots into the kitchen area where his empty, plastic bowl awaits. Young Levant follows him in there, takes the heavy bag of food off the cheap, mottled surface and overfills his bowl; some of the dried, meaty spheres fall onto the linoleum floor and roll across the other side of the room. He can lick those up later. A treat. Besides, he'll be hungry by the time Young Levant's uncle arrives.

Unfortunately for Ergo, his master will not be killing himself at home, otherwise he could feast on the worthless remains until someone realises that he's gone.

But that is not what was agreed.

He leaves the bag of dog food on the floor next to the washing machine in case nobody comes. If Ergo is hungry, he will find a way. He will survive. For a while.

Someone will find him.

People care about him.

Young Levant rubs Ergo's back as he moves from the unhygienic kitchen into the untidy living area. It's a small, tactile gesture to say that he loves his dog. And that he's sorry. Ergo continues to crunch on his nutritious meat pellets. His owner ate earlier in the morning: one piece of paper and four words.

13

EXPERIMENT

Cats become hypersexual through sleep deprivation; this is then followed by hallucinations and, ultimately, death. There was an experiment to test this that involved sitting an unsuspecting feline on a small plant pot surrounded by water; every time the cat fell asleep, its face would drop into the water and wake it up.

Seems pointless. Cruel, even. It may not be applicable to humans. Men certainly veer towards limp-dicked dysfunction without adequate rest.

But you have to try things.

You have to probe and assess.

Get things wrong before you get things right.

Even failure moves us forwards.

You win or you learn.

Take Milgram. Take someone off the street and tell them they can electrocute somebody else if the question they are asked is answered incorrectly. Watch as that person screams in agony. Tell the test subject that they will not be held responsible for any pain inflicted. See how they hate pressing the button. Now wait. Because they keep pressing it. They inflict more pain.

Take the Stanford Prison experiment. Or Bystander Behaviour. Think about self-interest and compassion with the Good Samaritan Test.

Call them unethical. Call them immoral. But don't call them worthless.

You don't get to Chelsea Bridge without some hiccups along the way. You can't make nine people do your bidding until you know how to control one.

Take this study performed on mice. There is a light box connected to a dark box. The mouse is placed in the light box but will always be attracted to the darker area. When they enter the darker box, once all four limbs have passed the doorway, they are given an electric shock. They are taken out of the dark box and the experiment is repeated ten minutes later. It tests how quickly they learn from an adverse stimulus.

The People of Choice always return to the dark box.

They never learn.

14

225–233

And we withdraw our gaze from the trains entering and exiting Victoria Station over Grosvenor Bridge. It is almost time. Nearly our cue.

Nine new members.

The bearded camera amateur at the southern end of the bridge remains oblivious, wasting his time, offering nothing of interest. It is his fault that the authorities will have to wade through thirty-two differing, hyperbolised testimonies. Some based on drama, others riddled with shock.

Now standing, we take a length of the heavy rope that caused us to perspire on our journey here. And we place it down carefully on the spot where we have been sitting.

And we breathe.

In through the nose. One, two, three.

Hold. One, two, three.

Exhale through the mouth.

No turning back now.

We don't look at one another. We don't speak. We don't have to.

The rope has a loop at either end, already tied to save time. One loop is larger than the other. We don't remember preparing this, or storing the bag in our home. But we did. This day has been coming.

We didn't know when.

We don't know each other.

Not really.

And we lean forwards, each facing our corresponding upright girder. It could be choreographed. Street art. Some deathly art installation. We pull the small-looped end round the pole and thread the larger loop through the hole. It is secure.

We turn back to the east. The derelict power station to the right looms large on the cityscape, casting a darkness where trains penetrate Battersea.

The next to emerge from the silhouetted spires will be our cue.

We won't have to say *go*.

Or *jump*.

Or count down from three.

We'll just know.

As the carriage appears, the words will not rhyme, the debt will vanish, the love will rekindle. As the brakes commence their screaming and the wheels cease to turn, nobody becomes less, nobody becomes less, nobody becomes less, and Young Levant is a success.

The doctor just wanted to help.

We gave you a parking ticket. We do yoga in the village hall.

We deliver political leaflets through your door. We denied your insurance claim.

And we stand facing the shadow that is our future, our eternity, the large loop in our hands held at our stomachs. The rope is still slack behind us. Cars pass but do not notice, do not care; The thirty-two witnesses are still safely tucked behind a building in the distance; the cameraman still films nothing worthwhile.

The nose of the first carriage ekes its way out into the light and we know it is time. We understand what we have to do and that there is no turning back. It travels forty yards, fifty yards, sixty, before the wheels screech as, brakes straining, they increase their friction against the rails, every passenger compartment now in view from our location.

If we can see them, they can see us.

The larger loop drops over the top of our head, the stray fibres grazing our face or rubbing our neck. We tighten slightly.

So we don't fall out.

Come loose.

Escape.

We are The People of Choice.

And our choice has been made.

EARLIER THAT DAY

15

225–226 – LOVERS

The boys sit down at the table, innocent and unknowing of their impending fate. Unaware that their parents are going to leave them. That they will make them orphans. There is still a chance to get out of this but it would need both of them to take it.

Because they are linked.

They come as a package.

But these lovers are on autopilot. And that is their problem.

She cracks the eggs and toasts the bread while he pours juice for the kids. They are well oiled in this procedure now; every Friday morning is the same: bad-breathed, sweaty-skinned, musty-covered morning sex interrupted by hyperactive, energised children, followed by scrambled eggs on toast with juice and the background noise of some high-pitched children's television presenter.

They do it without thinking.

Two cogs rotating, gliding past each other to create the same end result.

Unfortunately, this is the only way they seem to be able to tesselate any more.

Habit and reverie has killed them. Not the rope.

Their sons remain content and oblivious as they wolf down their usual end-of-week breakfast. Tomorrow, their grandmother will use this same time of day to explain what has happened. She will call it an accident but say that they are not coming back. They won't be home. She will lie and tell those poor boys that their parents are in heaven, that they will be looking down, watching over them. The boys will accept this explanation at first, but they'll grow and they'll wonder why their parents could not do in life what their grandmother claims they do in death.

He flicks the kettle on and smiles at her but she doesn't reciprocate.

It seems futile to chastise the boys for jumping down from the table the moment the last forkful of egg passes their lips, but they do. They are still their parents. And they make them return to their seats, sit down and ask politely to be excused.

Keeping it normal.

Like any other day.

'Can I be excused, please?' they drone in sulky stereo, elongating each word in monotone.

The so-called parents let them go. Immediately, the future orphans rush into the lounge, turn up the television before upturning boxes of cars and bricks and jigsaw pieces. The lovers look at each other. This time with the same expression.

Who are they to decide how their children should act?

Who are they to decide what is right and what is wrong?

Why can they not just love them enough?

The boys shriek with joy, there's garbled excitement, it's innocent play. But it doesn't flick a switch within their parents to bring them back to the reality of their world, and what they are planning to do; what they have been chosen to perform.

There's a twisted combination of phobia and wrath and abhorrence and it's beating out any kind of bravery or pleasure or adoration. And maybe that's the reason they ended up joining The People of Choice.

She doesn't love him anymore. And he hasn't loved her for even longer.

She may have grown to hate him. She certainly hates herself.

A high-pitched squeal compels them both to bolt instinctively to the living room, where their eldest son is mounted on the youngest's back, forcing his face into the sofa cushion while pulling at his hair and grabbing a toy from his hand.

Parental zombies.

It's their last day on this job. They explain that he should not do this to his younger brother, that he is supposed to protect and look after him. This is normal, regular discussion, but today is given weight by their future actions.

They want to say, 'Soon you will only have each other to rely on.'

But they don't.

They can't.

They play the role of concerned parents.

The boys are coerced into mutual apology. They continue with their exuberant toy-box bulldozing while the adults sink into the sofa with a hot drink and allow themselves to be entertained by boyish antics, losing time in a moment of thoughtlessness and enjoyment. Momentarily compartmentalising their fate. They project their love in the same direction. Letting the boys know, without words, that they matter to their parents and that they are important.

It is a perfect moment for tenderness, for one of them to put their hand on the other one's leg. To softly, affectionately, squeeze a knee, not even looking at one another. A simple touch would convey some contentment with life. That they got one thing right.

They know, they have been told, that it is the small things like this that could save them.

All of them.

But there is no subtle graze of the other's knee.

There's no glimpse from the corner of the eye to register the gratification they both feel in this moment.

No emotional reciprocation.

And the moment passes.

Another one.

So close.

16

231 – UNGRATEFUL

She holds her breath under the water for nearly a minute. Her hair splays outwards on the surface like a peacock tail. The torn credit-card bill swims over and gets caught up in her curls. But that's as close to sinking into her brain as the situation gets for today. Any day.

She could've tried to hold on longer.

Her eyes open and gaze at the bottom of the tub. It's the way she would look if the rope snapped, it's how they'd find her, washed up on the stones further east by the MI6 building.

Her lungs full of water.

Her banks empty of funds.

Drop. Splash. Cold. Shock. Gasp. Lungs. Burn. Panic.

That is no way to die.

Wake. Read. Cry. Sulk. Drink. Spend. Party. Sleep.

This is no way to live.

Just one more day.

The sound of a droplet falling from the tap into the water

sounds so clear, so loud. Her father lurks behind the door, waiting to detect more suffering, but the water around her ears closes her off from the real world. She feels a wave of heightened senses, like she could stay under there for ever, like she could breathe under water.

At first she does not hear her father's knuckle rap against the bathroom door as she rocks her head from left to right in the water, her knees becoming more uncomfortable as they rest on the slate floor, a line imprinting itself into her left knee where it pushes against the grouting that joins two tiles.

He taps louder against the door, this time with four knuckles. This time calling her name. The sound is muffled as she tries to recreate the motion of the sea, swooping from side to side.

Then he screws his hand into a fist and bangs the fleshy parts heavily against the door, this time shouting her name. He is worried. He thinks she could do something stupid. Her mother is gone so he has to take care of any parental intuition.

Her head springs backwards out of the water and she takes a deep breath in.

One, two, three.

Strands of hair stick to her face and water trickles down her back and chest before hitting the floor.

'Dad, I'm fine. My head was under the water, that's all,' she shouts back at him, not knowing what he said but understanding enough that he would have been worried.

He's always worried.

He is silent for a short moment and then speaks to her again through the door in his usual moderate tone.

'I'm off out for a bit, sweet one.' He always calls her that. It makes her feel young again. And protected. It's the same thing he used to call her mum. A million people probably use that phrase but it still feels like it's theirs. 'I just wondered whether you needed anything while I was out.'

She can't imagine what she would ask him to pick up for her. He couldn't choose a pair of jeans or sunglasses or products for her rigorous beauty regime. She doesn't want to talk about how heavy her flow is right now. He could go to the bank and pay off her overdraft; he could easily do that if she asked him. He'd do anything for his sweetheart.

That's the problem.

And she can't ask him to do that for her.

He knows how she will answer. It was just an excuse to check in on her.

Trying to catch her out.

'It's fine, Daddy. Thanks. I'm going out myself, anyway,' she calls back, picking at her face to remove the wet, tangled mess that sticks to her skin.

'Okay. I'll see you later for dinner then...'

'By-ee.' She feigns some kind of daughterly dotage, pushing out a chirpiness that doesn't really exist in her. Because she can't agree to dinner. She doesn't want to lie to him anymore. She loves him too much for that.

He walks away.

And that is the last she will ever speak to her father.

The last time she would have seen him would have been to not see him at all.

He is a voice through a door. A concern in the distance.

The answer to a question she should ask.

17

232 – POET

Back under his duvet, avoiding the ink spot, he kneels and touches his head to his knees.

He grips his hair and squeezes hard, wringing it out as though it's his mother's neck. More displacement. More avoidance. His mother isn't even the issue. He loves her so completely. It is not even himself that he despises. It's the person he is never going to be. The poet he cannot become. Because he's just not good enough.

There's no talent show to enter for poetry where a panel of alleged experts deal out truths. He has had to discover it himself. That the gift he thought he possessed does not exist. That he is shit at the only thing he wants to do. Yet, still, he persists. Hoping things will change. He does not want his father to be right.

He should be twenty-two tomorrow.

He shouldn't be living with his parents. He knows that. It's his own fault that he allows himself to exist in such an infuriating way. He's worse than those people on television who believe they can sing even when they are told they can't. But he's not deluded. He understands his limitations. Which is worse?

This is his choice.

This is every morning.

A moment of gratification followed by lingering torment.

He knows that he needs to take a breath and count and enter his thoughts into a diary to read at a later date, once he has calmed, to gain some perspective on how he feels; how irrational he can be. They are not against him. His mother is not against him.

The poet tells himself to snap out of it.

Get up. Just get the fuck up and out of the house.

He can hear the rattle of cutlery and crashing of plates as somebody empties the dishwasher. Undoubtedly his mother. She does the work while *he* sits in *his* chair and reads the newspaper.

Jeans, a plain white T-shirt, checked shirt and thin scarf that serves no function other than to look a bit like a poet, he snaps some oversized headphones around his neck, picks up a pen and notepad and opens his bedroom door to the stuffy old-fashionedness that awaits him downstairs.

He hears his mother's sudden gasp of panic as his foot hits that third step. And he senses his father's apathy as his right hand grazes down the bannister. She wants to get things back to order, ensure everything is proper. He just wants to forget.

This poet, he walks through the lounge past *him* – they do not exchange a glance or a word – and into the kitchen, where his mother is wiping down a surface, which looks clean already.

'I made you some breakfast, dear.' She points to a glass of pure orange juice next to a plate on the table holding two slices of buttered toast. And he wonders why he aims his wrath at her when hers is the only opinion that seems to matter. She tells him to follow his dream, do something that he loves.

Because she never could.

Her son is the only thing in the world she stands up to her husband about.

And this is what infuriates him. What kind of lesson is this? She does something thoughtful and pleasant and selfless and carries on as though nothing happened that morning, like it's the first time she has seen her son all day. She must want to ask him what he was doing or why he was covered in blue.

But she doesn't.

And the poet wants to confront her about entering his room without knocking, tell her that she shouldn't be seeing a person of his age naked whether she gave birth to him or not.

But he doesn't.

It's easier to bottle it up and pretend that they are functioning.

He is just as she is.

As bad as one another.

Crippled by the knowledge of their own limitations.

'Thanks, Mum,' he says, taking a bite of toast. He picks up the slices in his left hand and leans in to kiss her on the cheek. 'Got to dash. See you later.'

But he won't.

He's heading out to do what he does almost every day – wander romantically around the city, find an area of greenery, sit down and scribble some words that hint at the way he feels. Rhyming for catharsis.

Battersea Park seems ideal. It's close to the jump site. The leap-of-faith location. He can work on his new piece, 'Mother #47'. Then leave it on the grass or in a bin or throw it in the river before joining the friends he doesn't know on that stretch of concrete and steel.

He walks back through the living room where *he* is obscured by the newspaper. He crunches loudly on his breakfast and his father doesn't even flinch.

This is the last time they won't speak to each other.

It will be the longest period yet.

The rucksack containing his jumper and rope are in the cupboard under the stairs and his note is in the front pocket. He heaves the bag over his shoulder and twists the latch on the front door. And, in that moment, he pauses, wondering whether he should wish them well or say goodbye properly or just have it all out, get the issues sorted.

Best to leave it as it is. That's what they do. Nonconfrontational. The last moment with his mother was a tender one: a kiss on the cheek, a smile, the agreement they seem to have made to not mention anything indecorous, ever. She deserves that much.

And he can leave *him* wallowing in guilt,
At the poor excuse for a home *he* built.

18

TAKE THIS PILL

I can't sleep. I'm sad. Burnt out by work.

Never wanted that kid.

Can't lose weight.

Your local quack doesn't know what to do with this information. It's not a lump or scratch or itch or bleed. They are never going to suggest lavender on your pillow at night or acupuncture. They don't know enough about nutrition. There's an endless queue of sniffling kids and aching pensioners. There are bonuses for getting people off the cigarettes.

Take all those not-very-amusing *Doctor, Doctor* jokes you heard when you were younger; they all have the same punchline now.

Doctor, Doctor, I feel like a pair of curtains.

Take this pill. Disguise the issue.

Doctor, Doctor, it hurts when I do this *waves right hand*.

Take this pill. Mask the pain.

Doctor, Doctor, I think I'm addicted to brake fluid.

Take this pill. Obscure the problem.

The issue goes deeper. Why can't they sleep? What's causing it? Is it really sadness or something more sinister? Perhaps it is simpler. Why can't they discuss things with their partner? Are they scared? Are they taking in more calories than they are expending?

Pull yourself together.

Don't do that, then.

You can stop anytime.

There's a better way to deal with things. Get rid of the time wasters. Kill them off. Get them to kill themselves, if you can.

Doctor, Doctor, can I get a second opinion?

19

230 – DOCTOR

She once finished a shift at 6:00 am, travelled back to her apartment and had a glass of wine before the first segment of morning news had dribbled its way onto the television screen. Because it was the end of her shift. It was her version of post-work drinks. So eating a bowl of oats at 3:30 in the afternoon is in no way strange to the doctor because it is the start of her day.

And the letter in her mailbox tells her that it is also her last.

But she rolls up her new compression tights, pulls her vest

on, straps her phone to her arm and plugs in her earphones. Like she always does. The first song on her playlist is 'Stronger' by Kanye West. She's tried running music and rock music and house music and upbeat pop, but nothing gets her heart racing like an angry rapper.

The gym is two miles away. A boutique place that is over-priced but not overcrowded. She can afford it. She couldn't live without it. Inconspicuously situated beneath a railway arch, it takes her sixteen minutes to jog there. It's her warm-up. She has never understood the mentality of people who drive to a gym to run on a treadmill for an hour then drive back home. It's another reason she chose this gym: no machines.

She leaves the music blaring as she enters and nods at one of the male trainers. There's no need to sign in or swipe a membership card, it's not that kind of place. She moves to the back room and stretches in front of the mirror.

There are three other people working out: some pituitary-gland grunting as he presses too-heavy weights above his chest; a woman of indeterminate age is with the trainer, having a private session – her face pumped so full of chemicals that she can't express the pain of her workout – and an athletic man in his early forties, who is pulling himself to the top of a rope that hangs in the very centre of the main floor. The doctor has spoken to him a few times before. He's often there at the same time.

She's attracted to his physique.

And his discipline.

And today he decides to make his move.

The doctor is in the squat rack with forty kilos resting across her shoulders, about seventy percent of her body weight. She's being watched. Admired. And she knows it. And she likes it.

He smiles before approaching her. He's easy. Comfortable with himself. A simple 'Hello again' gets things moving. They talk about exercise. They move on to work and why they both go at that time. And everything seems to fit together.

Today.

It all starts to work out today.

And he gets a little more awkward as he builds the courage to ask her out. And she finds it endearing. And sad. It's the kind of morsel dropped in front of a person that might make them think, *I don't want to die.*

Her father would say it is a gift from God. That it is a sign. 'Thanks be to God that He sent His only son to die for our sins and rise again to give believers eternal life in Jesus Christ.'

Thanks, God, that sounds fucking great. And stupid. Dad, you sound ridiculous. Still.

Fuck you, Jesus.

He holds the back of her arm while he types his details into her phone that is still strapped to the front. She feels the touch of his hand as though it is between her legs. And she knows she is supposed to act like nothing is different, like this is everyday, but she thinks about fucking him in the changing room.

And she takes his number, knowing that she will never use it.

Then jogs home. Showers. Gets dressed. Eats her lunch while everyone else in London is preparing their dinner. And she takes up her bag, with the rope inside, and starts walking to Chelsea Bridge.

And there will be no eternal life. There will be cessation of breathing. And blood circulation. And brain activity.

Just another unused gym membership.

20

225–227 – NOBODIES

Think of a person in your office who you know of but don't really know. Now imagine one of the other parents in the playground staring at their mobile phone, waiting for a classroom door to open. Or the guy that's always behind the till at the petrol station, who says 'good luck' when you buy a lottery ticket. You might notice if they suddenly weren't there one day, but you're not going to miss them. It will register but it won't truly affect.

They're nobodies.

To you, anyway.

What do you do at six in the evening? Maybe you've just got in from your train commute but didn't have time to finish the last few pages in that chapter of the book you are reading, so you sit down on a bench before you go into the house in order to fold a paper corner in the right place.

That's what the Nobodies are doing.

Maybe you always sit down for dinner at half-five and you are scraping the last morsels of broccoli stem into the bin before you wash the dishes.

Just like the Nobodies are, right now.

Or you're running through the park, like the Nobodies. Or you're washing your baby in the bath, like the Nobodies. You're driving one of the kids to one of their clubs. You're getting changed for spin class. You're watching the early-evening news. You're lighting a candle at church. The online grocery delivery has arrived and you're emptying the bags and filling the fridge. And the Nobodies are doing the same.

The thing is, they know who they are. They don't think they're special. They don't think they're unique. She knows her father did her a disservice by calling her 'princess' while she was growing up because now her standards are warped. He knows he's stuck in middle management forever. Stagnating.

But they don't want your pity. That's what they say, anyway. They don't want you thinking about them. They're filling in the gaps. Making up the numbers. There for the spectacle of it.

They don't want you to give them a second thought. Because there's a doctor to think about. The Lovers have two kids. It's almost the Poet's birthday.

And they think they're just three shadows dangling between six more important people. People they don't really know. People in their cult, but people they think they have nothing in common with.

But they share something with five of the six people on that bridge.

Not one of the Nobodies wants to die.

Still, at six o'clock, while you rush to make your screening at the cinema or you're in the shower or playing the banjo or having an argument with your sister, the Nobodies are walking towards Chelsea Bridge with ropes in their backpacks and no stutter in their step.

21

233 – YOUNG LEVANT

Ergo pulls at Young Levant, jolting him forwards so he steps on one of the cracks in the pavement. And then he's cocking his leg to the lamppost and ignoring the traffic at the crossing and shitting on the grass. And his master is ignoring the defecation, leaving his hand in the pocket that usually holds a plastic sack for this exact event. And then he's tugging at Ergo's neck with the leash and dragging him away from the open parkland and back to the squalor of his flat, avoiding the cracks on the ground even though his father is not there to praise him for doing so.

Then they're back home.

Both of them deflated with a pseudo-claustrophobia. The dog mimicking its owner.

Young Levant wants to lie down in his bed again. He wants to jump under the creased covers and bury his head into the pillow, just as Ergo is trying to do right now with a stuffed toy.

To do that would be acting as though today is the same as always.

But he can't. His role is more important. People will be able to see him. He is in the light. He is visible. Different.

He is the face of The People of Choice.

The poster boy for their success.

The lowest shelf in the cupboard beneath his sink has accumulated a thick layer of dust and dirt through lack of use. The lids of the unopened and half-used products show a similar level of neglect. He finds two bottles of bleach that can be used on the tiled floors and an antibacterial spray for the surfaces in the kitchen and bathroom. Another bottle says 'Power Cream'.

Behind is a tub containing cloths and scourers and a plastic flask filled with a powder to shake on a carpet and vacuum up to give the illusion that it is clean and fresh-smelling.

It seems like more than enough to erase himself.

He agitates a spray, which is a mixture of water and corn

flour that an ex-girlfriend left behind. The corn flour grips the grease and shines up the window on the oven door without leaving tracks or smears. He turns to Ergo in amazement that it actually works.

The dog's chin rests sulkily on his stuffed plaything, the sides of his mouth hanging limply over his teeth, his eyes slightly glazed. This time, Young Levant's expression starts to mirror his dog's.

'I'm sorry, boy.' He speaks in something close to a whisper, either to come across as more genuine or through embarrassment.

He feels like he is killing the poor creature.

He's contagious.

He has made his dog depressed.

I bring everyone and everything down.

With The People of Choice, Young Levant feels like he belongs. All the members do. They are part of something greater than themselves.

Ergo does not move for the entirety of the bleaching and scouring and eradication of Young Levant. He's not even asleep. Just a slump. A daze of submission to the life that he has been given. His master swears he sees the dog sigh.

Young Levant shakes the sandy particles over the carpet, some dropping onto Ergo's saggy tail. The dog finally jumps when the vacuum is switched on and barks heartily until the job is complete. For that brief moment, he shows some energy but collapses quickly into apathy by the time the plug and cable have been wound around the handle and placed back into the cupboard.

The sad young man slides his back down the wall until he is perched next to his faithful companion, and rests his right arm along the dog's back.

The dog doesn't move.

They sit like that for over an hour. Young Levant strokes at Ergo's dark coat and stares out of the now glistening window, waiting as the night starts to draw in.

And Ergo stares at the wall, wondering when his owner will just leave him be. Asking why he can't manage to go through with any ideas he has had for self-culling.

Probably wishing I would just fuck off and die.

He wants to live but he doesn't know how.

He requires guidance.

Somebody to show him the way.

22

225–226 – LOVERS

The remainder of their final day is filled with commonplace and loose regime: a taxing lunch where one boy teaches the other about the evils of green food; the ensuing tantrums; the force-feeding; the empty threats; a daunting walk to the park fraught with dangers of the green-cross code; boys falling off swings; jumping off climbing frames; swinging from branches. All the while innocent of the fact that their parents are hardly speaking, that they are standing side by side with all the warmth of their wedding-cake figurines from eight years ago, five of which have been unhappy.

And with each act of the children's pure naiveté, they find themselves slipping deeper into withdrawal, further into self-loathing.

The boys, their boys, behave well in the bath for once. They splash together as their parents look on, crouched on the cold slate tiles, leaning against the tub, their hands dipping in the water to join in with the merriment. They are a Norman Rockwell painting. A still image of togetherness. They are the images you see on social media that make you feel guilty about your own family life.

But real life illustrates their falseness.

Their fake family.

Truth protrudes through the facade.

They take one child each and wrap them in a giant towel and help them get dried and into their pyjamas. And they carry them down the stairs even though they are capable of walking themselves and they sit them on their laps on the sofa and watch some television while hugging them until the bell rings.

And their grandmother arrives to sit in and watch over their sons while they go out for the evening to jump off a bridge.

From the moment they step outside their unhappy home, their den of despair and weakness, they are doomed. They may be known as The People of Choice but every inch closer to Chelsea Bridge eradicates individual thought. They are zombies now.

Followers.

And their final test will only come when they hit the edge that separates them from the cold. The drop. The snap.

The end.

The real moment of choice.

Separate but joined.

By the time they see the lights on the bridge, she can't even remember whether she kissed her children goodbye.

23

231 – UNGRATEFUL

At the mirror, she pulls at her nest of hair, stretching the skin on her face, and ties it back.

The way her mother used to wear it.

The way her *daddy* likes her to wear it, too.

It's the least she can do.

And she leans over the bath and cups her hands to collect some warm water to splash under her arms and between her legs. She's already clean. It's just a spruce. You never know who you might bump into, where you might end up, what might happen. She pats herself dry, wraps a towel around her, picks up her clothes from the floor and unlocks the door that leads back into her bedroom.

The air is cooler out there and her shoulders start to goose-bump. She tiptoes across the bedroom carpet, trying not to get it too wet, and jumps onto the hair towel she used last night, which is still on the floor.

She starts to reapply her make-up and forgets everything. The fact that she owes more money than she can earn is no longer troubling. It's out of her mind.

This *is* a day like any other.

For a brief moment it may seem that she forgets where she is supposed to be later. That she has been accepted into a very prestigious group. But that isn't the case at all. He has made sure that she will be there. That they will all be there. And that The People of Choice have no choice at all.

Ungrateful leaves her opulent Chelsea home, her purse bursting with credit, her attitude set to *shop*. She wants to buy something new.

Something to make her look better.

Feel better.

Something she will look great in, dead.

An outfit with a strong silhouette to complement her noose.

She spends her last day with her five favourite plastic, rectangular friends. She pushes them to their limit, not because she wants, selfishly, to punish her father, just because she wants to. There is no motive behind this at all. She wants to be able to do what she wants to do. These temporary moments of happiness lift her heart and work at filling the crack left by her mother's death. But all the shoes in the world cannot fill the hole that has been left.

And nobody looks twice at the woman dressed like she is attending a film premiere with an old backpack slung over her shoulder.

And nothing she has ever done or planned to do will matter when she drops towards the Thames using her vertebrae as a brake, plummeting to a place she never wanted to go.

She will hang in the dark with the three Nobodies.

She'll be one of them.

And her father's heart will fracture in a new direction.

She takes a left after the hospital and sees the bridge in the distance.

Look at all the lights.

In the next life, wherever she goes, she will be wearing new heels.

24

233 – YOUNG LEVANT

His jacket is strewn across the back of the single-seater. He throws it on and takes the woollen hat from the pocket to cover his greasy hair; easier than washing it. The action forces him to recall his ex-girlfriend and how she introduced him to the wonders of dry shampoo. He smiles to himself. A sad smile. Downcast.

All the pills and the talking and the support in the world, it can help overcome some personal demons or help a person come to terms with grief, but nothing can erase regret. It never leaves you.

His scuffed trainers are next to the doormat where Ergo's lead hangs on a single nail, hammered into the wall directly above. At the sound of the rattling chain, Ergo abandons his meal and skips over to Young Levant, jumping in excitement.

The dog forces his head into the nook of his owner's neck as he crouches down to tie his laces.

'Oh, boy, we've been out already today.' He strokes his one remaining friend. 'I need to go out on my own for a bit, okay?' He looks the dog in the eyes.

Ergo is a placid being but Young Levant senses something else in the animal.

He stands up and reaches over to his bag, which contains a note and a rope. Ergo grabs at it with his teeth and pulls.

'What are you doing, boy. Stop.'

This isn't like him.

They tussle for a few seconds. Ergo growls.

'Ergo, let go! Stop this. Stop it now. Let go.' He obeys. 'Don't leave it like this. Please.'

As he opens the door to leave, Ergo bolts towards him. He's not trying to escape. He's not trying to hurt Young Levant. He's keeping him busy. He's keeping him here.

Clever boy.

'Okay. Okay.' He smiles. 'One more.'

Young Levant takes the lead from the nail in the wall and walks back towards the kitchen. Ergo follows, affectionately rubbing his back against his master's leg, cocking his head to the side so the lead can be clipped on to his collar.

And then the other end of the lead is looped over a radiator pipe. And his master is walking back towards the front door. And the poor animal is confused. And Young Levant takes his keys from the nail beneath the one that used to hold Ergo's lead. And they stare at each other. One last time.

And it's shit. It isn't a day like any other. This wasn't the agreement.

But nobody will ever know that.

Nobody is watching.

Nobody knows who The People of Choice are.

They don't even know themselves.

25

230 – DOCTOR

She's the last to arrive at the bridge. Of course. You can't truly have control over people. There are too many variables to consider. They are complicated and emotional. And unpredictable.

And doubt is such a strong sensation.

But she's here.

She's the last. So she gets to see what they look like.

These followers.

Servants.

Acolytes.

The doctor stares down the length of the bridge as she approaches from the north side. The eight of them are sat staring out across the river they will eventually jump towards. Their choice.

They look pensive.

Thinking nothing.

The Poet doesn't ponder his final moments as a sonnet. The Ungrateful doesn't contemplate saying thank you. It is too late for the Nobodies to realise they are the Somebodies.

The Tired cannot daydream.

The Lovers only hate.

Young Levant is the first person she passes. He is the one to be seen. The one in the light. There's a space for the Doctor. Her place. For whatever reason. She doesn't think twice about taking it. She sits down on the cold steel box that extends the length of the bridge, the wire behind their heads straight up to the curved suspension cable. Nobody speaks. And she does not look at any of them again.

They know she is here. That she has arrived.

That the choice will soon arise.

She is no different from them now. They are all joined. They believe in the same things. She has become a nobody in this life and must move on to the next.

The Doctor takes her jumper from the bag, places her right arm in first, then her left, and finally pulls the hood up to protect herself from the breeze that is bouncing up from the water. The rope tickles and grazes her face as she slips the loop over her head. She tightens it for extra security. It can't slip off.

She doesn't want to land in the water.

She could live.

They would know what she had done.

The train pulls out from the shadow of Battersea Power Station and she hears it slow down. Or she feels it slowing down. Somehow, she knows it will soon come to a stop.

She is near.

They all are.

26

225–233

There is no time for last words, not out loud. The lights inside each coach illuminate the commuters, workers and tourists as the train starts to slow. But we do not see them. Some continue to read their book or newspaper, others drink coffee and tea. Thirty-two of them turn their heads to the left, looking up the river at the splendour of Chelsea Bridge at the exact moment that nine people speed five steps towards them, vaulting the railing in whatever fashion befits their personal fitness level.

We drop over the edge, a moment of free-fall and then a tightening.

And then a crack.

And then a change.

For we are The People of Choice, the ones now with courage.

And we choose not to fear.

The commuters with papers, the workers with books, turn at the sounds of horror from those who look left. The tourists with tea and coffee spill hot liquid without noticing and join the thirty-two witnesses, bumping shoulders and pressing noses.

The thirty-two, each with a variation of the same story, all staring at the nine flaccid bodies still swinging above the water, witness our choice, our decision to finally be brave.

Thirty of them do not understand.

Two of them have been selected.

Recruited.

They do not know this yet. They have not received their calling to make their own choices known.

Somewhere, opposite our limp, lifeless, stupid bodies, in the boxcars heading to Victoria, are two people like us; ready to subscribe to our pact.

Ready, like us, to choose to live.

Ready to be immortalised.

234 and 235.

27

YOU CAN'T TRUST PEOPLE

One of the stumbling blocks of any suicide cult is the fact that people have to kill themselves. Logistically, it becomes very involved.

There's always the danger that one of them could lose their head.

Take the Doctor.

230.

Throw her in the shower, fully clothed. Wait. Take her back out and get her to step on the scales in the corner of the bathroom. You'll be lucky if the digits click past eight stone. Calculations suggest that her rope needs to be 8' 6" long. Or 259cm.

So her head doesn't come off.

A few inches longer than that and the level of torque could decapitate her. It would ruin the imagery. An empty rope swaying in the breeze. Her head floating down the Thames. The rest of her body trying desperately to catch up.

No. That doesn't work.

They can't lose their head.

Take a Nobody. #3. 227. That rope has to be 5'8 1/2". That half-inch is important. To keep that useless brain in a pointless head attached to a purposeless spine.

Now take the Lovers. He weighs 13 1/2 stone. That means his rope is 5'3 1/2". Or 161cm. To keep him intact.

Hers is the same length.

Even though it should be 7' 2".

Keep it short. So that she can choke out. So that it takes a little longer. For the picture, the art.

Because she needs more time to think.

Then you have to add in the distance from the upright girder to the railings.

You can't trust people to just kill themselves anymore.

You have to do everything for them.

28

230 – DOCTOR

She's the last one to the bridge and the first one to die. Because she is fit and light and agile. When they don't say *go* or *jump* or count down from three, she takes four steps forwards, puts two hands on the railings and vaults over the bar in one swift and fluid motion. Justification for that expensive gym membership.

You wonder whether she contemplated God. Because of her pious father. Whether a verse from that good book she heard so much from as a child popped into her head.

The Lord is close to the brokenhearted and saves those who are crushed in spirit.

You wonder whether she is sorry.

Whoever believes and is baptised will be saved, but whoever does not believe will be condemned.

That's the kind of capricious bullshit that she always hated.

She's perfectly capable of condemning herself.

Maybe it was that guy at the gym who dropped into her mind. A missed opportunity. She wishes she could've fucked him or pulled his face between her legs. Maybe then she'd be okay with the dying part.

Or maybe she thinks of the patients she's left behind. The teenager with the broken leg. The family hit by the drunk driver. The father who won't wake up. The kid she knows is fighting for nothing. The parents who won't let go.

Did it all slow down? Did she see the people watching on the train opposite? Was she looking at somebody who was looking back?

It didn't slow.

She didn't think it was wrong until a split moment before the rope tightened and put an irreparable kink in her vertebrae. She opened her mouth to scream – there was enough time for that, but not enough for any sound to emerge.

And as she came to an abrupt stop, her open mouth clamped shut and bit straight through her silent scream.

Those who guard their mouths and their tongues keep them-selves from calamity.

29

231 – UNGRATEFUL

Her dad works hard for all his money. There's a lot of it. He's under tremendous pressure. As he should be. He's responsible. And he's successful. But now, everything he does, it's not for him. It's all for his two daughters.

He lost the great love of his life. Watched her body wither away, followed closely by her mind, her kindness and her mem-ories.

And he stayed strong while his heart was breaking. He took care of her. He looked after everyone. All the while, there was nobody around to take care of him. To ask how his day was. To see if there was anything he needed. The girls were too young. He was protecting them.

Of course it is difficult to lose a parent, somebody you are born to. You are supposed to love them. You kind of have to. But what about somebody you choose to love? Or that person you couldn't help but love?

Why wasn't her father drinking heavily or blowing his money on things he didn't need and women he didn't want? Why wasn't he lying on a couch and discussing his troubles.

After everything she put him through, how did he still love her so much?

These are all the things she didn't bother thinking before she dropped.

30

225–227 – NOBODIES

Their ropes were all the correct length for the long drop. Things got tight real quick. The spinal cords were severed. Within a second, their blood pressure had dropped to zero; the same level as their ambition, the same number as their contribution, the sum of people they believed would care if they were suddenly no more.

They lost their collective consciousness.

It was several minutes until three brains were irreversibly dead.

And they each thought of only two things before the drop:

1. The knot of the noose has to be at the side so that the head is forced backwards, breaking the neck.

2. They didn't want to die.

Nobody wanted to die.

31

232 – POET

Wouldn't it be great to think or know that, just before the knot shot his head towards the right, tearing his central nervous system apart, he remembered the line of that poem he was thinking of when his mother interrupted him in the morning?

That would be the best birthday gift.

That he finished another shitty poem nobody would ever read.

Even the best poets don't sell any books. Nobody is reading poetry anymore, because love and romance has been replaced by twenty-four-hour-a-day access to any kind of pornography you desire.

So the world isn't going to miss another sub-par rhymer, who couldn't recall his closing couplet. His pitiful mind didn't even have time to complete the thought, 'Oh, fuck' as he dropped.

Happy birthday to the low achiever.

Who didn't want to die today, either.

32

225–226 – LOVERS

They were holding hands. Looking like lovers. Some inseparable twosome. A partnership. Unbreakable. Even in death.

Bullshit.

He didn't want it to end this way. Leaving those boys. What did they ever do? He wanted the marriage counselling to have worked, not quit part-way through. He wanted to let go of his anger. He wanted to forgive her for what she had done. He never wanted to jump off a goddamned bridge.

And it wasn't that she was sabotaging the counselling sessions, it wasn't that she wanted a divorce, she hadn't even wanted to fuck that other guy. She was numb. To everything. She had been for longer than she could remember.

It wasn't that she wanted to orphan her two sons, she just felt nothing. A non-being. That meant she was no longer herself.

It wasn't even that she wanted to jump.

She just didn't care.

They jumped together, fell together, and like the seven strangers next to them, something snapped in their mind before it snapped in their neck.

His rope was the perfect length. Scream. Jolt. Crack. Swinging in the breeze.

Hers was the perfect length for him. Silence. Realisation. Choke. Swaying. Eyes bulging. Entirely aware of everything around her. That train in front with those people watching. Traffic above and behind, unaware.

And the idiots had held hands. They'd jumped together. What a team. So brave, right? Well, she couldn't let go of his stupid hand. She tried, but the small split in her vertebrae sucked any strength from the left-hand side of her body. She couldn't let go of him like she let go of her kids. With her right hand, she wanted to swipe at the rope. Maybe get her fingers underneath and stop herself from losing breath. In her oxygen-starved brain, she thought that was what she was doing.

She wasn't.

She shook a little. Nobody on that train noticed. It wasn't about her.

They died together, hanging hand in hand, but cracked in two.

33

233 – YOUNG LEVANT

Worry had made him lose weight. That rope should've been 3 1/4 inches longer, but it had done the trick. The guy was dead from the moment he'd left the house.

You think he gave Ergo another thought before he rolled over the railings. You think he wondered about his grandfather. Because they were close. But the old man will get to find out from the news on his television. Like thousands of people who never knew Young Levant. Like the other people who will know him as 233.

Or the one in the light.

That guy in the cult.

A person of choice.

There's a brightness on that side of the bridge. It's intentional. He can be seen. His head lolled to one side, the same way his dog would beg for food or affection.

It's theatre. Tableau.

They are one. Another way to take away their identities. Making them all into nobodies. Whether they're shadows or illuminated. Whether they wanted to die or not. One voice. No voice.

And the notes that were flushed or burned or eaten or torn into fifty pieces were all correct. Nothing important happened today. But the *other people* aren't unaware of this. They will buy into it. They'll drink the Kool Aid.

And a dog is tied up in a kitchen and some kids lost their parents and a father is down to his only remaining female relative. And while so many people focus on the darkness of this act, there are *others* who will be pointing towards Young Levant's light.

34

NO NAMES

Here's a secret: Turn them into numbers.

Take any livestock farmer. They are not trampling around fields calling for pigs by name. They're rounding them up apathetically. They're not patting Carrie the cow on the back and telling her to 'Walk this way', because 'this way' is the direction of a room where a man waits, ready to put a bolt into her head.

And sometimes, that bolt only stuns the cow, so they're still alive when they are hung up by one foot and slit across the neck to bleed out. Sometimes, they're conscious as the skin is peeled away from their head.

You can do that to a cow.

But it's harder to do that to Carrie.

People don't want to eat Carrie. People don't even want to eat a cow. They want to eat beef. And each of those is a very different thing.

If you read in the news that twenty-something Dinah Faige has jumped off a bridge and died, you may feel empathetic to that. You may later learn that she was clinically depressed and unable to function fully due to the untimely death of her mother and her inability to grieve that loss. You may feel worse knowing that. You may think you understand her pain. But, if you want to run a successful cult, give her a number, label her with a personality defect or archetype.

Call her *Ungrateful*.

Tag her as *231*.

Take any large company. Something the size of Dell or Pepsi

or Mars. You're not Peter Flaws, you're sales or marketing or distribution.

You're an email address.

You're a barcode.

A dial tone.

A SKU number.

It makes it easier when they have to let you go, when they have to restructure or dissolve an entire department.

Take 225–226. Don't call them parents. Don't call them post-natal depression. Don't call them anxiety or panic attacks.

Don't call the Poet talented or driven or abused.

Because you might end up caring that they died.

Or that you have to kill them.

35

It's tucked away on the South Bank. Behind the National Theatre. You'd never know it was there unless you were looking for it. The road is quiet. Odd, considering the amount of people who walk or jog along the river only a hundred yards away.

There's a barrier that remains open. A signpost says that the speed limit is ten miles per hour, and the speed bumps reinforce that. Turn right at the bottom of the road and park outside the first set of doors.

London is suddenly out of sight.

The brass plaque is etched with the word ERMA. Beneath that, four brass buzzers. Each with a name beside it.

Erickson.

Rossi.

Milton.

Artaud.

In that order.

Then, a windowless box, a drop in temperature, another set of glass doors, an unmanned reception desk to the right. A man appears, older, athletic, a tidy, trimmed beard flecked with grey, and white at the ends of his moustache.

Then, two flights of stairs and a long corridor and some words about *Erickson and Milton being away at the moment* and a wooden door and an uncomfortable entrance and a hand gesture to guide you into a safe space.

You wouldn't know it was here unless you'd been told where to go. Unless you'd been given detailed instructions about the barrier and the bumps and the door and the correct buzzer to press.

Inside, it's wood. Everywhere. Halfway up the walls with a dado rail around the entire room. The giant oak desk. The wooden plate that says the doctor's name is Artaud. The coat stand in the corner. Some more words. *It's pronounced ah-toe.*

Outside it's black. It's colder. There's screaming on a halted train as it overlooks a scene of mass suicide. Outside, nine strangers hang from Chelsea Bridge by their broken necks.

And inside, it's wood.

And it's cut off.

And it's silent.

Because Detective Sergeant Pace doesn't want to talk.

Detective Sergeant Pace still sees black flames.

Detective Sergeant Pace cannot run fast enough.

36

They've got the best seats in the house. Those thirty-two people on that train carriage.

And they all react to what they see in a different way.

There are those who completely buy in to what they are witnessing, they watch it from start to finish. The cascade of bodies as they drop over the edge of the bridge.

One. Crack.

Two. Snap.

Nine. Split.

The sharp intake of breath as they register what could be happening. People jumping towards their own end. And then another. And another. It's so absurd that it has to be real. Some are screaming. Some shout *no*. One person hits his fists against the window like the people outside might be able to hear him. As though it could stop them. But he's too late and he knows it.

Two people are crying.

Then there's shock. The ones in disbelief. It can't be! They're dead. They killed themselves. There are nine of them. What the fuck is this? Are you seeing what I'm seeing?

And there's apathy. Of all things. Indifference to death. If they're selfish enough to kill themselves then maybe they deserve it. The classic misunderstanding. Why weren't they thinking of their families when they stood on that railing?

Maybe they glimpse the scene as it ends. A momentary break from the screen of a mobile phone, eyes flitting to the bridge before turning back to their game or a text about dinner. Can they pick some wine up on the way home?

Selfish annoyance emerges, too. Another goddamned

jumper making me late home from work. Like a day in that glass prison of an office wasn't bad enough. The carriage is packed and hot and it's stopped on the track. And now this. Fuck my life.

Somebody spills their coffee.

There's calm in one corner and hysteria in another.

Some continue to read their books. For escape. Through lack of empathy. It doesn't matter. Not everyone has that morbid urge to slow down as they pass a car accident. Though a minority seek out these situations because it turns them on.

However they react, there are thirty-two differing testimonies on one carriage alone.

The train begins to move. The driver is unaware of the image down-river, he has been waiting for his signal to pull into the station. He wants to get home for wine and food, too. Maybe his wife will want to get intimate tonight.

There are three other carriages with passengers. And some of those passengers are witnesses. But this carriage is important because there are two people here, they are not sitting with each other as they do not know each other. But, in the next week, these strangers will meet on the Millennium Bridge with a rope and they are going to jump. And they are going to die.

37

225–233

We didn't say *go*.
Or *jump*.
Or count down from three.

We just knew.

For we are The People of Choice. The ones now with Nothing.

And no voice to hear.

Only now do we see the truth behind the words. Only after the fall, crack, black, do we understand when and where our paths have crossed, how we were chosen, why we came to follow the ambition and ideology of a single figure.

We know what we have in common and we realise the choice we should have made.

We had to want to die in order to live.

Then the Lovers could still have their arguments, their silences, their loveless morning copulation, their children. They could live a lie as somebodies. The Poet would have more opportunity to rhyme and hone and fail. There would be more time to ignore his father and continue to love only his mother. The Nobodies may realise that they were always the everybodies, while Ungrateful could continue to spend and credit and contest her father's approval in a competition with a sister who has no idea such a rift exists between them.

Maybe the Doctor would find some faith. In her work, in a God, in somebody else.

And Young Levant would learn to live up to his responsibilities.

But this is not the end.

Nor is it the beginning.

For us it is empty solitude. Eternal nothingness. This is not absolution.

In Chelsea, a widowed father is brought closer to a daughter who never competed for his affection. He still has to pay off the debts amassed by her frivolity. South of the river, a grandmother explains to two small boys that their parents won't be coming home. She will lie about their love for one another. She will never understand what has happened. And back across the bridge, another mother, left alone in grief, still bakes a cake for her dead son's birthday while an emotionally absent father reacts in a manner that would surprise the boy. That boy who opted to dive from the bridge into the everlasting ambience we now all inhabit.

We are simply nine deaths.

Nine corpses.

No problems.

No choice.

Nowhere.

We are nine nobodies.

And the cycle of recruitment has already begun.

38

YOU WANT TO HELP

When you start your own cult, the first question you have to ask yourself is, 'What do I want it to be?'

You have choices.

Maybe you want to help other people. Get them to live a healthier lifestyle. Have them think about the consequences of their actions against the planet they inhabit. Make people aware of their imprint on the environment.

Take veganism. Take CrossFit. Take that animal product off your dinner plate one day a week. Embrace meat-free Monday. Decrease your risk of getting certain cancers. Have more energy for yourself and the people you love around you. Run around the garden with the kids. Run for a bus. Run up the stairs. Lift something heavy. Try some fucking quinoa.

Maybe your guiding force is the idea of power or money. You want to be the head of a family. You want a Rolls-Royce. You think your ideas are worth hearing and your music is worth playing. You're sick of having a boss. You want people to listen to you.

Take a religion and hit a part of it until it splinters. Take that sliver and build something of your own. You can spread peace and love. Or you can tell them that Jesus talks through you. Don't be niggardly with your application. Confidence is power.

Build a following.

Maybe you want to get laid. Maybe your mum didn't let you suck on her tits when you were a baby, you went straight on the bottle. So now you want to suck on all the tits you can find. You might want to fuck your friend's wife. You might decide that you want all the women to be your wife and all their daughters to blow you. Perhaps the men can suck your dick, too.

You could get thirty people in one room. Take their clothes off. Get them drunk. Give them drugs. Light some candles. Tell them that freedom comes through sexual expression. Knock down their inhibitions. Let them choke, hit, bite, suck anything that writhes around near them.

Sometimes you can start out wanting to help those less fortunate, but *other people* become involved and they start to say that what you want is the power. Or the sex. And to the outside world, it looks that way.

There are options.

What is it that you want to achieve?

You want to help?

You want the power?

You want to fuck everybody?

Maybe you believe in the things that you preach. But maybe you just want to kill a lot of people. Or you want to see whether you can get them to kill themselves.

Helping people is the most difficult. Eventually, if you get things right, all cults lead to power and sex. If you get things wrong, if you let the *other people* become involved, people will have to die.

So, maybe it's easier to start there.

Get killing.

39

And the train pulls into the platform. And the doors to each carriage hiss open. Passengers step over one another to get away from what just happened. Others sit in silent shock.

They call the police.

They call their families.

You'll never guess what I just saw.

The operator at the other end of the line is asking, 'Sir, can you tell me where you are, please? What *exactly* did you see? How many? Are you hurt in any way?'

Can you stay where you are? The police are on their way.

Some people feel more comfortable staying on the carriage and letting the chaos exit. It feels safer inside, away from that scene of hanging desperation. But the shock is far weaker than the intrigue. It's only a few minutes before the witnesses to this crime, the ones who saw nine people drop off the side of

Chelsea Bridge, are clambering, not to escape, but get out and get back. On foot. In a cab. They want to take another look. Maybe even snap a picture on their phone. Or a short video. Perhaps even open up one of those apps that will film the bodies swaying in the breeze and then play it on a never-ending loop.

Or they'll make a meme that will go viral. Nine crudely drawn stick people on a white background.

This is The People of Choice.

The People of Choice are selfish.

The People of Choice kill themselves.

The People of Choice are stupid.

Don't be like The People of Choice.

But maybe they just need to make sure that it's real, that it's not some ill-taste art installation or political protest or television magic trick.

It's very real. And they are all very dead.

The People of Choice have arrived.

This is not how you start a cult, the hard work has already gone into that; the instruction manual has been written.

This is how you grow.

This is how you build a following.

40

BUILD A FOLLOWING

Take social media.

Take these millennials.

Take shitty parenting.

And thank them for making everything so easy.

Calling your daughter 'Princess' is setting her up for failure. If you are telling your child that they can do anything they want to do with their lives, if you are saying that they can be what they want to be when they grow up, you are doing them a disservice.

If they are going to school and a medal is given all the way down to last place, you are killing that child. Not me. How does the kid in first place feel? The one who trained or had some natural ability. The one who tried hard. You've just devalued the reward of that person. The one who could have made the difference, the impact, that your entitled little shit believes they are going to make just because you kept on telling them that they were special.

It's not even their fault.

You send them out into the real world and they are going to struggle to get a job. And they certainly aren't going to get the one they want, the one they feel they deserve. And they'll soon discover that they are not a princess. That they are not special. That they can't have anything they goddamned want just because they goddamned want it.

And there's no prize for last place.

And this is great for any wannabe cult leader because you've managed to burp out a generation that has lower self-esteem than the previous batch of dot com dicks and property pissants.

They just want to feel like they belong to something.

And they do. Because, now, everybody is depressed. Or they're being told they are. They're being convinced. By doctors and writers and celebrities, who are telling them that it's okay. But they're all just treating the symptoms. Putting a plaster on a broken leg.

It's made worse by likes. And thumbs-ups. And smiling faces with tears streaming from the eyes. Because everything is filtered. They sift through the events of their lives, commenting and sharing only what is good. The pictures are clarified and refined. They attempt to decontaminate their existence of all that appears negative or ugly. And they are left to deal with those things themselves.

And they can't.

Because they're not special. And they are ugly. And they are not getting another medal for being shit.

Thank Zuckerberg and Dorsey and Systrom that your child is hanging from a bridge.

But don't forget the impact that you made.

Now take Apple and Samsung and Google and Huawei, who provide the technology that ensures these millennials can always feel awful. They can access that emotion at any time through the addictive, dopamine-inducing, glowing screen inside their pockets.

They've messaged five friends and are waiting for one of them to reply in order to get their next hit. But all of their friendships are superficial. They can't form meaningful relationships with anybody now. That was taken away by the wrong parenting approach and social media and ever-advancing technology.

The very things that were supposed to protect them, nurture them, liberate them, and bring them closer together has only brought them closer to The People of Choice.

While social media can be a tool for spreading motivational quotes and messages, it is also ideal for disseminating hatred and mayhem.

So, the other way that this all helps anybody wanting to get into the business of the cult is that you can spend months, years, planning an event like this. You can be the hard worker putting in the effort, the one who deserves that winner's medal, and, within minutes, it pays off.

In a moment, the world knows who you are.

41

Twelve minutes after the Lovers' brains have been completely starved of oxygen, this happens:

Two Thames River Police boats haul up on the water beneath the nine bodies. They're used to finding corpses that wash down the river fairly frequently. It's not always suicide. It can be murder or drunken stupidity. It can even be accidental. But this is different.

Officers stare upwards at the ghostly mannequins swaying in the wind.

They call them *jumpers*.

Chelsea Bridge is shut down at either end. Local constabulary are guarding the entrance and exit. Two detectives stand between the strings of that nefarious, giant harp created by nine ropes attached to the bridge's suspension cables.

They look down at 225–233.

They look down on them.

They call them *fucking idiots*.

The media are here. National news with the cameras pointing at the spectacle. Reporters manoeuvring through the crowds that have formed, writing shorthand notes and digging for the story.

They call them *victims*.

The crowd call Young Levant *the Man in the Light*.

He already has his own social media page.

Three hundred followers. Eleven thousand by morning.

There's a page for *Chelsea Bridge Jumpers* and *The Chelsea Nine*, too. Some amateur satirist has set up a profile as one of the ropes. He also runs a page as the president's hairstyle and a piece of tissue stuck to a celebrity's shoe. They're not funny. And the latest seems to be in particularly bad taste. But it's getting clicks. So who cares, right?

People call him *sick*.

But he gets the hits, the likes, the exposure.

There's an account for The People of Choice but nobody is following yet. And the legalities and guidelines on social media make it difficult to shut down a private group of paedophiles, let alone unlock the privacy of a personal profile.

Young Levant receives the greatest public attention. Because he is the one revealed. The other eight are shadows. Including a woman who has saved more lives than the ones hanging beside her. Another who has spent more money in the last three months than the couple would have earned in a year.

Young Levant is illuminated. It's deliberate. He has to be seen. He has to be first. He's Beyoncé.

At homes across the country, men, women, pensioners are watching the news as it breaks. It doesn't have to contain much information, entertainment is enough. And the simultaneous death of nine strangers on a major bridge in the nation's capital is entertaining as hell.

They call it *insane*.

They say it's *fucked up*.

They ask *why? Why would someone do that? Why would they do that?*

Nobody has said the word *cult* yet. But they will.

An elderly man sits in his lounge, among the papers and empty beer cans and TV dinner trays.

And he cries at the image on his nineteen-inch screen.

He doesn't say anything.

But he takes in the tableau of those nine dead cult members. He sees the dangling silhouettes. And that *man in the light*.

He calls him *nephew*.

42

And Detective Sergeant Pace has no idea what is happening.

He's on a comfortable sofa. Not talking to Dr Artaud.

His superior stated with confidence that Artaud was the go-to guy. That he had been used countless times for officers dealing with post-traumatic stress. Those men and women who had dragged dead bodies from the underground on 7/7 or searched the carriages at the Potter's Bar crash, amid the never-ending ring of mobile phones as families desperately tried to contact dead relatives that would never pick up, the officers who couldn't deal with what they had seen and experienced, they went to Artaud. Or one of his colleagues.

But Pace doesn't want to speak.

What's he going to say? That bad things always happen around him? That he sees black flames creeping over his walls and ceiling? That, recently, he has been seeing this more and more? That he stayed in contact with a woman from his last case? That he gave her his card and, two weeks after her husband had died, she called him and asked him to come over?

At the bridge, they gasp.

They hold their breath.

They roll their eyes.

In here, it is quiet. Cold. Removed. Pace is uncomfortable. Artaud speaks.

'Detective Pace, as I'm sure you are aware, nothing that you say in this room will go back to the police. I cannot forward particular information. That is between us. Unless you are contemplating an unlawful act or impart some illegality that you are complicit in, which seems unlikely considering your profession.'

And he waits. He doesn't want to give his client too much. Simply build some rapport and then allow the client to fill the silence that is so expertly left to linger.

'Sounds like I could've just gone to confession.'

'Do you have something you wish to confess?'

'No. Of course not.' Pace's answer comes quickly, this time.

'Then I'm sure we will achieve more than five Hail Marys would give you.'

Pace controls the smirk he knows the doctor is hoping for. That moment of lightness that is supposed to take him off his guard so that he starts talking.

'Not a religious man, then, doctor?' And Pace looks around the room for any kind of signifier that Artaud believes in a god. A cross on the wall. A bible among the many books on the shelves. A picture of the doctor with his arm around the Pope.

There's nothing.

The walls are clad in wood, though there are three framed certificates detailing his qualifications. The shelves are filled with psychology texts. There's a well-worn copy of Oliver Sachs' *The Man Who Mistook His Wife for a Hat*, that stands out against the leather-bound volumes. There's not even a picture of his wife or children on the large oak desk, which obscures the lower half of his body.

'I believe in helping people come to terms with their griefs and aggravations, detective.'

Pace allows himself a smirk, this time.

Then Dr Artaud proceeds with a series of inane questions about Pace's sleep patterns and whether he drinks coffee and how much alcohol he takes in each week. Questions that require more than a yes or no but nothing that will demand Pace talks about himself for too long. Artaud's voice is low and slow, and Pace feels his shoulders drop a little because the answers he has to give are not taxing, they're not asking him to delve into the darker recesses of his mind.

It's nothingness.

He is inside a nondescript building on the South Bank, talking about his diet with a stranger. He's doing nothing. And while he is doing nothing, he is missing out on the biggest thing to turn up on a bridge in London since John Christie.

This is not his case.

43

The two detectives on the bridge, standing between the ropes, it's their case. They'll need to work with the people below on the boats, of course, but it's theirs to fuck up.

This is the crime scene:

Nine dead bodies – nobody has checked to see if they are still alive. Eight unseen due to their angle and position within the darkness. One seemingly spot lit from the side of the river. Identifiable only as a white male in his late twenties to early thirties.

Each hanging corpse is wearing an identical black hooded top. The ropes are identical in style though differ in length for each jumper.

On the ground, beneath each rope, is a blue rucksack. Again, identical. Seemingly used to carry the ropes to the destination, which has to have been prearranged.

The bags are empty.

Except the one beneath the rope of the Man in the Light. There's a piece of paper in there that hasn't been torn into small pieces or thrown in a bath tub or set alight on the stove or chewed up and swallowed.

There's a single piece of white, folded paper in that one bag that says:

> We are The People of Choice
> The ones now with courage
> And we choose not to fear
> This is one solution
> It is not the end
> Nor is it the beginning
> There are always more who choose to live
> There is but one certainty

Only two people have been granted access to Chelsea Bridge.

And one of them just said *cult*.

44

The psychiatrist says it's the end of the session and that some decent progress has been made, and Pace is thrilled to leave that giant-cube coffin of a room with a firm handshake from an older man and no idea what progress he could possibly be referring to.

'I can see myself out,' he says, confidently, trying hard not to look as though he is desperate to leave.

'Are you sure?'

'I remember the way, thanks.'

'Fair enough. Don't be startled if you see anyone in the building. Erickson often stays around longer than the others.'

Pace nods.

Artaud nods in reply and sits back down at his desk.

There is nobody else in the building.

The door clicks shut behind him as Pace exits. One down, he tells himself. Keeping the boss happy. A tick in the box.

Over the speed bumps and through the barrier, he finds himself back in the familiarity of the South Bank, parallel to the Thames. There's a little more vibrancy than there was an hour ago. He checks the time on his phone. An hour. Has he lost time somewhere? What did they talk about for that long?

One down.

Pace turns right, passing behind Royal Festival Hall, and continues in that direction. If he'd have turned left, he'd have eventually discovered that parts of the roads were closed off, that something was going on. Something interesting. Sinister.

Detective Sergeant Pace has five sessions left.

So, Detective Sergeant Pace turns right.

This is nothing to do with him; it's not his story.

Detective Sergeant Pace is the man in the dark.

45

STAY ILLUSIVE

And, if you're still interested in running your own cult, you need to think about a number two.

Somebody who believes in your cause wholeheartedly. Who has a similar drive to you. Somebody who will get drunk on power. Who will carry your message.

A person that you can trust to fulfil the requirements of your group's ideology, no matter what you ask of them, no matter how dark or depraved things become.

Somebody that you can throw under the bus when things become too heated. When the net draws in. They take the blame for the sex rituals or child brides or multiple wives or whatever it is that excites you about the lifestyle.

I wanted peace, they wanted guns.

I wanted freedom of sexual expression, they wanted twelve-on-one gangbangs.

Deny to the end.

Take Ma Anand Sheela. Official spokesperson for the Rajneesh 'movement'. She held the press conferences. She appeared on the TV talk shows. At first, she was peaceful, agreeable, yet strong and determined.

Then she didn't agree.

She dropped the peace.

All the while, her guru is sat in the background, allegedly meditating, thinking, teaching about ego and the mind. She gains a reputation for her brutality while the man who preaches about stepping away from a materialistic world buys himself another Rolls-Royce. She is left to deal with the legalities of the formation of their community while he takes more drugs and touches more women with his gnarled, arthritic hands.

And when the shit hits the fan, she is the one who is forced to flee, the one blamed for the poisonings and the deaths. She is the one who went 'off message'. Not the drugged-up, bearded, horny wannabe Gandhi.

She is the one that is excommunicated and imprisoned and forced into exile, while he is allowed to exist a few more years in an opiate-induced haze of pop-psychological ramblings and adolescent fondling.

The fate of the loyal henchman.

As the leader, you need to stay illusive.

Take The Children Of God. David Berg kept himself away from his people. He communicated with a newsletter or comic that he created and distributed to his followers. There was the occasional video reminding them to recruit by flirting, that sex was divine and should be experienced with as many people as possible. That the videos of children stripping or masturbating was beautiful. All the while, he was never there.

If you want true power, if you want to wash everybody's brain, give them a date that the world will end. That way, nothing they do really matters. And you get to decide how long you can play the game.

But, if you want to keep it pure, not look like the sex-starved sociopath that you undoubtedly are, get a number two. Somebody to take the fall when things go south. Because they always do.

And if you're smart enough to start a cult where nobody realises that they are a member until it is too late, then you've probably already realised that you can also have a number two who has no idea they've been given that illustrious job title.

46

Don't confuse him with Young Levant.

Selfish Levant.

Idiot Levant.

His fucking stupid nephew Levant.

He calls his uncle late one evening, sighing out a hello that immediately indicates his frame of mind. Something that has become all too common. Old Levant senses the fight leaving his nephew's body. It's been a struggle for the last few months, years, since his painful orphaning.

They only have each other now.

Old Levant was deep into his daily routine – falling asleep in front of the news – but his nephew's dreary salutation has flicked him to alert.

The old man has received this call before. A few times. He'll have cut himself, fallen off something, crashed his car, or taken too much of something he shouldn't have. But this kind of call hasn't happened for a while now. It seemed he had found some strength. Turned a corner.

Then there's a silence. But it's not awkward. It's usual. Familiar.

'It's almost eleven o' clock.' Old Levant holds the phone away from his ear and coughs.

'Oh, so I can only wonder how my uncle is doing at midday or just before dinner or—'

'It's okay. I'm fine, I'm fine.' He cuts his nephew off. It sounds like he is pushing for an argument, and his uncle is the only one left that he can call to have a fight with, now. But it isn't the case. He wants some reciprocation. Somebody to ask how *he* is doing, how *he* is getting on. He is desperate to tell somebody what is going on inside him; he just doesn't know how to communicate this. So he creates a conflict to give him the courage to get out what's really on his mind.

Old Levant lowers his voice to a whisper, hoping his soporific subtlety will calm and sedate the future Man in the Light. 'I was just sitting in my chair watching the latest headlines. Something about drones stopping flights from Heathrow. Sounds to me like the government want us to look the other way while they do something they shouldn't.'

Young Levant just listens.

'And the latest on those murders. Looks like they caught the woman who did it.' He keeps it general but honest.

'Yeah. I saw that. I thought of you.' A glimmer of the tenderness that used to be there between them appears. Young Levant knows that his old uncle still follows these cases; he associates him with them. He thinks of him.

'Same old, same old, with me.' He switches emphasis. 'How are you getting on, boy?' It doesn't take long to diffuse the tension because the old man knows what his nephew wants. He needs this. Sure, it's a little more of an effort between them, but he is all he has.

'Yeah...' He thinks for a second. 'Yeah...' Another pause. 'Yeah, I'm doing reeeeally well at the moment, actually.' His voice raises in pitch as he attempts to disguise his invention.

'Well, I'm very pleased to hear it.' The old man smiles as he says this, despite talking over the phone, somehow imbuing his falseness with a drop of sincerity.

Of course, he knows his nephew is not really well.

That something is on his mind.

He wants to tell his uncle. What other reason is there to call somebody at this time?

But he doesn't tell him. He doesn't open up. They talk and talk about nothing in particular. The boy raises his tone, he lies, then lies again. His uncle is complicit, going along with it, just as much to blame. This will all, eventually, manifest itself as guilt.

Guilt kills more people in a year than cancer.

Old Levant hits the mute button on his remote control just as the day's sport is rounded up by an attractive thirty-something woman whom he judges to be unqualified based on her appearance. Old dog, no new tricks.

'So, Sunday then?' the uncle confirms with a question.

'Sunday sounds great. See you then.'

But he won't see his uncle then. Sunday obviously doesn't sound great. Because the next day is Friday and he will be busy jumping off a bridge with eight friends from his ignorant cult.

Young Levant, the Man in the Light, will be otherwise engaged on Sunday, lying inside a drawer, on a metal tray with a broken neck. He has made previous arrangements to be a little bit dead on Sunday.

That is self-centred Levant.

That is Young Levant.

His uncle hangs up the phone and allows his heart-rate to slow again, flicking the sound back on to catch the tail-end of a programme he doesn't care about.

The last thing his nephew said to him, the last thing that self-absorbed half-wit uttered was, 'Get some sleep.' Like he cared.

Tonight is going to be the last time Old Levant gets anything close to real sleep, genuine rest. Because when they find those inconsiderate heaps of self-loathing flesh dangling over the Thames, when he realises that the thoughtless, uncaring one sagging on the right-hand side is the fool, Young Levant, there is no time for repose, no opportunity for recovery. All the old man can seek is closure.

Somehow, when he finds out that he has died, his dolt of a nephew truly becomes all that Old Levant has left in the entire world.

His last case.

His final investigation.

47

Artaud leaves shortly after his final patient of the day. He doesn't see Erickson, either. Not working late tonight, after all. He is the only psychiatrist in the office. He locks the doors and leaves. Gets into his Audi. Negotiates the speed bumps. And turns left.

Towards the mayhem.

The pavements are eerily devoid of life for this time of night. But Artaud is not concerned by this. He wants to finish his work, go home, pour a glass of wine, light a cigar and read. It's not too much to ask, surely. To leave the office and not have to drive an extra five miles at a laborious pace. To not go past the bridge he usually takes across the river and drive all the way to Albert Bridge to turn back on himself. To find more irritating cones.

He sees the crowds as he nears Chelsea but he can't see what they are looking at. He doesn't want to. He's been caring about other people all day. He wants to sit. Not talk to another person. For once, not listen.

Dr Artaud wants Châteauneuf Du Pape.

Dr Artaud wants a Cohiba.

Dr Artaud wants Murakami.

Dr Artaud has diversions and circling helicopters and society's morbid urge to stare at death.

Eventually, he arrives at the police station for his debriefing. The bedlam inside far eclipses that which he passed on his elongated journey north of the river.

'What is going on out there?' he asks, after being ushered into the clinically grey office of the equally ashen inspector.

'You haven't heard?'

The doctor shakes his head.

'Bunch of jumpers on Chelsea Bridge. Some kind of suicide pact, it seems. Fucking mayhem. That, out there, that's our pool of witnesses. Fat lot of good it'll do us.'

The doctor looks over his shoulder out of the doorway. There must be twenty of them, he thinks.

There are thirty-two.

'Anyway, you're not here for that. How's our boy? Saying anything?'

There was the whole 'anything you say in this room goes no further' speech but it's bullshit. Artaud's job is to get to the bottom of Detective Sergeant Pace's problems and neuroses. He has been given a specific set of tasks to ensure that the detective is in the right frame of mind to continue his work, to make sure he is not stepping too far over the line.

'He's one of our best, doc. We give him a little leeway, but he can't go too far. Any news on the woman?'

He's referring to Maeve Beauman, a widow whose husband turned out to be a three-time murderer that ended up with a bullet in his chest. Rumour has it, Pace has seen her more than once since the case ended.

'It was the first session. I haven't delved into that matter yet.

I'm just establishing trust. He's cagey, but that doesn't mean he has anything to hide. He doesn't seem overly paranoid. He's weary, of course. He doesn't think he needs this. And perhaps he doesn't. At this point, I don't have any worries about him continuing in his position. This may change as we progress.'

They talk a little longer about Pace, about a former patient with PTSD, who has adapted well and is back to work. They discuss a few nothings.

There's a knock at the door.

'Sorry to interrupt,' he offers. It's one of the detectives from the bridge. The overweight one who wheezed his way around the suicide scene with the grace of a wounded bison.

'No, no, come in,' his superior instructs. The doctor stands up. 'Sergeant Paulson, this is Dr Artaud, psychology expert.'

They shake hands.

'I was just leaving,' the doctor explains, looking awkward.

'Psychology, eh? Maybe you could shed some light on what makes someone do this kind of thing.' Paulson rolls his eyes.

'What kind of thing?'

'These people. Jumping off a bridge together. For what? Some pact? To make a point about what? It screams of cult mentality, doesn't it? What makes people do it? How do you get people to do that kind of thing? It's baffling to me.'

The inspector looks at the doctor like he expects him to posit a theory.

'It's not really my area of expertise, but in order to exert that kind of control over somebody, or a group of people, you would need to be looking for somebody highly intelligent, articulate and methodical. Somebody inspiring, likeable, motivated and, above all, passionate. This person must have the ability to instil credence in their followers, their fellow believers. If such a personality could convince themselves that the words they preach are true, that their own fabrication becomes fact, then an impressionable, suggestible subject will accept what is being said without question and be indoctrinated into a similar line of thinking.'

'I can get my head around that idea, but to get nine people to end their life at the same time, without one of them backing out...'

Dr Artaud take his keys out of his pocket and asks the detective to hold them out in his hand. He does as is requested, screwing his face slightly towards the inspector in confusion.

'Now, as I bring my hand closer to yours, you will begin to feel the keys start to throb within your grasp.' He speaks assertively and directly to Paulson and moves his hand slowly towards the clenched keys.

As the doctor's hand nears Paulson's fist, Paulson senses something and looks at his inspector.

He says that he can feel them pulsing like a heartbeat.

'Thank you, Detective.' He takes his keys back and explains. 'Of course, the keys were not throbbing in your hand. It is a combination of my words telling you that they *definitely* will throb and the pressure of standing in front of your peers and not wanting to look like you are getting something wrong.' Paulson fidgets, displeased with the dissection. 'Part of it is that I have also taken time out of my day to come here and you don't want to embarrass me or make me look stupid.' This salvages some of the detective's pride. 'This is cult thinking in its very simplest form. It's a cheap trick to demonstrate my point and I should apologise for exploiting you like that, but it would have worked on almost anybody for exactly the same reasons.'

'So, for example, if somebody believes they are Jesus, I

mean really and truly believes it, then other people will believe it?'

'That is at completely the other end of the spectrum to this silly key demonstration and would require a great deal more skill than I have just shown. But the principles are the same. Yes. Put someone in the right situation and it is possible, of course.'

'If you could explain that to the thirty people outside this room, it might help,' he almost jokes.

There are thirty-two.

'My work here is done, I'm afraid. I have a bottle of wine and a good book waiting for me at home. Inspector, I shall see you again in a couple of weeks. I'll need two more sessions to make some proper progress with your man, if that works for you?'

'Absolutely. Thanks again for your time.'

Dr Artaud returns to his car and negotiates the slow-moving traffic, though the crowds seem to be dissipating. He looks at the clock on the dashboard; it's later than he wants it to be, he should be supping something French and inhaling something Cuban while ingesting something Japanese by now. He sighs. He was only supposed to give information about the detectives he has been tasked to analyse. *Everybody wants a piece of me*, he thinks.

He kicks his shoes off, walks to the wine rack and takes what he wants. Then he moves to his office, opens the humidor and takes what he wants. His book is already in place on the side table in the lounge beside the lamp, just as he wants.

Dr Artaud does not turn on his television. He doesn't want to know about the thing on the bridge. He doesn't want to think about the people who jumped. He doesn't want to contemplate all of those witnesses or the police investigating the crime.

He has red wine on his teeth, his eyes on the page and a

pungent blue plume of cigar smoke rising two feet in front of his face. It's everything, right now. He is happy.

He's not like those people on the bridge.

The keys would never throb in his hand.

48

234–235

We won't have to say *jump*.

Or count down from three.

We won't even speak.

What are we supposed to do, stop for a chat? Introduce ourselves to one another?

Hey, stranger, hold this rope, there's a good boy. Lovely to meet you. Fancy jumping off this bridge with me? Great. I don't want to die, either. Let's do this.

For now, we wait. In this dismal police station. It was crazy on that train carriage, carnage on the platform, but it's concentrated in here. People are biting at their nails and scratching at their arms.

And we wait. We wait as thirty other people talk to one another about what they saw through that window. As some shy away to a corner and relive it in their mind, hoping their name is not called next because they are not ready to speak about it out loud. Some hoping to get into an even more confined space with the morbidly obese police detective so they can recount their own version of events as quickly as possible then get home or to the bar or to their dealer or to a whore or a fuck buddy.

We wait. As time serves only for the embellishment of testimonies. Witnesses who picture the event in their minds as a movie or television drama and add details that were never even there in order to make it their own, to make it more interesting. Because nine people jumping off a bridge in front of our eyes isn't captivating enough. Because it can't just be their story.

Another status.

Another profile picture.

Another filter.

So, we wait. We wait as the room begins to empty and the noise starts to die down. As the level of shock diminishes and the adrenaline fades. As thirty-two becomes seventeen and that becomes six. And all we can do is recite our own unfortunate event.

The train came to a stop, as it often does. We looked over at an illuminated Chelsea Bridge. Nothing out of the ordinary. We looked around the carriage. May have even seen each other. Couldn't tell you. All we remember are the silhouettes, running towards the edge. They ran at the same time but they fell at slightly different intervals because getting over the barrier was more difficult for some than others.

It was silent.

But almost every person says that they felt the ropes tighten. And they feel as though they heard the necks crack. *And people started screaming on the carriage.*

Then the wait is over.

Thirty people have told their story and are now drinking or fucking or smoking the poison out of their minds. We may do that, too. But we are not like them. We were when we arrived here, disturbed and afraid, but we leave one foot in the door of The People of Choice.

One step closer to Millennium Bridge.
Where we will finally meet.
And make our choice to live.
By having the courage to die.

49

By morning, the Man in the Light has more than twenty thousand followers. There is only one post. A picture. At least the account holder has taken the time to doctor it. A monochrome lynching with a technicolour hero at one end.

This is the world.

Double tap.

Click the heart.

Thumbs up.

And video footage is surfacing. Not from the man with the camera who was on the bridge; he was pointing his curiosity down the river. Nobody caught The People of Choice in the act.

The first grainy, fifteen-second short documentary was directed by a nobody on the carriage opposite. And it doesn't even show the jumpers. It's a shaking *cinema verité* piece that encapsulates a pixelated fear. It's a screaming mess. It's not information. Its purpose is to shock.

Hashtag followback.

And another video file sold to the highest bidder shows the bodies being hauled up to a tent that had been erected on Chelsea Bridge to house the victims.

The news anchors refer to them as a *group*.

The River Police were not prepared for what happened. They're used to pulling bodies from the water. Fishermen have little use for ladders. They couldn't get high enough to loosen the ropes from the top. So the lifeless lumps were carefully pulled back onto the bridge, lifted over the railing they launched their potential from and laid in a marquee before being zipped up and transported away for examination and identification.

It was so unnatural. Slow. Deliberate. Sinister. And somebody stayed around to capture it. And sell it to a tabloid or put it on their YouTube channel. People can't find the time to go for a run or call a relative or text a friend back, but they can wait by a bridge on the way home from work and use up precious megabytes they were saving for the next Selfie Saturday on a dead body being dragged under a tarpaulin shelter.

That guy who created a profile as one of the ropes took down his page before the country woke up to the news footage, realising his momentary lapse in judgement had undermined his previous online success as a satirist.

Maybe it was the outrage. People love to be outraged. Especially when they can hide behind an online persona that is not mirrored in their real lives.

By noon, the BBC has an expert at the desk while viewers are spooning in soup and squeezing salad cream into their sandwiches, and the *group* of nine *victims* are 'displaying a cult mentality, aren't they?'

And the expert explains that 'These people had prearranged to meet at the same time in the same place. They committed the same act. It was planned. They knew what they were doing. They believed in the same things.' The expert repeats with hand gestures and beats between the words, 'They believed in. The. Same. Things.'

Whether it was confirmed or not, the word is out there now.

Along with the usual buzzwords like *terrorists* and *extremists*. But none of that matters. Because the nation's trusted broadcaster and an armchair psychologist have just created *other people*.

Now the nine misunderstood corpses have their label.

And The People of Choice page has a four-year-old status that just received its first *like*.

50

Old Levant thinks about Ergo.

His nephew has an inch-deep ravine in his neck; the rope caught hold of some hair at the back and imbedded it into that ravine that can only be caused by a long-drop hanging, and the old, retired detective is worried about a dog.

Starved of sleep, the old man spent most of the night cleaning his flat and watching reheated stories on the twenty-four-hour news channel.

He lit a candle. Not for the safe passage of his nephew's soul, but for the smell in the living room. An attempt to burn away month-old curry and stale alcohol. The small amount of beer left in the bottom of some of the cans has leaked out of one of the bags onto the carpet that saw its first vacuum in weeks.

You'd think he was decluttering to clear his mind, ready for an investigation of his own, but you'd be wrong. It's for the dog.

The upright cushion on his favourite seat is a different colour to the rest of the sofa, where his back sweats so much. He sits in it, watching that expert pontificate about nine people of whom he has no personal knowledge. And the news anchor thanks him, like he's performed some kind of public service.

He forces his weight forwards and stands up. He hits the television button with the fleshy part of his fist to turn it off and goes into the kitchen. The drawer beneath the one where he keeps his cutlery is filled with tea towels and plastic bags and broken tools and lighters. But, at the back is an unused lunch box containing keys. Spares for the flat, his garage, his bike lock, and the set he had cut after Young Levant last worried him with his mood changes and nihilistic telephone chatter and that three-day disappearance.

Old Levant can't stand the idea of that Alsatian been hungry and alone.

The old man walks down the stairs, two full bags of rubbish in each hand – he's old but he's still strong – and he throws them into a storage cupboard at the bottom, ready to put out on Wednesday night. Then he takes the bus to the ground-floor flat his dead nephew recently cleaned.

Ergo barks excitedly as the key turns in the lock. Like he's hoping his master didn't go through with it.

'Hello, boy,' says the old man, disappointing the dog, confirming that he has been left alone.

He kneels down, strokes the thing, unhooks it from the radiator and fills a bowl with dried food. Ergo eats. He obliges. He knows the dead boy's uncle well enough not to feel threatened.

With the dog pacified, Old Levant picks up the telephone – he can get it cut off tomorrow – and calls the police to inform them that he knows the identity of the Man in the Light.

Then he takes Ergo back to his own flat that still smells like the bins at the back of an Indian restaurant. And he sits in his favourite chair and sweats against the cushion.

51

The newscaster reads out the note from Young Levant's ruck-sack.

It doesn't take long for these things to get out.

'We are The People of Choice
The ones now with courage
And we choose not to fear
This is one solution
It is not the end
Nor is it the beginning
There are always more who choose to live
There is but one certainty'

The letter is displayed on the screen and relayed in perfect received pronunciation, pausing slightly at the end of each line, giving it the gravitas it surely deserves.

That middle-aged, white man furrows his brow on cue and lowers the tone of his voice, feigning concern, remaining detached as he tells the doctors, the poets, the dilettantes, the nobodies, that '...authorities are yet to release the identity of the nine alleged cult members as several are yet to be identified, though family members have been contacted in most instances. The note was found in the rucksack belonging to the Man in the Light.' He says this part so casually, like everyone is referring to the dead young man in that way. One of those catchy marketing phrases that somehow sticks. Like *Yes We Can* or *Got Milk?* or *Brexit*.

'Police are following up leads that suggest he may have been the leader of this small and wayward group...' He trails off. They don't have anything that really constitutes information.

And what they do have appears to be wrong.

Wayward? Maybe. But small?

The online presence of The People of Choice is trending. Their page is getting hit after hit. Click after click. And like after like.

Comments are emerging every minute. Some positive, some inquisitive and some more abusive.

'It's a solid mantra but what are the beliefs behind it? Who is your God?'

'This group is fucking sick. Did they not think about their families?'

Several people write 'hang on...' followed by a laughing face.

But these queries pale in comparison to the number of people asking 'Is there a website? How do you become a member?'

What that newsreader failed to acknowledge was the scale and severity an action like this can have. He insults the organisation when he refers to The People of Choice as *small and wayward*. And, if anybody dared to read the note properly, they would understand that the nine people on the bridge was not a single event. It was not the beginning. Nor will it be the end. They wanted to feel like part of something. And now they are.

It is becoming a *movement* – somebody will call it that in the next two days – and it is bigger than anybody could have imagined.

52

The next day, they're calling it a Kubrick party – something that passes for humour in academia. It's a lecture and interview with a self-confessed cinema expert who has written a book on the film director, followed by a viewing of *Barry Lyndon*.

Some party.

Starts at 19:00. May go on past 23:00.

Ines Dupont is a film lecturer at the Université Bordeaux Montagne. Young, unorthodox, with an encyclopaedic knowledge of the moving image and an off-beat beauty that suggests she fell straight out of a black-and-white movie herself.

It's the kind of party she loves, that she never misses.

During the lunch hour, she hands out leaflets saying that she killed herself after her last lecture. She smiles at the students – some that attend her classes and others that know of her – and they smile back at another of her quirks.

Three hours later, her auditorium is packed and the projector is ready to roll. She shows clips from *Harold and Maude* and *The Death King* and *The Fire Within*. She talks and everybody listens. She asks questions and hands shoot up to enter into a dialogue with her.

It's not just about the films, it's about love and death and the choices we make. It's about the party later and whether or not she will tell the author of the book that she thinks Kubrick is overrated and that Stephen King is right to hate the movie of his book, *The Shining.*

They stare at her, laugh with her, watch the screen and make notes.

She clicks the remote control to move on to the next slide then places it on her desk.

The students read, white font on a black background.

Nous sommes Le Peuple de choix.
Ceux maintenant armés de courage.
Et nous choisissons de ne pas avoir peur.

And before most of them have reached the end of the sentence, Ines Dupont has reached into her top drawer, pulled out a loaded handgun and shot herself in the head.

Roll credits.

53

Outside Stuttgart, in the town of Neckarsulm, Harald Yeoman sits in his beat-up Polo, waiting for all the other cars to leave the Kaufland car park.

He could've parked up in his garage and attached a hosepipe to the exhaust. He could have slowly drifted towards death in a fume-filled haze. But that doesn't always go so well. It doesn't always work. Then you have to explain yourself.

Herr Yeoman reads the newspaper. He starts at the back with the sport and works his way to the front. Borussia Dortmund are looking strong this season. He drinks a carton of apple juice. And he watches as the final employee leaves the building.

Five minutes after the manager has driven away, Harald Yeoman exits his vehicle. He takes the thirty feet of rope that has been lying on the back seat the entire time and he loops it around a sign that tells customers where to place their trolley once they've unpacked their shopping into the boot of their car.

It's night. It's dark. It's cold. His car is still running. The driver's-side window is open. He sits back down, fastens his seatbelt and then threads the other end of the rope through the open window, dropping the loop over his head.

He tightens the noose and takes one look at the passenger seat where he left the folded newspaper. Beneath the old news is his message.

Das ist eine mögliche Lösung.
Es ist weder das Ende.
Noch ist es der Anfang.

He revs the engine twice and looks straight ahead. Then pushes the accelerator into the floor and releases the clutch. The car bursts forwards. The rope starts to unravel. As it reaches its limit, the car is travelling fast enough to tighten around Yeoman's neck and take his head clean off.

The car continues forwards for another twenty feet before coming to a stop. Yeoman is headless in his seat. His face rolling across the concrete outside. His love letter to The People of Choice on the seat next to him.

He'd filled the tank with unleaded the day before.

54

Since the sixties, Sweden has been perceived as having the highest rate of suicide in the world. US President Eisenhower even bleated out this notion in the early part of that decade. And it stuck.

Eventually, a more standardised measurement of this cause of death was introduced internationally, and it was found that Sweden was lacking. Lacking in men and women who were dying at their own hand. In fact, its rate has remained steady over the last decade; twelve people in every hundred thousand die from suicide.

Scandinavia is getting a raw deal about their identity due to some questionable maths and research. Even though we know they earn money and they're happy and their healthcare is heavily subsidised and they look after their elderly citizens. Somehow, a loudmouthed American politician says what he wants and everyone buys into it.

You'll find a good sixty-five countries above Sweden on a list that details a country's suicide rate. Including the US. And a hundred or so that are higher up than places like Denmark and Norway.

And, somehow, dentists received a bum rap, too. Like they're the most depressed profession on earth.

So, when Noah Holmgren, a dentist from Linköping, slits his wrists and sucks down a few lungfuls of nitrous oxide to ease his passing, it could look like a bad joke.

While Swedish people would take this very seriously, the rest of the world may not even notice. Because they think that Swedish dentists must be offing themselves every five minutes. That the population of that country has such poor dental hygiene as a result of this phenomena, the majority are walking around with a smile that looks like a burnt fence. But there's probably not that much smiling, anyway.

The story would have stayed in Linköping. Dr Holmgren would have gone down as one of twelve people in a relatively unknown statistic. But nine people had hung themselves from a bridge in London the day before and, prior to his decision to laugh through his blood loss, Noah Holmgren had written something on the wall of his operating theatre in five-inch lettering.

Det finns alltid fler som väljer att leva.
Bara en sak är säker.

There are always more who choose to live. There is but one certainty.

It's growing.

55

Ergo will get fat.

230 – Doctor would tell you – if she wasn't resting in a metal drawer – that overweight people have overweight pets. They also tend to have overweight children. She'd say that these people usually put it down to genetics or bone density, but it's not that; it's that the modern western diet is one of sugar-filled convenience. It's a culture of bad habits and either insufficient knowledge or nutrition information over-load.

Old Levant is overweight, therefore his new companion will soon follow suit.

He happily chows down on his third bowl of wet food today. Chicken with sweet potato and apple. He's also devoured salmon with sweet potato, and apple and some lamb, again with sweet potato, and cranberry. There is also a bowl of dry pellets in the kitchen to snack on throughout the day. The rest of the day, Ergo has been lying next to his new master.

Old Levant sits in his chair, his back sweat further bleaching the cushion behind him. He has a box of his nephew's paper-work between his feet that he is working through for clues. Any indication that he was part of a suicide cult and anything that may implicate him as the leader of the sect.

The news plays quietly in the background. Old Levant is finding it difficult to concentrate on two things at once. He is also comforting Ergo.

In the background he sees text on the television.

It says *Ludzie z wyboru*.

And Люди выбора.

And *Arbitrio populi*.

Languages from every direction you can travel shouting that they are The People of Choice.

And, though the television is almost muted, Old Levant can hear the shouts, he can hear it getting louder as more voices join the cause.

Then Ergo sees a picture of his former master on the screen, bathed in a light that his friends cannot touch, and he stands up on the chair and begins to bark. He's sad and angry and hopeful. He doesn't understand. But the bark adds to the crescendo of sounds in the old man's head. And it builds.

He sifts through letters that his nephew wrote to his ex-girlfriend but never sent, and some notes to himself. There's a bank statement that shows he had little money but wasn't in any debt.

And Ergo barks loudly and the television says *Mense van keuse.* And the old man finds another envelope in his box of random trinkets. And the colours swell. And the sounds merge into a deep hum. And he does something he hasn't done for more than twenty years.

He blacks out.

56

DEAL IN CERTAINTY

When you're the leader of a cult, when you're killing a lot of people, the key is to focus on the things that you can control.

Take Bordeaux and Neckarsulm and Linköping and mark them down as free marketing. They're building the brand. But you can't control what happens everywhere.

Think locally, act globally. You know this.

Take ten high-school students in Tinley Park, Illinois. Stand them around the centre circle of their sports field. Feel pleased with yourself that all the horrific school shootings have not dented or infringed your rights to keep and bear arms. Give these kids a gun. Each. Have them stand around that circle and hold the gun to the head of the person on their right.

They don't have to say *go*.

Or *pull*.

But they do have to count down from three.

And when they are found slumped around the scarlet-and-gold school logo, crimson clashing with that sacred emblem, you notice that nine of them have a small hole in the left temple and a larger exit wound to the right. But one has a hole in the back of their head where some weakling didn't have the gumption to pull the trigger on their friend and left them with the sight of nine dead peers and the task of choking down on their own barrel.

And this is how you know they are not the real People of Choice.

Because they had one.

Everybody on the bridge was always going to jump.

It is controlled and crafted.

In Sweden, there was no *839 – Dentist*. He was Noah Holmgren.

In France, there was no *621 – Lecturer*. She was Ines Dupont.

So take your Harald Yeomans and your not-future-leaders-of-America and use them for what they are: free publicity; spreading the word, broadening your reach. By having it out there, everywhere, everybody watching, waiting, it keeps you hidden. If you focus on what you control.

None of these people count.
All that counts now is 234–235.
And they're in.
Almost ready.
A little more work to do.
Take a couple of weeks.
Ride the wave.

TWO WEEKS LATER

57

234 – WITNESS

One of the girls he lives with nearly kills herself by accident.

The communal kitchen is on the top floor, the third floor. Seven of them live below. Four on the ground level, himself included, and three on the second, who have slightly larger rooms. He wakes up and heads straight to the kitchen for coffee and a bagel, and his three female housemates are already around the table eating toast and drinking giant mugs of tea.

One of them is reading a magazine article out loud. She is wearing a white T-shirt with a pattern that is obscured by the magazine and a pair of loose, blue cotton shorts. He can't help but stare at her smooth legs and, as she lifts her foot up to rest it on another chair, he catches a glimpse of more than he bargained for before breakfast.

Perhaps she knew he was watching.

He wonders how she got that small bruise just above her knee.

One of the other girls jolts him back to the real world, waving something at him as he pushes down the lever to toast his bagel.

'Sorry, this is yours, I started opening it by accident,' she smiles and hands across a white envelope with his name clearly printed on the outside.

'Oh, right. Thanks. No worries.' He takes the envelope from

her hand; she rejoins the others, who are laughing at the article, and he tries to capture one last look at the pink he saw between that blue cotton and the milky white skin of her legs.

She has no idea how close she came to killing herself.

She could have been next.

What if she'd read that first page?

The kettle boils and he makes himself a cup of instant coffee with cream and two sugars. They call that *regular* where he's from. He spreads a thin layer of butter on the bagels, lashings of cream cheese, and takes it back to his room with the un-opened letter gripped to the bottom of his plate.

'Later, ladies,' he utters over his shoulder, opening the door with his foot.

'Lateeerrrrr,' they respond, exaggerating his American accent and laughing again.

In his dormitory, he places his breakfast on the desk and flicks on his laptop to check emails: his family back west will be asleep for another few hours.

The computer takes a moment to boot up and he swings back on his chair, scanning the room he currently calls home. The pin board he never uses. The walls he is not allowed to affix posters to. The overflowing trash can spilling over with balls of screwed-up essay trials.

He leans left and fingers the curtains apart to see if anyone is outside. The launderette is close and he often watches people trail there with baskets of clothes and bags of sheets. But not today.

Nobody is there.

Just the empty world covered in the grey wash of London.

The laptop makes a tinny tone that says it's awake, and he opens his emails with one hand while reaching for the bagel with the other.

He scrolls. Nothing from his parents or his younger brother. Just junk from websites he has visited and some book recommendations and cheap flights to places he doesn't ever want to visit.

The bagel is finished in a few bites. He pulls the envelope out from beneath the plate. The corner is slightly torn where his housemate mistakenly started to open it.

She was so lucky.

She can choose life to live.

He reads the first page, the four words that tell him that his time has come.

Nothing
Important
Happened
Today

The second page looks exactly like the one he has seen on the news.

The witness screws the notes into tiny paper balls and aims them at the overflowing garbage of lecture notes and discarded ideas. The first one lands on top, and he mockingly punches his fist in the air as if scoring the winning basket.

The second misses. He's supposed to keep that one.

Then he's on his knees picking up spilled papers, placing them with the others, tying a knot in the top of the plastic bag and dropping it from the top of the stairs onto the other rubbish bags below. They'll be collected sometime next week.

He sees his neighbour returning to her room with the magazine tucked under her arm and the form of her buttock in those soft shorts draws his gaze downwards.

She smiles to herself – he sees her ears lift slightly from behind. She knows what she is doing.

And he knows what he must do.

Nothing.

Not act on his impulses.

Not buy what she is selling.

Like any other day.

No point in changing things now.

The only way this day is different from any other is that he will not return to his room after lectures. He won't have the opportunity to read a note from his mother or father or brother. He has to go to a bridge and meet briefly with somebody he has never really seen before and commit himself to something profound.

His last email from home was three days ago and he can't even remember what it said.

58

235 – NOBODY

There's not much to say. His life has been fairly unremarkable.

The best thing he'll ever do is throw himself off a bridge attached to a stranger whom he assumes feels the same way as he does. That they were both affected by what they saw that night.

He wasn't always this way. While most of his friends went off to university to further their academic education, he started out on a measly basic salary trading currency. The company was small, the commissions were substantial and he moved up quickly. He had money, friends, a life. He was somebody.

But The People of Choice are everywhere.

They can get to anyone.

This Nobody wakes up, as he usually does, whenever he wants. No alarm clock or buzzing of a mobile phone. He stares up at the ceiling or sideways at the bedroom door and wills himself to get out from beneath the covers. His eyes are open. He won't go back to sleep.

'Get up, you loser,' he speaks aloud, psychotically, and clenches both fists as though that will adrenaline him into action.

But he remains enveloped by the quilt and the recognition of his own inadequacy.

It's normal for him now.

Regular.

Vanilla.

Blah.

He dreamt of them again last night. For the final time. The image of them dropping, falling, jumping, vaulting, flopping, slipping off the side of the bridge.

Descending.

Cracking.

Ending.

It replays in his head like a deeply scratched vinyl record. No sooner have their necks snapped than they are back on the ledge preparing to leap. And he can't click out of it. He can't wake up. He can't get out of his bed.

In his waking state, they are on his mind. Not replaying their final choice to move on to another state of being. Not their decision to extinguish their existence. But they are there.

Just there.

Always there.

And he sympathises with them. While others were aghast on that train, or screaming in shock at the sight they only wished they could forget, he felt a release of pressure. Like he had nine new friends outside that carriage window.

So, when he reads those four words on the first sheet of paper in the post, it may as well say:

You've.

Won.

The.

Lottery.

But he's not interesting. Not worth talking about. Don't discuss him.

He's not one half of a loveless marriage or a struggling artist, a poet who believes his words are worth hearing or reading. He's not a spoilt little girl with everything in life she could need, pissing away her future, worrying about things that need not be worried about; his values are not a pretence for attention.

He's a guy that was in the wrong place at the wrong time, took the wrong path, wrong road.

He's a Nobody.

Perhaps every act of The People of Choice requires the attendance of a Nobody.

Someone who thinks this is a good idea. Someone who wants to do it.

Until they step up to the edge.

59

It wasn't anything major like the 7/7 bombings in London.

And there were plenty of events in the eighties that were similar. The IRA were bombing Harrods and fast-food restaurants on Oxford Street. More explosions occurred in Hyde Park and Regent's Park during military ceremonies. The Lockerbie plane bomb. The Iranian Embassy siege. Another explosive at a Conservative Party conference in Brighton attended by the prime minister.

But it was none of these.

It was an everyday call-out. 1982, Old Levant – who was a younger Levant, then – and another officer were called out to investigate some railway vandalism and graffiti. It was routine. Nothing to worry about.

But it all happened so quickly.

One moment they were laughing as they walked along the platform, the next, Levant's partner must have slipped or fallen or something, because the old man heard a slap, then a gargling, and before he could react, his friend had been electrocuted and was dead.

And Levant froze.

Then he blacked out.

That was the first time it happened.

It kept happening, though. Every time he got anxious about something or was faced with something he hadn't been completely prepared for, everything went black.

He beat it. It took time and effort but they stopped. Until his nephew threw himself off a bridge and the dog barked incessantly at the television image of his decomposing former master and the newsreader said The People of Choice in five different languages and he found a piece of paper in a box of things he took from Young Levant's flat and it said *225–233* and the old man did the maths and came up with minus eight and associated it with the bridge incident and decided that his idiot nephew wanted to take eight lives with him and the news had suggested that the Man In The Light may have been the ringleader.

And black.

With the dog still barking and the news still humming and his back still sweating.

60

To the public, the nine cult members now have names. The police and the press think that it makes them more real, it provides some kind of attachment. But names are so forgettable. People remember stories and details. It's much easier to remember Ungrateful or Doctor or Lovers.

Poet's parents say things like, 'Oh, he was so creative. He wanted to become a writer. Ever since he was little.' Even his father chips in with the occasional supportive grunt. The mother looks withdrawn. Like she has been crying for weeks. Like a parent who has outlived their child.

They mention their thirty-nine-year marriage but neglect that only two of those years were happy. The father doesn't mention his lack of relationship with the boy or that he found him to be 'a bit of a weirdo'. The mother doesn't speak up about her worry concerning the dead boy's probable sexual deviance but she does help to explain the blue ink all over his body, telling them about the explosion on the bed sheet.

The last thing they want to do is attach strange sexual practices to their son and a cult.

So they lie. To protect his memory. To keep themselves safe.

Ungrateful's father is far more benevolent with the personal information. He tells the authorities that she has found it tough to move on after her mother died. That she has run up a considerable amount of debt trying to find out who she is without a mother.

And that's the part the police dig their teeth into. The money. It makes people so desperate. And desperate people do stupid things like rob a bank or jump off a bridge.

You can tell the parents that care the most, that find it toughest to deal with, because they continue to talk about their dead child like they are still here; in the present tense. Poet's father is more of a past-tense guy.

For those looking on like they are watching their favourite soap opera, it's the Lovers who garner the most empathy but also the most vitriol.

That poor grandmother, having to bury her own child and take care of those two little boys.

How could they do this to her?

How could they just leave their kids like that?

Something must have been seriously wrong for them to take that way out.

And that poor grandmother doesn't want to say anything bad about her own son or her daughter-in-law. She doesn't know for sure that they were struggling, but she had an idea, some intuition. But never did she think it was this bad.

And all their friends are shocked. The Lovers were looked at as paragons of love and commitment. The couples they hung out with all wanted to be like the Lovers; they looked up to them.

Someone says, 'I guess you never really know what goes on behind closed doors.' And while it's with great sadness that they have to deal with the loss of their friends, and they feel terrible for those innocent boys left behind, somewhere within all of them, there is a happiness, a smugness, that the Lovers weren't perfect and their own lives aren't as shit as they once thought.

Take a look at your happiest friend. The one who is always bloody smiling. All the goddamned time. The one who always seems so pleased to see you, even though she saw you on the school run in the morning and has just bumped into you at the supermarket. You know the one, she's got the most friends on social media. There are pictures of her kids and her baking and her crazy nights out. She goes on holiday and takes selfies of her and her husband kissing on the beach. She gets on with her mother. She is sociable, always out having coffee in the day and prosecco at night. She finds time to work out and hashtag her 'fitfam' with a picture of her new leggings.

You think she is blessed. That she leads a charmed life. That she is lucky.

Luckier than you.

You accept it because it is written down. The camera doesn't lie, right?

What if you didn't just accept it as true? What if you dug a little deeper? Maybe you'd see that loads of friends means they are all surface relationships, that the happiest person in the world has nobody to share their deeper emotions with. Perhaps you'd notice something in the family pictures that suggests they are more content with their children than they are with their partner. Or you'd work out that going out so much means the children are often neglected – she's not taking pictures of them fighting or shouting at her and not doing as they're told.

Your happiest friend is lying and you are buying it.

So who's fault is it that you don't understand her guilt at

having an affair? Is it her for not telling the truth to the world, or is it yours for not taking the time to notice and dig a little deeper?

How are you to know what the Doctor feels like when she loses a patient or how one lover deals with his wife's one-time indiscretion? How do we get to the bottom of the Poet's Oedipal complex?

How can we help anyone when so many people are lying?

To themselves.

About themselves.

And now everybody is lying about those nine people who jumped off that bridge. For the same reason they lie about their own life. They don't want you to see the worst in them.

Seeing the worst can mean seeing the truth, seeing the beauty.

It's the only way this is getting cleared up.

61

Detective Sergeant Pace is at his third session.

Detective Sergeant Pace has started to talk.

'And your relationship began to develop into something more personal?'

'That's what they want you to find out, right? Whether I ended up fucking the wife of a suspected murderer? See if I've compromised myself somehow and can't be trusted to do my job properly.'

'That's not something I would have to consider passing on to your superiors, Detective,' Dr Artaud lies. 'I don't believe that would constitute breaking any laws.'

'Look, I didn't even meet her while investigating the case. The first time I saw her was to inform her that her husband was dead. I gave her my card and she called me a couple of weeks later. So it would hardly be a conflict of interest if anything had happened between us, which it didn't.'

He also lies.

It's a pandemic.

Detective Sergeant Pace has three sessions left with Dr Artaud. Three hours to convince him that there is nothing psychologically wrong with him and that he is capable of continuing in his position, that he isn't fragile. Three short hours to avoid talking about those black flames he can't seem to get away from. Three more sit-downs to circumvent any discussion of his paranoia. Or that thing that he thinks is following him.

'It can't be that bad. I'm not sat behind a desk; I'm working a case right now.' Pace pleads a little too forcefully.

'The thing on Chelsea Bridge?'

'No, no. That's nothing to do with me. Mine is a lot less interesting, I'm afraid.'

Artaud crosses out something on his notepad.

'Okay, let's talk some more about where you grew up.'

'Hinton Hollow? Small village in Berkshire. Very typical, I'd say.'

It isn't.

'You know, one of those places where everybody knows everybody.'

That's true.

'There's a real sense of community.'

That, too.

'It was a great place to grow up.'

He lies.

And he can't stop. Because he doesn't want to share that, either. It wasn't his choice to come here. He was made to do it. So he lies about his childhood and the small town he came from.

Artaud listens to the lies and writes down: *Ran away from something. Needed to escape.*

62

234 – WITNESS

This stop, Embankment.

Next stop, death.

Mind the gap.

The witness walks through the underground barriers for the last time. When he free-falls for that split second, when his third vertebrae snaps and his airways are clamped shut, when his life can't even be bothered to flash before his eyes, he still has £16.30 left on his Oyster card.

He walks across the bridge to the South Bank. This is not his side of the river. This is for Nobody.

He stops and looks across the river at a ship called *Wellington* and recalls a drunken, one-way conversation with a guy in a bar lecturing about how *Great Britain is no longer great*. He spoke fondly about ships and bridges and how *we just don't build anything ourselves anymore*.

His welcome to England.

The ship is white. He doesn't know whether it was always like that or it has been painted but it makes him think of his mother and their home and selling their house and how you have to neutralise in order to appeal to a larger market and make it easier to sell. But he still can't remember the last thing he said to her.

Probably *goodbye*.

He hopes it was *I love you*.

He hopes she believed him.

Passing a red phone box, he recalls how his father asked him to send back a photo standing next to one. *Get a picture with one of those double-decker buses, too*, he asked enthusiastically. Of course, this witness obliged and emailed digital copies across the Atlantic. But he can't recollect his father's response. Or the message he sent with them.

He has forgotten his gratitude.

The world has dulled.

This is his grey mile.

He walks by another ship turned into a restaurant turned into a themed Mexican bar turned into a nightclub turned into an insult. The life preserver has been taken from its housing on the wall outside.

From this point on he cannot be saved.

63

235 – NOBODY

One-hundred and eleven steps back from the spot that he will leap from he is blinded by the brightness that edges itself above the tower of the Tate Modern, and it almost snaps him out of the frame of mind to jump and die.

But it doesn't.

He has no choice.

Before he walks up the hill to the mark where his vision is impaired by sunlight rising high above the gallery, a City of London policeman walks past him, swinging a white motorcycle helmet at his side dejectedly, his steps devoid of bounce, his heart omitting passion, his mind elsewhere.

Nothing he can do.

Oh well.

Thanks for not trying.

One minute behind the ignorant, uncaring policeman, this Nobody is stood outside the City of London School watching the gaggle of children emerging from the double doors in their white T-shirts and shorts, embarking on a riverside run in the direction from which he just came. They smile at one another and jostle for position, energised before their daily prescribed session of physical activity.

Unaffected.

Unaware of the things that this nobody witness has seen.

Uncomplicated.

Prior to wrenching his vertebrae and crushing his oesophagus, before the apathetic helmet-swinger. Behind the carefree, uncorrupted school kids, he was counting lampposts. Nine of them. Each offering an opportunity to turn back. To save two lives.

At lamppost nine he is yet to encounter the policeman who could stop him, search him, find a rather long length of rope in his backpack with a noose at either end, locate the suicide note in the zipped pocket.

Make it seem like his job actually means something.

All the nobody notices is another bridge under reconstruction; so many of them are in decay of some kind that it takes away from the beauty of their passing. It detracts from the poignancy of their deaths.

The first time he notices the location on the Millennium Bridge is the moment he ambles past lamppost seven. There are so many people crossing the river from either side but it never enters his mind that this will not work.

Nothing will enter that can send him off course.

The only way to stop himself is to truly give up.

He's no quitter.

No white flag here.

At lamppost six he takes the time to stop and watch two boats cross paths: the Cyclone Clipper and Moon Clipper. They are identical apart from their first names.

The policeman is just ahead, he hasn't seen him yet. The carefree kids with no responsibility other than to have fun and enjoy learning are still putting on their plimsoles before jogging past.

A woman swoops by at the fourth post, overtaking his leisurely amble along the waterfront. She swings one of those hessian shopping bags that supermarkets are encouraging everyone to use now. Bags for life. And they make you feel guilty if you ever forget it and have to ask for a regular plastic carrier bag, like you are the only reason the world is so polluted, you personally contribute the greatest percentage to landfill sites.

Her bag has a picture of a giant poppy on one side so he knows that she has had it since November, maybe a little earlier. There always seems to be some theme to these life bags. Whether Easter or Christmas or an annual charity telethon that the supermarket supports.

Previously, at the second lamppost next to the river, just before the poppy power-walks past Nobody, many paces earlier than his admiration for river vehicles, prior to lifting his head to the view of the place he will drop, crack, engorge, and ahead of the overly joyful adolescents and lethargic officer of the law, his attention is grabbed by a woman.

Her hair is blonde but not naturally, and neither her lips nor her breasts can boast that fact either. She wears pink. Bubble-gum pink. A tracksuit of bubblegum to match her bubblegum bike, bubblegum phone and bubblegum nails. She is not riding the bike, just pushing it as she talks on her phone.

He looks around to see whether anyone else can see this vision of synthetic anti-beauty but nobody seems bothered, perhaps it is mirage. Maybe his eyes are playing tricks on him. He looks over his shoulder but everyone seems to be facing in the opposite direction apart from the smudge of a woman in black swinging a bag in time with her legs, which has a giant poppy painted on its surface.

Beyond where he stands, waiting for the apparent apparition to pass by, his eyes focus back on the jiggling behinds of the overweight joggers who passed him at the first lamppost.

None of these people are linked to him in any way. He's not sure he would have even noticed them on another day. Perhaps they are all here to give him a second chance, a million second chances to just turn back, make this day like any other, when he despairs and he can't yank himself from his cesspit of a bedroom where he constantly relives the nine lives lost on Chelsea Bridge and he moans and he's cynical and everything around him is the problem, not himself.

Everything he sees leads him one hundred and eleven steps onto that bridge, it pulls him there, it thrusts him in the direction of death. They say they are The People of Choice, the ones now with courage but none of them want to die. None of them want to be here.

Leading up to the very first post, before he even digests the things around him, the death site, city police, guiltless children, fake plastic bimbos, Olympic shoppers and lunchtime workout buddies, he takes a moment to heave the rucksack into a more comfortable position on his shoulder.

Under the bridge a sign says *Safety Starts Here*.

64

VICTORY IN NOTORIETY

I'm not in control of these people. This is not a dictatorship. I can't make them do anything they don't want to do. They are free.

This is the kind of thing you end up saying to news reporters after your lawyer has completed their closing remarks and the gagging order has been lifted. It's the kind of thing that people expect from a cult leader.

It's boring, predictable shit.

Take Strong City. Take Michael Travesser, also known as Wayne Bent, also known as the Messiah, also known as the second coming of Christ, also known as inmate 470204. Let this guy show you how not to run a cult.

Every movement starts with a funky notion that people can get behind. You form the group, you talk to them about ideas, they get on board. That's not a cult. It's the community bingo club or monthly weavers meeting.

If you really want to mess thing up, you have to Strong City the fuck out of that Women's Institute jam-of-the-month conference.

Don't tell them that you're God; that would be ridiculous. Maybe just that God can speak through you. That'll get their attention.

'What's he saying, Wayne?'

Stop calling yourself Wayne. That was the name given to you by your Earth parents. No, you are Michael, now. That is what God calls you.

'Michael! Michael! The Lord has named him Michael.'

Get some sub-mental hippie wearing a skirt made out of a curtain to write a song on her guitar called 'Michael, Let Us Be Your Servant'. Give them wine and campfires and a voice to praise you with.

Now give them a date that the world will end. Maybe. Or, better yet, say that God has told you that you have to see your brother's wife in your bedroom. Now fake some kind of seizure that God has induced, which means you just can't resist climbing on top of her and fouling her with your dick. Perhaps you could drop to your knees on the rug for added poignancy. Howl at the moon. Question your Lord. Then sink a few inches into your sister-in-law.

That God, always working in such mysterious ways.

If they accept it. You've got them.

You can start dancing around the compound, naked, whipping your back with long strands of rosemary – the Lord's herb – and your people will sway in time to your hairy, pious ball sack.

Here's the thing: you're ridiculous. And even among the most devout followers, there's going to be someone with an ounce of sense, some brother with a chip on his shoulder about sharing his wife. And they'll leave. And they'll tell a bunch of people. And while you're inviting six virgins to lay with you naked, four of whom are underaged, the authorities are on their way. And before you know it, God has left you to sit in front of a jury while your daughter-niece shows them where you touched her on the doll.

You give *cult* a bad name.

You. Mumbling a bunch of stuff about nothing.

But the line is so thin.

Are the successful cults the ones you have never heard about? Are the best serial killers the ones who have never been caught? Or is the victory in the notoriety, the infamy?

That final number.

You tread so carefully, trying to do what you think is right, what you believe in, but the power does corrupt. And it can make you flashy with the cash or brag at your conquests or grope some teenagers.

Maybe you operated for decades, under the radar, and now you want some recognition for your efforts. Maybe you put on a show. Maybe two. Maybe you want to go out with a bang.

Maybe you tell yourself that the power comes from being known.

Because that's what you want to hear.

And that's what a cult is, right? Telling people what they need to hear.

Also, if nobody knows about you, you can't call yourselves a cult. Because that's the way we get other people.

Without the other people, you're a boot camp. You're buggy fit. You're a mums and toddlers sing-a-long with the bear. You're pensioner's Pilates. You're the tombola at the primary school Easter fete.

It may go against everything you've been taught. The cautionary tales you have taken and digested and pointed at as mistakes; well, they're the mistake that you now have to make for yourself.

Because you don't exist if nobody knows you are there.

65

In Oviedo, Spain, David Mendosa plays his last gig – solo guitar outside a packed wine bar to a captivated crowd. He is paid in cash and has three glasses of Rioja on the house before packing his instrument into the car and driving home.

When he arrives home, he drinks another bottle of something red and picks at those nylon strings with effortless dexterity. Then he goes to bed with a glass of water and bottle full of pills. The wine used to help him sleep, but if he swallows enough of the pills down, he knows the rest will be the best he's ever had.

When his mother discovers him in the morning, she knows what has happened, she knows he is gone, but she shakes him and screams his name and shouts at a God she is about to stop believing in.

She takes the note next to his bed, the one that says he is a person now with courage, who chooses not to fear, and she screws it up. That wasn't her boy. No way. This will go down as an accidental overdose. A kid who took too many sleeping pills.

She is his mother. She'd know if he was depressed. He never said anything.

He was not a member of The People of Choice. He just wanted to feel part of something.

Eighty people listened to him playing the guitar the night before he died and all David Mendosa craved was to be heard.

66

Ergo's scent has bedded itself into the fabric of Old Levant's place, already. Who's to say whether it is better or worse than the stale alcohol and tikka masala? It doesn't matter, there are no visitors.

The news plays. The dog gets stroked. The favourite chair fades a little more under the weight of back sweat being massaged into its cushions. It's the new routine. Ergo seems to have forgotten about Young Levant even if the public are still hanging on to that image of the Man in the Light. Thinking he was the leader.

A narcissist.

Guiltless.

Whatever spin they're putting on it this week.

The smell stops at the threshold of the spare bedroom. Ergo is not allowed in there. That's just for the old man. It's the one room he looks after. It should be the second bedroom but there has never been any need for that. There's not that much need for the first bedroom; he spends most nights on that clammy sofa.

There's a long desk in the centre of the room that's partially covered in paperwork. There's an old laptop that runs slowly to anyone with the latest iPhone, but for the old man, it does exactly what he needs. There's a printer at one end that he uses for his work.

On the wall is a crude, almost childish squiggle that is supposed to represent the rough shape of the River Thames. Where Chelsea Bridge is located, there is a drawing pin. Nine pieces of string spiderweb outwards and each strand is attached to a photo of a dead person. Below each cult member is information. Some have more than others. Young Levant has the most. The Nobodies have the least.

And you'd be forgiven for thinking that this is the work of a retired police detective, looking into the unfortunate death of his nephew, trying to crack the code of who is behind The People of Choice, because it looks exactly like that. It looks like the work of a former professional. Gathering information and evidence. Questioning. Cross-referencing.

Unless you want it to mean something else.

Obsession, maybe.

Planning.

Plotting.

The careful recording of information by a faithful number two.

The next pin to go into the map will be at Millennium Bridge.

The old man will require two pieces of string.

The People of Choice will only need one.

67

She could tell that something wasn't right. Even without talking to her son. Mother's intuition, maybe. Or a firm grasp on a person she had shaped over two decades.

There was a quiet desperation to the emails the family had been receiving. A little surface chat about university and a lot of questions about what was going on back home. She sensed he was holding something back.

Her husband had transferred extra money to try to alleviate any stress that was bringing.

The move to England was supposed to be an experience to remember. Character-building. The kind of thing any parent wants for their child.

'The distance is killing him,' she had said one evening to her husband. 'It's more than homesickness. He's our son and we are having a video conference every two weeks.'

Her despair was less quiet. She'd seen the news about Chelsea Bridge and didn't quite understand how these incidents had already spread to her side of the world, too.

The next day, her husband returned home from work and gave her a plane ticket. 'Pack your bags, I'm driving you to the airport in two hours.'

'Wait. What? No, we can't just...'

'We can just. Now go and throw your clothes and products in the case while I make some coffee.'

She cried. She was smiling hard but crying all the same.

Then she's upstairs with the case on her bed, looking online at the weather in London and packing appropriately. And she's running back downstairs to kiss her husband and thank him again and share some coffee and ask him how his day has been.

And she says, 'I'm so excited.'

And he says, 'It's going to be such a big surprise.'

Then they're at the airport and kissing goodbye at the gate and she's waving her ticket at him and smiling still and he is heading back home for a beer.

And with all that intuition and grasp, a message to say that she was on her way may have brightened the mood of 234 – Witness, but it wouldn't have changed anything.

Then she lands at Heathrow and collects her bag and her

mobile phone provider sends an automatic text to inform her of how much she will be charged for making calls and using data overseas.

Then the icon lights up to tell her that she finally has reception.

Then six missed calls.

Two from the university.

Four from her husband.

68

234–235 – WITNESSES

We don't have to stop moving.

Or speak to one another.

Or arrange the direction we will face.

We just know.

For we are The People of Choice, the ones now with courage.

And we choose not to fear.

It has been fourteen days since our train was delayed, stranded above the water, an inopportune moment to prophesise our own fates.

We watched them jump.

Nine people, the same as us, each of them given the choice between life and death.

Leading the way.

Our journeys are long and solitary. We walk on opposite sides of the Thames, both heading east to Blackfriars Bridge, where our paths cross. We pass each other but there is no need to stop, or converse. We just know.

We trade riverfronts for the final stretch of our journey to give ourselves a different viewpoint; plenty of time still to back out. We each count the steps as we round onto Millennium Bridge, one at the north end, one at the south. This is how we know where to meet.

There are plenty of people around us; many using the bridge to cross to the gallery or cathedral. Enough people will see it. They will experience things in the same way that we did. They could join. They could be next. We are recruiters.

We are everywhere.

It's growing.

We step onto the bridge. Neither will make it to the opposite end.

It is quick and fluid. We do not meet in the centre of the bridge because there are too many obstacles. Steel design flourishes, cables, all hindering our descent. People have tried jumping from this bridge before but the lattice structure around the outside, in the centre, gives them long enough to have a second thought.

We cannot risk that.

So we meet slightly closer to the South Bank, just beyond the mid-point of the bridge.

We count the steps.

One takes one-hundred and eleven.

The other takes one-hundred and three.

This is enough to avoid the main part of the suspension.

We walk, one on the right and one on the left.

One hundred and eleven steps past couples holding hands, seagulls perched on the cables and a mother pushing her small child in the pram while the older child stands on a board attached to the back.

One hundred and three steps past two joggers, a man in a wheelchair and more seagulls resting on the far reaches of the structure, allowing themselves time to relax and dream.

Then we meet.

Ninety-seven steps; I take one end of the rope and place the loop over my head.

One hundred steps; I take the other end from the backpack and hold that loop in my hand; the bag holds the weight and length of the rope. Nobody even notices.

Nobody cares.

One hundred and three steps; I place the loop over his head as he hits the mark.

We don't stop moving.

This is our moment of choice.

Like a choreographed dance move we turn in opposite directions from each other. One facing Southwark Bridge with Tower Bridge looming magnificently in the distance, the other having a view of the scaffolding and tarpaulin-covered Blackfriars.

And we speed towards the edge.

Too spontaneous for a bystander to attempt to intervene.

Too late for us to stop ourselves.

The choice has been made.

The rope is unravelling.

We leap from the rails on either side of the bridge, dropping through a gap between two steel rods, disturbing the resting gulls around us. The rucksack containing the main length of rope is dropped in the centre of the walkway and, as we fall to our fates, the rope springs upwards out of the bag, becoming taut as it wrenches our necks on either side of the structure, instantly transforming us both into nobodies.

There are screams that we do not hear as our vertebrae dislocate, as our brains die and our airways are viced. The line of rope splits the walkway into two sections of equal mayhem and pandemonium. Some Londoners are too busy to stand around and watch, they do not want to be involved, they have their own lives. Many are rooted to the spot in shock. Some turn back from the direction they came, others duck under the rope and continue their journey.

All are afraid of the bag left behind. Some think it could be a bomb; others are fearful of the unknown.

It is empty, almost. Just a sheet of paper with a short note to explain ourselves. Everyone knows what it will say. They've seen the news. They've scrolled through their feeds every hour since the last nine jumped.

The first nine, they think.

And we continue to dangle here, not fulfilling our ambitions or making good on our promises. And we leave behind confusion and resentment for our families as a result of our nefarious act. And we mock the art and religion that bookend our demonstration.

The focus is on us.

Nobody dares to touch the rope, to try to help. They may still have some time to help. Whoever they 'saved' would not have the capacity to shed any light on the cult. But they're not thinking that far ahead. They're thinking of themselves.

There are more than fifty people on Millennium Bridge, and they are frightened. But it's a strange fear. If there was a madman brandishing a weapon, they could fear for their lives. Yet, nothing is happening. Nobody is threatening them. And that scares them.

They should be scared.

Because any one of them could be next.

They'll never know.

And it is almost finished.

He only needs four more.

69

HELP BY KILLING

Take four names and see if they mean anything to you. Anything at all.

Tex Watson.

Susan Atkinson.

Linda Kasabian.

Patricia Krenwinkel.

How many Krenwinkels do you know? You think you'd remember that one, right?

It's midnight in California. The year is 1969. The address is 10050 Cielo Drive, Beverley Hills. Tex Watson climbs the telephone pole and cuts the cables. On the way up the path that leads to the house, he stops an eighteen-year-old student driving away from the property, slashing his hand open with a knife then sinking four bullets into his chest and stomach while the three women hide in the bushes.

They break into the house and massacre four people they don't even know.

Five if you count the unborn child.

And you should.

Another four names: Jay Sebring, Wojciech Frykowski, Abigail Folger and Sharon Tate.

Sebring and Tate are sat on chairs and tied together by their necks. Sebring is shot, left a while, then stabbed seven times to stop his moaning. Frykowski is kicked in the head. When he tries to escape, he is beaten with a gun, shot twice and stabbed fifty-one times. Just to be sure. Folger is only stabbed twenty-eight times, but that'll do the trick, too.

Sharon Tate, the name most people remember, is eight months pregnant and pleading to save her child's life. She'll do anything.

It doesn't help.

They are devils and they are here to do the Devil's work.

She is stabbed sixteen times.

Her blood is used to write *Pig* on the front door of the house as the murderers leave.

It's bloody and brutal. And it changes the landscape of an entire country. Politically and artistically.

Here's the kicker: they were just doing what they were told.

'Totally destroy everyone. As gruesome as you can.'

And Charles Manson, who wasn't in the house on Cielo Drive that night, is eventually tried and charged with several accounts of first-degree murder.

He made them do it.

And they're counted as his kills.

Now take a nineteen-year-old undergraduate. A smart kid. Bilingual kid. Dissatisfied kid. Directionless kid. And show him this atrocity. Let him watch all the videos of Manson. Let him read all the newspaper and magazine articles. Let the idea fester in his sharp but wicked mind.

Manson almost had it right. He had an idea. He had people who believed in him. And he had the other people, the ones who made his way of life into a cult. And he could notch up all those kills without ever having to physically harm anyone himself.

But the notoriety was his endgame. He wanted to be known. He wanted to be famous. And that shit is easy. Blow up a school. Cut up some prostitutes. Drive into a crowd of peaceful protestors.

Manson got what he wanted. But take that nineteen-year-old undergraduate with his ideals and thrust him into a decade of counter-cultural revolution. Make sure that his endgame is to help the world, help as many people as he can. Spark his imagination with a Manson, a Kemper, a Bundy.

Now wait.

Because he is going to do this by killing as many people as he possibly can.

PART TWO
KILLER

70

You can feel it. When somebody jumps off a building and hits the floor, you can feel it.

It's the noise. You don't expect the noise.

You think it'll be a splat. But it's not. You throw a bin liner filled with yoghurt off the roof of a car park, you get a splat. That's the sound. But you don't feel it. A human body: eight pints of blood, a skull, a brain, 206 bones, a heart, intestines, that's a thud. It reverberates through the ground and you feel that in your own chest.

Maybe it's the weight of life.

The burden of existence.

A bag full of yoghurt doesn't have that.

And there's that idea that you die before you even hit the ground. The notion that fear of your imminent death causes shock or a heart attack or asphyxiation. There's no time for that with a 213-foot drop off the top of Tower Bridge. The thing that kills you is decelerating so abruptly as you hit the floor. You weigh more by the time you connect with the concrete. Your cells can rupture. Your aorta can disconnect from your heart. It won't take long until your brain is starved of oxygen.

It's not always messy, either. Injuries are often internal. A movie might have somebody turn to liquid and spatter the on-looking crowds with blood, but the crush of organs can happen on the inside. The cracking of the skull doesn't always mean that your brain dribbles out.

Now multiply that by twenty.

It's worse that they don't all land at the same time.

The Nobodies.

The Teachers.

The Broker.

They drop in a crescendo, like giant hailstones that once had hopes and ideas. The weight as they connect with the floor comes from their experiences. You hear it and feel it because they have loved somebody and fucked a few more and failed exams and had first kisses and watched their grandparents wither and eaten bad sushi.

And hitting the water can have the same effect. It doesn't cushion the fall. From that height, liquid can impact a body in the same way as a solid.

They don't all land on the road. Some hit the Thames.

The Salesperson.

The Fighter.

The Au Pair.

They are The People of Choice. The ones now with courage. And they choose not to fear.

In the middle of the bridge are the last three to go. One whose hip hits the concrete with full force and opens a point in the abdomen that allows an easy escape for part of the large intestine. One who lands, feet first, with a snap of both femurs that sounds like a tree branch breaking in a storm. And one whose *thud* acts as a poignant full stop to the morbid charade. They are the last black lines on a barcode. They are telephone-hold music.

The Shrink.

The Chef.

The Detective.

This is one solution. And it is now the end.

71

DON'T GET SLOPPY

The trick to being a successful serial killer is to not get other people involved.

Because other people have a way of fucking things up.

Take the diminutive Donald Henry Gaskins. Insult him. Call him *Pee Wee*. Stick your thumb out on the side of any highway in North Carolina. And wait. Wait as 110 people are murdered. Many of them hitchhikers. Let him refer to them as *pleasure kills*. See how he gets away with it by working alone.

Now watch as a van breaks down on the side of the road and he is forced to take three lives at once. See how he can't move them on his own. Watch as he calls an old con friend to help. Then brags about his other victims and the graveyard he has for the remains. See how long it takes this associate to roll over when questioned by the authorities.

Take Denis Nilsen. Undone by a local tradesman. See how burning bodies and flushing parts down the toilet is not the best way to dispose of your victims. Because the drains get clogged and you have no choice but to call your plumber. And he has no choice but to call the police when the blockage he finds appears to be caused by human flesh and bone.

Or take Keith Hunter Jesperson – The Happy Face Killer – and let him know that murdering your girlfriend is the stupidest thing you can do. You have to watch out for these other people. They have links to you. They get you caught. Stick to randoms. Don't shoot at politicians or stalk famous actors or off a member of your own family.

There's a reason to choose hobos and prostitutes.

And don't believe that Zodiac Killer hype. Taunting the police is getting other people involved. It gets you found out. DNA will eventually show that this Zodiac guy died or ended up in prison for something else. He didn't outsmart anybody.

Forget the associates, the partners, the girlfriends or boyfriends.

Don't get sloppy.

Don't get caught.

You want to rid the world of more than a few college campus stoners; you have to be creative.

Take Harold Shipman. Doctor Death. Marvel as he uses his knowledge as a general practitioner to administer lethal doses of morphine to his elderly patients and his position within the community as a medical professional to cover up his tracks.

Watch as he works alone, year after year. No ex-cons to snitch on him. No accomplices that can take a deal to deliver his head on a plate.

See how he doesn't have to get rid of the bodies – he makes it look like an accident or natural causes. The victim's families end up paying for a burial or incineration of the evidence. No chance that a plumber or plasterer will come across a hair sample or bone or tooth.

Learn from his thirty-eight-year marriage to one woman. Who he didn't have to kill. Who would never lead the police to their doorstep.

But note his complacency. And his greed. Pay attention to his mistake of trying to steal the inheritance of a victim, forging documents that would leave her estate to him in her will.

Harold, you are a killer.

Not a thief.

Not a forger.

Harold 'Angel of Death' Shipman. With 238 confirmed kills and a further twelve unconfirmed.

Harold 'The Good Doctor' Shipman. Who got greedy. Got sloppy.

Got caught.

Harold Goddamned Shipman: The greatest serial killer of all time.

Until now.

The real trick to being the biggest serial killer in history is to learn from all the other fuck-ups. No accomplice. No dependents. No mistakes.

And the best way to do that is to set up a cult that doesn't really exist.

72

The double-hanging on the Millennium Bridge tips The People of Choice page over 100,000 followers. The majority are based in the UK but believers and haters all over the world are clicking their *like* buttons and joining the discussion.

There have been instances across Europe and North America, Japan and Australia. It's possible for the page administrator to run the figures on how many countries are involved in dialogue about the cult, the same person could respond to some of the messages. Not as themselves, not opening up their identity as the invisible leader, but as the collective voice for The People of Choice.

But that can't happen. The page was set up more than four years ago under a fake account, which is dead and unused. It's not hard to set up an account under a name that isn't real, on a public computer in a cafe or library, then create a page for people to follow and never return again. Never log in from a different Internet location. Never have a sneak peek from your phone.

Just leave it.

Wait.

The Branch Davidians page only has 197 followers. And it's clear who runs it.

The Peoples Temple has 910 followers. That's eight fewer than the amount of people who died in Jonestown.

The Charles Manson Official Music page has up to 15,000 subscribers. Charles, you were better at the guitar than getting away with murder.

Understanding Bundy: 22,000.

Scientology: 662,000.

This is what people are judged on now. This is their impact, their contribution. They all just want to be liked. They want to be followed. Everything is a cult now. Everyone is a leader.

The leader of The People of Choice doesn't care about followers. They are the *other people*. They are there to promote the brand and validate the cult. That's as far as it goes. Other people ruin things. They get in the way.

The only number he cares about is the 238 people that Harold Shipman killed.

After Millennium Bridge, he's only three behind.

73

There's a drawing pin pushed into the Millennium Bridge. Not in the centre, a little closer to the South Bank, that's where they jumped. A piece of red string is wrapped around the pin, one end is fastened to the left, and one to the right. To the right, Old Levant scribbles the word *student*. That's what it said on the news. To left he writes three question marks.

???

He hears Ergo scratching around at the door.

'One second, boy. You know you're not allowed in here.' He speaks fondly, never taking his eyes off the map. It's really coming together. Every victim has a picture rather than a silhouette. Every jumper has a name rather than a number. On the far left there are three photos: Ines Dupont, Harald Yeoman and Noah Holmgren. The three European cases of alleged People of Choice suicides. Beneath that, a circle of teenagers, shot dead in Illinois.

No strings. No attachments.

The old man sits behind his desk, papers strewn across its surface, and he swigs from a can of beer. The last two members came at just the right time. The police would be closing in, uncovering information; it was something else to deal with. More manpower. More brainpower.

He looks at the nine pins on Chelsea Bridge, focusing on that one at the bottom. Where the one in the light was hanging. His mixed-up nephew. And his hand starts to shake. Just a little, but it draws his attention from the wall. Not enough to make him spill any beer but it worries the old man. He takes another shaky swig.

And he looks again at his wall, the faces and names and pins and crudely drawn river crossings. He glances across at the European fans, who have nothing to do with The People of Choice – they're not part of the number – and lastly at the rectangle that represents Tower Bridge.

It's not big enough to fit twenty pins.

His anxiety rises.

He goes to drink, thinking it will calm him. But he blacks out again, hitting the floor with a thud that Ergo feels in his chest.

74

Her classmates described her as quiet, intelligent and conservative. She read law at King's College London on a scholarship, before attending the University of Southern California, where she graduated in photography, fine art and gender studies.

She went on to direct a movie that was her vision of the William Gibson novel *Neuromancer* before settling in California to work as a web developer.

But nobody cares about the finer details of Grace Quek's existence.

They remember that on 19th January, 1995, she called herself Annabelle Chong and laid back as 251 men were filmed fucking her, which was, at the time, the largest gang-bang ever.

Because people really only care about the numbers.

There were nine victims on Chelsea Bridge.

There were two on the Millennium Bridge.

That's eleven People of Choice.

The others that have been reported in America and Cambodia and Estonia and all the other countries this suicide virus has spread to; those people who have cut, hung, shot, jumped then left a note in their native tongue pertaining to the mantra of a cult they believe they have joined, they're nothing to do with the members from London. They're not the same.

But the news organisations seem to care less about the facts than they do about the figures. Because it only took four days before there were more worldwide People of Choice deaths than there were men who had stared into the business end of Annabelle Chong on 19th January, 1995.

The amount of bloody baths and handwritten letters had doubled in the next three days.

The news channels are just waiting for Meeteru Tokuhara to leave the one thousandth note.

And they would have missed the point of The People of Choice entirely.

Just as they failed to realise that Ms Chong's motivation for taking a couple of hundred dicks in one sitting was her desire to challenge gender roles.

75

The police are looking for a ghost.

There is no splinter protruding from the side of any organised religion. They can't find a town hall that is being used for meetings of The People of Choice. But a church doesn't have to be a building. A church is a group of people who believe in the same thing. Like a cult.

Yet, there is no community. The members of this suicide cult are not going around with one another, talking about their plans to die. They meet for the first time moments before their lives end. It's impossible to find a person who is ready to take the leap and stop them before they step over the edge. This is what the police require. Somebody to shed some light. To defect.

Every cult has members who become disillusioned with its practices. They have people who end up leaving. Sometimes, parents escape and leave their children behind. Sometimes the other way round. The genius of The People of Choice is that no member can ever leave because nobody knows they are a member until it is too late.

And where is the compound? Why have they not segregated themselves like a good little cult? Why are they not behaving how they should? Where the fuck are they?

It is a waste of time for the police to look for the leader, because he doesn't exist. There is no point searching for current members, because neither do they. The focus must be on the victims.

Nine from Chelsea Bridge.

Two from the Millennium Bridge.

How are they linked? How did their paths cross? What would make them do this?

Before Dinah Faige became 231 – Ungrateful, she was sweet and caring and studious. And she had a mother. And that mother had a cancer.

And that cancer had a doctor.

And that doctor jumped off Chelsea Bridge two weeks ago.

76

And the police hear Ergo barking as they bang against Old Levant's front door. The old man has awoken on the floor again, the chair tipped over on its side, Heineken spilled. He's worried. He couldn't handle the blackouts the first time around. He's older and more unhealthy now. Physically. Mentally. But he has enough in him to get up off that floor, get out the room – locking the door behind him – stroke his new companion and answer the knocks.

'Sorry about that,' the old man dithers, making himself appear even older.

'Mr Levant?'

'I'm sorry, you are...?'

'The police, Mr Levant. Mind if we come in?' They flash their badges. They didn't need to. Old Levant could tell they were detectives from the cheap crumple of their suits and the black bags beneath their eyes and the scent of coffee and alcohol on their breath.

Ergo barks.

'It's okay, boy. It's okay.' Levant pulls the dog into his leg to reassure him. 'Please take a seat. I just need to fill his bowl. Can I get you anything while I'm in the kitchen?'

They both decline. They stare at the untidy lounge, look at each other, back at the lounge, then walk towards the sofa, where they sit and wait. They can hear the old man pouring food into a bowl. He is mumbling to the dog. At one point they hear him whistle a tune. Then they hear the kettle boiling.

The old man is trying to buy some time. He knows they are here to discuss his nephew, to put some padding on their theory that he was some kind of evil mastermind. He would rather that his nephew was remembered as a follower, a victim, not a cult leader. The quickest way to fame is to kill somebody. The simplest route to infamy is to kill even more. The old man wants his nephew to be forgotten. So he needs to push the focus on to somebody else. If he can.

He returns with a cup of tea and sits in his favourite chair. A few perfunctory exchanges later and they are on to the subject of Young Levant.

'But there have been two more victims. My nephew is dead.'
Old Levant almost pleads. He thought that the Millennium
Bridge incident would clear his nephew's name.

'Often, the legacy can live on a little longer than the leader,
in these cases, Mr Levant.'

'These cases? How many of *these cases* have you worked on?'

'Well...' They falter.

'It's already been two weeks and you're only just getting to
me. The media has been badmouthing my nephew that entire
time. Where the fuck have you been?'

The detectives are put on the back foot at the outburst.

In this situation, it is easy to jump straight back in with an
answer, but the Old Man would pounce on that. So they wait.
Let the old man catch his breath. He's clearly out of shape and
they can smell the drink over the flat's natural dog stench.

The larger detective, Paulson, explains to Old Levant that
the police are not the same as the media. Journalists are pur-
suing one direction while the authorities are looking into other
avenues. The newspapers are seeking blame.

'We are working with the River Police and medical exam-
iners to see if there is any kind of link between the victims. They
may all be victims.'

He goes on to explain that Dinah Faige had crossed paths with
Doctor Alden. He asks the old man whether Young Levant had
ever been to that hospital, whether he had been treated by Alden,
whether a relative had been to see her, whether he, himself, has
any reason to visit that hospital. The detective asks what happened to Young Levant's father. Did the kid have any money
troubles or debts he was finding difficult to pay off? Did he have
a girlfriend? An ex? Did he go to church? Was he member of any
clubs? Had there been a change in his recent behaviour?

No. No. No. No. No. His dad was a deadbeat and disappeared. Not sure about debt but he lived a simple life. He has an ex, doesn't everybody? No church. No clubs, he stayed in mostly. He seemed happier over the last couple of months.

The old man takes Paulson's card. 'In case you think of anything else that might be useful. You know how it works, right?'

Levant nods. He ushers them towards the door, eases them out, locks it behind them and returns to his office.

From the drawer in his desk, he takes out more string. He links Ungrateful to Doctor with a piece of yellow string. With the blue string he forms two lines. One between his nephew and the doctor, and the other between his nephew and the ungrateful woman everyone refers to as Dinah.

Then he looks through the box of items he took from the dead boy's flat because he needs to find out who this ex-girlfriend was.

77

Detective Sergeant Pace sits at Chelsea Bridge, the monolithic power station looming ominously to his right, and he waits for the train to emerge opposite. When it pulls into view, he stands up. The train stops, as it always does, to allow another to leave the station. Pace walks to the edge and looks over at the black ripples beneath.

He looks left at the light that illuminated one of the jumpers. Just a boy. Mixed up in something he probably didn't understand. It's not his case but Pace has looked into it and there's no way the kid was behind it.

It was weeks ago so the bridge is open again and people walk and drive across like everything is normal. If you went to buy a house and found out that the previous owners had been murdered there, it would turn you off, no matter how big the garden was. But nine people died on this bridge and it's almost like it's forgotten because remembering might be an inconvenience.

His mobile phone vibrates in his pocket. He takes it out and looks at the screen. There's no name but he recognises the number. He doesn't want to program it in until everything has blown over.

The train opposite sets off to pull onto the platform.

'Hey,' he answers, looking around over his shoulder, but nobody is there. Nothing is there.

She wants him to come over. Stay the night. He has to explain again that he will, there's only a couple of sessions left and it'll be done. She feigns understanding. She's frustrated. She wants to fuck him. They leave the conversation; this is no time to get into it.

Detective Sergeant Pace needs to get home. He's not even sure why he came to the bridge. It's nothing to do with him. He finished his fourth session with Doctor Artaud and turned right instead of left.

He still won't open up to the therapist, to the idea of therapy, but it's more comfortable now. The time went by quickly this time. Pace can't even remember half the things they discussed. But it certainly wasn't Maeve Beauman or Hinton Hollow or the nagging paranoia that bad things happen wherever he goes.

He can't really remember. But it wasn't any of that.

He doesn't recall but it couldn't have been anything important.

Pace has two sessions left.

Then everything can go back to normal.

78

236–255

There are people everywhere below us.

They don't want to see us die.

They just want to watch us kill ourselves.

Switch the phone to camera. Swipe to video. Upload when ready.

We don't look down. We can't see the crowds, or whether there are already police vans at either end, trying to cordon off the area. It's too late, anyway. It's almost time to jump. Or step over the edge. Or shut our eyes and lean forwards.

We take our cue from the Teacher. People will be hypothesising about her forever. She jumps alone. Then we wait for the scream. There's always a scream. One when she takes flight. Another when she crumples into the concrete.

That's our siren.

That's when we all go. Follow.

Peppering the pavement, the road, denting a car roof, breaking our neck on a bumper, hitting the river and washing away.

All of us.

Doing as we are told.

We are the final People of Choice. The last ones with courage.

Below, they point upwards. They gasp because they think they should. They tap each other on the shoulder and mouth their shock because they're too afraid to speak. They have watched as nine of our people leapt from Chelsea Bridge. They were shocked when it happened again with the two members that cooperated so perfectly on the Millennium Bridge. So they know we are going to jump.

And so do we.

Because we don't want to.

Yet, below, nobody leaves. Why are they waiting around? Nobody is trying to help. Nobody tries to stop us. Negotiate. Talk us off the ledge. Nobody. All these nobodies.

And up here, it's cold. But it's beautiful.

Look at all the lights.

Our fingers are numbing, our heart rate is steady.

We are waiting for the Teacher.

79

Meeteru Tokuhara leaves work at the Nippon Travel Agency exactly on time. She smiles as she says goodbye to her fellow workers. They say they will see her in the morning. She does not answer.

Directly across the road is the Matsue Station ticket office. She has never missed her train.

She has time to wander around the shops, pick up some food for the evening and some toiletries that she doesn't really need but doesn't want to run too low on.

She orders a coffee, sits for three minutes and scrolls through her phone. Pictures of the kids. A couple of texts and a missed call from her husband. She wants to get home but part of her dreads it. Her day doesn't stop just because work is over.

From her handbag, she takes a small pad and a pen. She writes something down, tears the page out and puts it in the shopping bag. She sips her too-hot coffee, blows into it, then stands up, her handbag on one side, her shopping bag on the other. Plenty of time to make the train.

Meeteru Tokuhara waits on the platform, smiling. You can see it on the CCTV footage. As the train nears, she calmly places her handbag on the floor on her left and her shopping bag on the right. She doesn't run. She doesn't panic. She doesn't second-guess.

Meeteru, mother of three, hard worker, smiler, walks calmly to the platform edge, lowers herself onto the track, lies down and shuts her eyes. She doesn't even flinch at the sound of the oncoming locomotive. She does not wince.

The train cuts straight through her neck and shins. Because it was so casual, so slow, so deliberate, nobody tried to stop it. They were confused.

The Japanese police watch the video footage over and over. It's eerie. It's as though she was possessed. They find the note inside her shopping bag with the mantra for The People of Choice.

For the people of the Chūgoku region, it is a tragedy. But there is also a culture of tolerance for a person responsible enough to take their own life.

For The People of Choice, it is a lie.

She is not one of them.

She does not count.

Dupont. Yeoman. Holgren. And now Tokuhara. They're not real. They're not part of this. They're different to every single member of The People of Choice. Because they had a choice.

They are dead because they want to be.

80

230 – DOCTOR & 233 – YOUNG LEVANT

Technically, she is limited to working forty-eight hours in a week. But these hours are averaged out over twenty-six weeks. So, it is possible to, sometimes, work twelve days in a row. Sure, you get the next four or six off to recover, but that doesn't help you when you're in the hospital on a shift that spans half a day and you are supposed to be caring for people with life-threatening illnesses.

Throw in the pressure to work some extra hours that are not recorded and it's a recipe for mistakes. Overlooking a detail on a patient record, accidentally sewing a piece of surgical equipment inside a person when you close them back up. But the simplest of all must be the forgetting; seeing so many people in a week that require your best bedside manner while you float around the wards, not knowing what day it is or whether the sky outside is black or light grey.

The Doctor is energised from a forty-five-minute high-intensity workout, followed by seven minutes of high-intensity masturbation and a protein shake to finish.

Two hours into her rounds and she has spoken to more cancer patients than should be normal, and the natural high from exercising has dissipated.

Another four hours and she is relying on caffeine to pull her through to the second half of her shift. It's night-time but that doesn't mean it's quiet. She is dragged from oncology to help consult on a patient and maybe rule out the possibility of symptoms being caused by a tumour.

And she is pulled aside to assist with some drop-ins and she needs another break already but there are four hours left and the young man she just saw could be any one of a million young men who find it difficult to say what's on their mind but find some release in the cuts they administer to their arms and legs.

And again, she wonders how much she is really helping. Is she preventing anything? Are her reactions even worthwhile?

The mother of the young man is crying outside the ward. She's upset that he's still cutting but also relieved that he's not dead. And the doctor thinks to herself: *If he wanted to die, he could do it. All he's doing now is wasting time and taking up a bed. If you're not going to go through with it, then you should choose to live. And live fully.*

Any guilt she should have felt from such a thought evaporates when the next problem comes hurtling around the corner, and she's back to shrinking tumours and hair loss and lumps in places that there shouldn't be lumps.

Young Levant's mother stops crying and returns to the bed her son should not be taking up and a completely different but equally fatigued doctor tells her to keep a close eye on him but that some therapy might help, too. He knows that the mother isn't listening and the boy will probably be back in a month or so, maybe even in a body bag, but he hands across the leaflet he knows she will not read and he moves on to the next bed.

The next time he sees the boy with all the cuts, he has become the Man in the Light. And he recognises one of the shadows hanging in the picture as a colleague from work, but he can't remember her name, either.

81

233 – YOUNG LEVANT & 232 – POET

The wood on Albert Bridge is rotting. They say it's through the amount of dogs that stop and take a piss as they walk to Battersea Park.

Ergo always stops.

Young Levant lets him. It gives him the opportunity to open his mobile phone with his thumb print and swipe away at something. He tugs at the lead if anybody walks by, pretending to discipline his dog, worried what other people might think. As soon his feet hit grass he lets Ergo run free and stretch his legs.

The boy with all the cuts throws a stick or a tennis ball. In the summer, he tries a frisbee. The dog gets to run around and expend some energy. Sometimes they get as far as the Pump House Gallery before they turn around.

The walk back is always more controlled. Back on the lead and at Young Levant's pace.

This one morning, he's tired. Sometimes it takes everything to get out of the house.

'You mind if I sit here?' Young Levant asks the wispy young man with the scarf and notepad, occupying most of the bench.

'Sorry. Of course.' The Poet pulls some crumpled pages closer to his leg to make room for the stranger.

They don't speak for a few minutes. It's not uncomfortable. Young Levant strokes his best friend and says *well done* for the normal things that dogs do, and they catch their breath and regroup.

The Poet is secretive. Young Levant tries to catch a glimpse of the page but can't make anything out. He looks ahead of the Poet to see what he is staring at.

'Are you an artist?'

'I'm sorry?' The Poet takes his pencil away from the paper and turns it upside down on his lap.

'I mean, are you drawing something? Sketching? Just that we are right near the gallery. I thought you might be an artist.'

'Oh, no. I'm not drawing.' Young Levant expects the stranger to embellish. He doesn't, at first. Then, 'I'm writing.'

'Oh, you're a writer.'

'Well, I wouldn't quite say that. But I am writing.'

'A novel?' he probes.

'Er, no. Nothing so grand, I'm afraid. Poetry.'

'So you're a poet.'

'Again, I'm not sure the title befits my status. But I am writing poetry.'

'If you are sat here on a weekday morning when all the no-bodies are at their desks selling something people don't really need, and you are writing poetry, then I'd call you a poet.'

The Poet fights back a smile. 'That's an interesting viewpoint. And who might you be, stranger?' It's unlike the Poet to be so sociable, but he doesn't feel as awkward as usual.

'There's not really anything interesting about me. I wouldn't want to find myself in one of your poems. Just call me Dog Walker.' With that, he stands up from the bench, wishes the Poet luck, and heads back to the piss-drenched Albert Bridge.

The Poet's mother reads through all the scraps of paper with half-words and scribbles left by her dead son. She even reads the one about the dog walker. But she doesn't think it's any good and she doesn't think it's in any way important because it's not one of the forty-seven she found that were written about her.

No words explain why her boy chose to leave.
Her husband, downstairs, refuses to grieve.

82

240 – FIGHTER

He was tough, there was no doubt about that, but to his daughter, he was gentle and silly and fun and energetic. To that eight-year-old girl, the Fighter was the man who would change the words to songs on the radio to make her laugh as he sang along with her on the school run. He was the guy who would never be quiet; he was whistling or tapping the spoon as he poured her cereal. But her favourite thing about her dad was the way he always made songs up about her on the spot, just to make her smile.

She loved that about him.

It made her sad when this went away.

The day before that white envelope dropped through his door, the Fighter was shaking as he pushed his finger against the doorbell. His daughter had shown no such nervousness. She bolted for the door, overtaking her mother in the hallway. She could see the outline of his athletic frame through the window.

When she opened the door, he was already singing.

His finger was pointed at her as he held out a long, over-drawn *ooooh*. And she knew he was about to launch into her favourite song – the one he'd made up about her being his 'favourite person in the whole, wide world'.

'Hi, Dad,' she said, then hugged him, waiting until he had finished his ditty.

'Hello, sweetheart. Ready to go?'

'Almost.' She let go of him as her mother appeared in the doorway.

She greeted the Fighter with a smile he had almost forgotten then said, 'Go inside and get your shoes and coat on.'

The favourite person in his whole, wide world ran back inside and the Fighter was left on the doorstep with his ex.

'I'm really glad to see you back on your feet.' She sounded genuine.

'It's taken longer than I'd hoped. But things are looking up.'

'She's missed you.' There was something in her sincerity that lead the Fighter to believe that perhaps his daughter wasn't the only one to have missed him. He didn't want to push it. He was only there for the girl.

And he spent the afternoon with her, driving around, running in the park, eating ice-cream before they ate dinner. And that tough guy put her on his shoulders and walked around because he knew she loved being up that high even though she was a little bit scared.

He didn't buy her toys or spend lots of money on her. He just gave her his time and attention and it was all the therapy he would ever need again.

After dropping her back with her mother, he returned to his own home and emailed Doctor Rossi to thank him for all his efforts and instructed that he would no longer be returning to the ERMA offices because Thursdays were, once again, the day he spent with his daughter.

Then he threw on his favourite, grey hooded sweatshirt, jogged to the gym, and threw punches at his shadow for thirty-five minutes.

This was his comeback.
He could have it all.

83

SHUT UP AND LISTEN

The law of attraction suggests that you get back what you put out into the universe.

Take positivity. You look on the bright side of everything, you turn the sourest experience into a chance for learning, you see opportunity where others see failure, and you will attract others like that. And you will attract opportunity for yourself.

This is horse shit.

Just because you've set up an online account where you post motivational posters twice a day, or worse, quotes from people who had the gumption to stand up and be counted, it does not make you an inspirational mentor.

It only works if you really believe it. You can't quote Martin Luther King Jr – 'Love is the only force capable of transforming an enemy into a friend' – then bitch about your kid's teacher or the whore in the playground or your old personal trainer. Because what you really believe in is putting other people down to try to make yourself feel better. And, if all this is to be believed, your negativity is going to magnetise others like that to you.

Without realising, you've become the mean girls. Or guys. And you're surrounded by people like you. They're not adding anything to your life. They're not enriching it in any way.

You've become everyone around you.

You're a nobody now.

Here's something to believe in: shut up. You have nothing important to say.

If you are quiet, if you can shut your own mouth for just five goddamned minutes, you will attract the people who have something they need to talk about.

This is the great power.

This is what connects us.

You can use it to attract a mate, a friend, a business partner, a member of your sports team. Or you can use it to recruit members into the armed forces or your wacky sex cult or you can get them back to your Volkswagen Beetle and smash in their skull with a hammer before sawing off their head as a trophy.

Wisdom is the reward you get for a lifetime of listening when you would have preferred to talk.

84

225–226 – LOVERS

Both of the boys are scared of dogs. So, when they go to the park to play, they stay away from areas where they might get too close to one, or the person walking it.

And the idea of stranger danger has been drilled into them from birth. So, even if they met the most timid man, keeping himself to himself on a bench, doodling away in his spitty little notepad, they know not to speak to him.

She never joined buggy fit or a boot camp or the local bitch 'n' stitch club. The kids were home birthed, without complication. Doulas and midwives are not nobodies.

There was only one time they ventured outside of the protected microcosm they had created.

That's all The People of Choice need.

It's almost midnight on Christmas Eve. The last one they will have before they jump off a bridge. The boys are fast asleep. The stockings are hanging on the bottom of their beds and are now filled. A bite has been taken out of the mince pie and half the carrot has been eaten by a reindeer. The Lovers are wrapping the last few presents and putting them under the tree. They've been drinking.

'Oh, God. Have you seen what Vanessa just posted?' he calls to her in the kitchen.

The post is nine minutes old and already has more than eighty responses. Comments. Crying faces. Angry faces. And selfless offers to help.

He explains that Vanessa was finally sure that her three kids were asleep, so she went out into the garage where she had hidden all of their presents, and it was empty. Somebody had broken in and stolen everything. Her children were going to wake up to the worst Christmas ever.

Then the social-media machine kicks in. That same place where photos of Christmas trees had clogged up everyone's timeline on the first of the month, where even the shiest of people have a megaphonic political voice, where people go to remind themselves that everything is shit, it kicks in. It does what it was designed to do. It brings people together.

Within an hour, Vanessa has more gifts than she had bought in the first place. They may not be everything the kids asked for, but it's better than an empty stocking. Parents who keep a cupboard filled with random toys for when they forget they have accepted a birthday invitation, fill up bags and take them over. A community comes together.

The power it wields is used for good.

While he runs over with two identical Lego sets, she reads Vanessa's post, then scrolls through her private messages and stupidly responds to an advance. It isn't somebody she knows. She thinks it might be funny. But she is intrigued. Not feeling herself.

That's when they get her. That's the moment she is taken out of her world. The one she always wanted.

That's when she killed her family.

You can't tell that everything is perfect for you when everyone around you is telling you that they've got it better.

85

236–255

We emerge from the lift in staggered packs. It costs eight pounds to come up here. That's £160 we have contributed to Tower Bridge, just so that we can throw ourselves off the top.

There are films playing at either end of the walkway. Both in black and white. Both with an English voiceover and English subtitles, though many of the tourists at this attraction are not native London dwellers.

We all are.

We all live here.

We all die here.

Seven people from a previous tour while their time away in front of an old photograph of the bridge at its completion. We don't care about that. We have our eyes on the spiral staircase. A lethargic guardian of the heritage is slumped on a chair near our exit. But he won't be a problem.

It should be harder to get outside.

It will be after today.

Paying patrons hold their cameras and phones up to the glass of the long tunnel, which overlooks London, and snap blurry, grey-washed shots of buildings they do not know the names of. Nobody has realised there are strategically placed shutters that open for taking pictures without your camera focusing on the dust and grime of the windows.

The Teacher talks to the bored guard. She drags him off towards the stairs, asking him questions. He's out of shape, already wheezing a little from the short journey.

He tells her that if she follows the blue line on the floor, it will lead her down into the engine room.

He's distracted.

We make our move.

Several collapsible tables clutter the area around the bottom of the spiral stairway and some unused display flats divide the area off from the public. The Detective takes the fire extinguisher from the wall in case we need it to batter something open, a door we shouldn't pass through, a padlock we have no key for.

We squeeze through a gap in the boards, move up the stairs and emerge at the top. There was no need for the fire extinguisher. It's discarded.

We keep our feet wide for stability on the initial incline of the passageway roof.

We're out.

We line up along the top of the walkway, smothered in London. It isn't long until somebody spots us from below. Us, the ones now with courage. No ropes. No bags. No notes. You know who we are. And we are ready to jump.

As soon as she gets here.

86

People take their phones everywhere. They're glowing in the darkness of cinema screens. God forbid you miss a text message in the ninety minutes your mind gets to wander or escape or you give yourself some time to decompress.

They're everywhere.

Sat at the traffic lights for twenty seconds? Might as well scroll through some messages. You wouldn't want to miss Katy's latest cake creation.

A thirty-second rest period in your exercise class? Quick, Jim has another outspoken political view that you don't want to miss.

Sometimes, you're grateful that some teenager was filming themselves walking along the road and caught someone crashing into the back of your car before driving off. It's useful. Or that picture you took of you with all your girlfriends shows some guy in the background spiking one of your drinks.

Way to go, camera phone.

Or some guy plants his feet outside the pharmacist's on the high street and starts preaching. And you video a portion of his speech. And he says things like:

'Be strong and courageous, for you must go with these people into the land that the Lord swore to their ancestors to give them.'

And, 'There is a way which seemeth right unto a man, but the end thereof are the ways of death.'

Or, 'Who is going to harm you if you are eager to do good? But even if you should suffer for what is right, you are blessed. Do not fear their threats; do not be frightened.'

Somebody heard what was being said and it resonated with

them. Not because they believed it, but because it echoed the mantra of The People of Choice that she had seen on the news so much recently.

She thought about those nine people in Chelsea and the two young men who had just jumped off Millennium Bridge together. All she could hear the preacher say were lines about *choice* and *courage* and *not fearing*.

And she could have alerted the authorities with her concerns and somebody would have gone down to check things out. Instead, she took the footage home and edited it together with music. She added subtitles for every time he said, 'Fear not'. Twelve in all.

Then she uploaded it to The People of Choice page and typed 'LEADER?'.

And waited for the Internet to blow up.

87

FIND A ROLE MODEL

Success is a strange word. What is a successful cult? What is a successful killer? It's about getting from where you are right now to where you want to be. And how you bridge that gap.

You can do that in two ways. You can have your own vision, or you can steal from somebody else and do it better, do it faster.

Either way, you're going to need a role model. Somebody who has done it before that you can learn from. Take their successes and their failures and put them to your own use. To make you better.

If you want to kill more people than anybody that ever lived, you've got to look at the people who have done it before. Their moves will have been documented, they're there for you to see. You have to look at Shipman and Bundy and Nilsen.

You want to start a cult, you must examine Jones and Koresh, you have to understand all the different gods that have been invented for people to follow.

Looking to invest? What would Warren Buffet do? How did he get to where he is now? He didn't do it by sitting around and hoping, waiting for an opportunity.

Victims, followers and money aren't just going to fall into your lap. You have the vision, you just need a strategy. And you can take that from someone who has experienced success in the area that interests you.

Or you could steal.

Take Steve Jobs. A bright visionary. A man with a gift for reducing complicated things to their simplest form, ready for mass consumption. He brought the world the iPod and the iPhone and is attributed with the creation of the computer mouse.

Of course, he didn't invent the mouse. Xerox did, in the seventies. A three-button controller for your computer that cost $300 to make. It was innovative but it was costly. Jobs succeeded by taking that idea, reducing it to one button, meaning he could get it made for $15. He knew where he was and where he wanted to be. He learned from his role model and he took what he wanted.

Still, how hard is it to be successful with computers during the dot-com bubble, or housing around the property boom, or a serial killer in the seventies?

You want a role model, somebody you can really look up to?

Find somebody who became a billionaire during a recession. When your government are pulling all kinds of tricks that alienate segments of society and there are very few jobs, when people are at their most pessimistic – if you can thrive in that time, that is true success.

This world is going to shit. There are a hundred white men who have more money than the rest of the world put together. We are destroying rainforests to graze animals for our consumption because demand outstrips supply when you can buy an entire chicken for less than it costs for a cup of coffee. You can buy a book without breaking a note; only coins needed. And women still don't earn the same as men and men are being judged for loving other men or having darker skin. Still. And everyone wants to take when they should be giving something back.

If you can succeed now, when the world is at its most pessimistic, its most depressed, when you can say *this is not how it has to be*, you are a visionary. A success.

That is The People of Choice.

You can take what has been done, use them as your role models, create your own path. But do not stand on a street corner and preach as though it was your idea. Do not steal from The People of Choice.

You can take the ideas, but the kills will never be yours.

88

At his fifth session with Dr Artaud, Detective Sergeant Pace is going through the motions. Artaud says that he is satisfied with his patient's state of mind and will report that he is now fit to return to his regular duties.

They just have to go through the full six sessions to sign off properly on the paperwork.

The Doctor still makes notes in his pad as they speak. Habit, partially, but also covering all the bases.

'It's insane. How did they come up with the idea to be attached to either end of the same rope?'

'Well, Detective, I'm sure you could Google 'weird deaths' and come up with a hundred other ideas that would eclipse the unfortunate end those young men met.'

'Yes. Quite.'

They talk about the latest People of Choice because Pace opened up and told his shrink that he'd visited Chelsea Bridge after their last session. It's not his case but he feels drawn to it.

Artaud scribbles *fulfilment?* in his notes. He writes *chasing the next high?* beneath that.

The clock moves slowly. They continue to talk about nothing important. Killing time.

He's safe. Five sessions and no talk of Maeve or Samaritans or paranoia or black flames.

Detective Sergeant Pace has one session left.

Detective Sergeant Pace goes home.

Detective Sergeant Pace Googles *weird deaths.*

Just as Artaud told him to.

Volcano, router saw, chainsaw, cobra, molten iron, entombed alive, self-mummification. All these make The People of Choice so vanilla.

The one that stays with him, though, is *the lonely death.*

89

Dinah Faige.

231.

Ungrateful.

She was not the ex-girlfriend of Young Levant. It's a dead end. The old man should cut the string. But he doesn't. It's not confirmed that they're not linked. He's not accepting that. Not yet.

But, then, if Young Levant was not linked to the ungrateful girl, that must prove that he is not the leader of The People of Choice. Perhaps it would be easier to demonstrate that these people were not linked to his nephew, rather than finding the common ground. The old man doesn't have to solve the case – it's not his – he just needs to clear his nephew's name.

So what if he glanced at the Doctor?

Who cares if he rubbed shoulders with one of the Nobodies?

If you can't prove that God exists, you have to show how other people can't prove that He does not.

The police are no further ahead. They've linked Ungrateful to Doctor, and that's it. They chase up on the video of the street preacher but it's like everything else. It's coincidence. Or piggybacking. Or mixing up the real message.

The leader has remained invisible so far; he's not going to suddenly stick his neck out.

Forget how these people tesselate, how they have managed to weave their lives together somehow to meet at that bridge.

Ask a different question.

Why would these people want to kill themselves?

Don't ask how the Lovers may have known the Poet. Ask why a couple would want to hold hands and leap from a bridge with ropes tied around their necks. Ask why a young man with so much life ahead of him would want to jump towards the Thames, knowing he'd never make it into the water. It doesn't matter if he bumped into the Man in the Light once or twice in the park.

And the student on Millennium Bridge, was he homesick? Missing America? His family? Was it triggered by seeing those other nine strangers hang themselves so publicly? The man at the other end of his rope, that nobody, it was the first time they'd ever met. They didn't even see one-another on the train carriage. Or at the police station when they gave their testimony of what happened.

Is ingratitude enough of a reason to end your own life? Is it the millennial curse? Does seeing death every day prepare you for the end? Does it make you less afraid?

They are all members of The People of Choice, but stop looking at them as a group.

And it's not Pace's case, either. He shouldn't care. But he finds himself on another London bridge, staring into the abyss below, trying to understand. Between the sound of the rushing water and people passing by, he hears whispers, words in his mind that he doesn't want to listen to, shadows behind him that he cannot get away from.

Detective Sergeant Pace asks, 'What would make me jump?'

90

Twenty letters need to go out.

So they know to meet at Tower Bridge.

The Nobodies.

The Teacher.

The Broker.

Twenty letters, so they remember to pay their eight pounds to go through the turnstile and up to the top in the lift.

The Salesperson.

The Fighter.

The Au Pair.

Twenty letters so they understand to distract the guard in order to get out on the roof.

The Recruiters.

The Youth Worker.

The Pharmacist.

Twenty letters instructing them to line up along the top of the walkway, and jump to their death in front of crowds of people and officials, who are nowhere near solving this case.

The Human Resources Manager.

The Legal Secretary.

And the Detective.

Twenty white envelopes telling them that they are the latest People of Choice and that nothing important happened today.

91

The problem is that people lie.

Everybody lies.

If your son walks out of the house one day with his wife, leaving you to take care of your grandchildren, then decides to commit suicide, and a police detective asks you whether he was having troubles anywhere, you don't say that they were struggling for money. You give them platitudes about how expensive children are. You manipulate a comment into a half-compliment by saying that they worked hard to ensure that the boys never went without.

'I look after the kids so that they can work. I like doing it.'

Well, they're your responsibility now, grandma.

When you are questioned about their relationship, you don't tell the police that your son confided in you about the affair his wife had. A mistake they were trying to work through. You don't tell them that you started to babysit on a Tuesday evening while they went out for an hour to marriage counselling. You don't mention that. Because you don't want anyone to think badly of your boy. Though they already do after he left those poor kids behind, fucking them up forever, ensuring they'll need some kind of therapy, themselves, somewhere along the line.

'You couldn't find a happier couple. Ask any of their friends. They were great together.'

You're hurting. Your children shouldn't die before you do. That's not how it goes. That's not how it works. You don't want to have to explain the situation to your grandchildren. That's not your job. You're supposed to teach them how to cheat at cards. You're supposed to take them for lunch and ensure that sugar makes up eighty percent of every meal. You're supposed to get them into some kind of hyperactive state then hand them back to be dealt with while you head home for a sherry and a cigarette.

This isn't right.

But you can't say that, can you?

How does it make them look? How does it make you look? You want the kids to think that their parents were happy. They didn't jump off a bridge. They'd never do that. They loved each other and their children too much to do something so stupid, so selfish.

No. It was that bad man who ran the cult. He must have brainwashed them into doing it. Tricked them, somehow.

So you tell the kids that they were perfectly happy.

And you tell the police they were absolutely content.

You tell yourself you're doing the right thing.

But the river authorities are swimming in circles and the detectives you fobbed off are running in circles while The People of Choice dance circles around them.

All because you couldn't give it straight.

If you could have been honest, no filters, you could have said that things were rocky in the marriage. But you still could have saved face by telling the detectives that the Lovers were having counselling because they didn't want to throw their lives away.

You could have given them the address of the ERMA offices and led them straight to Dr Rossi and this could all be over.

You could have prevented twenty people jumping from the top of Tower Bridge.

But you chose to lie.

92

Or you choose to tell the truth, but not the whole truth, and nothing like the truth.

Maybe your wife died a few years back. Some cancerous mass on her brain meant that she didn't always recognise who you were when you visited, and sometimes you'd be visiting a person that you didn't even know. Somebody mean. Spiteful. Abusive. You told yourself that the thing in her skull was pressing on parts of her mind and making her act that way.

Sure, you can forgive her for that but you can't forgive yourself for telling the doctors that you wanted her to die there, not at home. You didn't know who she would be, day-to-day, and couldn't put your daughters through that.

Only you know that you instructed the hospital not to resuscitate her if she crashed again. And it was only a gesture when you agreed that they could cut her brain straight out of her head to examine after death but they couldn't have her heart. A small consolation that something might be discovered that would go on to help others in a similar situation in the future.

Her heart belonged to you and your daughters, though all of your actions demonstrate that you loved her with every bit of your brain.

Then you ploughed everything into those girls and your work and you never allowed yourself to grieve properly, so, when the detectives come knocking, you say that *Dinah took it the worst when her mother passed away*. Like that explains why she would join a suicide cult.

You brush it off like it accounts for everything.

'Did Dinah have any new friends that have come into her life recently?'

'She was out a lot, meeting people. She took it the worst when her mother died.'

'Did Dinah drink a lot or do drugs that you know about?'

'She liked to party, blow off steam. She really did take it the worst when her mother died.'

'Were there any money problems? Did she owe anybody anything?'

'You see, her mum died a couple of years back and she took it quite badly so I've loosened the reins a little on her and I cover her expenses when she gets a little too carried away.'

You downplay your wife's death and it loses its weight, its meaning. So the police look into the drugs and the partying and the spending.

'Sir, was your daughter an ungrateful sack of shit, who walked out one morning to meet with some cult friends and bring London to a standstill by diving off Chelsea Bridge with a rope tied around her skinny little neck?'

You have to say *no*.

You can't admit that. It would be like admitting that you didn't want to see your wife near the end. Or that you prayed for her to be taken away from you. You can't show that your broken heart left you weak and that Dinah following her mother into nothingness has all but killed the man you were. Because you still have to be strong for your other daughter.

Fake it for her, now.

Devalue the passing of the woman you once loved so completely.

You could have shown how much you cared for your daughter by explaining that you had sought out some grief counselling for her. Because you didn't want her to end up like you. Tell the police how far she had come, how well she had been doing, how much she had progressed with her outlook and her breathing exercises and her mindfulness.

Let them know his name. Clear your conscience a little. And allow them to do their job.

'Yes, he was very good. Dr Rossi.'

How difficult was that?

But you don't say any of that.

So you let your wife die, your daughter die and twenty strangers die.

This is what happens when people are given a choice.

93

How about the outright lie?

You watch the detective make a note in his pad when you tell them that your son was a bit of a loner.

'He wasn't weird or unsociable,' you go on. 'He just liked his own company. He wrote poetry, you see. It's something of a solitary profession.' And you smile. Like you're proud of the man he never became.

They ask whether he wrote professionally and you have to say no. And it hurts you because you know what it meant to him, and it scathes a little more because your husband is silently pleased with himself for being right about the kid all along. And part of you wishes that he was the one to have jumped; it could have been your way out.

You can't even remember how you got into this or why you ever loved him. Why can't he show some emotion? Why won't he shed a tear for his son? How does he go on like nothing happened?

Then you feel as though you let your son down by hanging on to him so long. You know why you did it. You were selfish. You couldn't imagine being alone with that man for the rest of your life.

But now that's exactly what has happened, and you have no son. So you are trying to preserve your dignity as much as possible. You're trying to make your boy sound creative and passionate and driven, but the police see him as lonely and awkward and maybe even depressed.

They look around at the dated decor of your lounge and see your husband fidgeting with his newspaper that he is just dying to get back to. And they make another note in their pad. And they look at one another as though they know something you do not.

They ask, 'Was he okay?'

You say, 'What do you mean by that?'

'Well, you often find with these creative types that they need to go to some very dark places. You know, for inspiration? It can often mean they don't feel great about themselves.'

You wonder why your husband has suddenly decided to join the conversation.

'He loved all of that dark and broody stuff. Thought it was all part of the process. Made him feel like a writer, but it wasn't real.'

You tell yourself that he's trying to protect his son but also getting in his daily dig.

'I apologise for being blunt but your son took his own life very recently, so I'm not sure how much of that writerly angst was posing for pictures that weren't being taken. We're trying to get to the bottom of that.' Then it comes. 'He never spoke to a professional about how he felt?'

This is the part where you tell the police *yes*. You let them know that you found a group of therapists and one of them offered counselling sessions on a means-tested basis. That he would work outside his regular paid office hours to do pro-bono sessions if needed. Maybe it was his way of giving something back. Dr Eriksson was a good man, who offered to listen to the Poet whine about his art and his father once a week for a fraction of his usual price.

But you don't want that stigma, do you? That you couldn't parent well enough and your son was in therapy.

So you let your husband chirp up again.

'Headshrinkers are for rich people with more money than

sense. He never needed that. And if he did, we couldn't afford it. All he needed was for someone to like his poems.'

This cuts you. Because you can't understand why he behaved that way to his own son when he clearly understood what the boy needed. And you blame him a little more, which eases your own guilt. It's not all your fault.

But it is your fault that you held information back from the police. And it is your fault that you didn't push back at your husband's lie.

It's your fault that the police are nowhere.

And it's your goddamned fault that twenty people will receive a letter telling them that they're fucked.

94

On the sofa, she hands him a shoebox filled with tin, hand-painted jockeys riding their horses, individually wrapped in kitchen roll.

'Nan, what's this?'

'Nice, ain't they? Reckon they could be worth something.' She says this somehow as a question and a confirmation.

'I don't know. I mean, they look old. So, maybe...'

Her flat was filled with trinkets she'd picked up on her travels or from the market. She loved the market. She'd once shown him a bag of CDs and proudly pronounced, '50p each.' Then nudged her grandson with her arthritic elbow.

'Nan, you don't even have a CD player.'

'I know, but what a bargain.'

It made her happy.

It kept her busy.

'Look at this,' she announces, fishing around beneath some letters on the coffee table. And she gives him another box, this time small but heavy.

Her grandson takes the lid off and looks inside. It's a high-quality paperweight, inscribed with his grandmother's name, her beloved London borough and some words about her work in the community.

'The mayor gave it to me. It was in the papers.'

'The mayor? Wow.' He humours her but part of him is proud of her.

'Yeah. Indian fella, but really nice.' It had taken her fifteen years to warm to the West Indians that had found a home in the East End, but many had become her friends. Now she was annoyed with the Somalians.

This is often how his visits went. He would go around and make her a cup of tea and she would hand him treasures she had discovered. He'd play cards with her. She would cheat. He'd make her something to eat, they'd have another cup of tea and he would leave her, often with a plastic bag of miscellaneous items she thought would bring him some money.

Then she hands him a letter.

'Can you just read that for me, darling, it's from the hospital and I haven't got my glasses.'

Her grandson does as he is told. He reads every line of the letter. Twice. To be certain.

'Nan, this letter is from nine months ago. It says you have cancer and that you probably only have six months to live.'

'I know. I've read it. I didn't know how to tell you.'

She looks well to her grandson. And she has outstayed her welcome according to the doctor's estimate. But he's worried that she's finally telling him because she knows she is going to deteriorate quickly.

She isn't. She has another year in her.

'Can you tell your brother for me?'

He agrees but doesn't want to do it.

Then she says, 'Go over in that corner. There's a banjo. I paid twenty-five quid for it. Gotta be worth double that.'

And when she does die, there are plenty of people from the community at the funeral. West Indians and all. And there are flowers and hymns and tears and she has a name.

But there is another community that she belongs to that nobody knows about. Where she doesn't have a name. She is known only as 139 – Paperweight.

95

IF THEY DON'T WANT TO DIE, THEY HAVE TO

Too many people. That's the problem.

7.7 billion of them.

And they're all so precious.

History tells us that we will be wiped out at some point. We get to start all over again. But, instead of waiting for a flood or a meteor to hit, we are imploding. We are killing ourselves. We are shitting in our own house then sitting around in it and complaining that there's shit in our house.

Some disgruntled world leader could press a shiny red button at any point and wipe out half the world's population. And the people twenty miles underground will be the brightest and the richest. That's who will be left. And maybe they'll emerge from the ground having learned from the mistakes of man. Maybe they'll screw up what we have left.

What they care about is preserving the top. Skimming the foam off the consommé so all that is left is clear. Pure.

The other way is to kick out the dross. Begone with the time-wasters and complainers. The moaners and the outraged. The ones who sit on that sofa and say how hard things are. Who cry because their girlfriend left them for somebody with a full-time job and the only friend they feel they can rely on is a dog. When the hardest thing they have to come to terms with is filling out the returns label for a pair of shoes they bought that pinched.

Daddy doesn't love me.

Daddy loves me too much.

I lost another patient.

And the thing you hear the most is that *nobody would even care if I weren't here.*

Take a gun and bite down on that barrel. Take every pill in the house and wash it down with every millilitre of vodka you can find. Don't take six paracetamol then stick your fingers down your throat. Because that goes against what you have told your therapist. Find the tallest building you can, don't jump off your second-floor balcony.

If you want to die, you can die. There are so many ways.

If you don't really want to die, head over to the ERMA offices. We can help.

We have ropes and rucksacks.

You can't pull the trigger, we will squeeze it.

Big enough to handle, small enough to care.

The US President might be able to squash Cambodia at the turn of a key but this takes focus. To take a specific set of people and erase them from the Earth. One by one. Nine by nine. Twenty at a time. It's a commitment.

Two hundred and fifty-five people is nothing compared to the population of South Korea but it's more than Shipman. And there's nobody around to talk about that nuclear holocaust because they're all gone. There's no legacy to that.

This will live on.

The People of Choice live on.

And this is what you tell them: 'When you get to the edge of the bridge, you just have to ask yourself one thing – *do I really want to die?*' If you do, if you have been sitting in that wooden room pontificating over the intricacies of your existence because you truly believe that you should step away from it, you will click into reality. You will walk away. You can be helped.

If you have been talking about yourself because you like to talk about yourself, because your followers are not listening, because your social-media friends are not responding, taking the bait, because you want to be like everybody else with a problem that isn't really a problem, you will ask yourself that question. And you will realise that you want to live.

You may not understand why, but you will know that you do.

That's when your choice is taken.

That's your trigger.

That is the design.

Here's the trick, they all want to live.

Because we are good at what we do. We help the ones who need it. And we kill the ones who do not.

96

236–255

Tower Bridge looks smaller than it does in the pictures.

It's still a long way down.

It will work.

A woman at the nearest set of traffic lights scratches her backside, thinking that nobody is watching. The usual wave of joggers trot by. Everyone else is a tourist with a camera.

Everyone but us. The People of Choice. All courage and no fear. That's what we say. But we don't mean it. We don't know what we are doing, who we are.

A group of kids on a school trip whizz past us, smelling of fast food and body odour. Then three women with naturally olive-coloured skin head in our direction, wearing sunglasses on this grey London day. They are followed by an Eastern-European family all wearing woollen hats and scarves.

All of them are walking in the wrong direction.

They will miss the show.

The water is less calm at this end of the river. Every part appears to be moving. Every wave has a ripple, every ripple has a crease and every crease a small fold. Three of us will hit the Thames. Maybe break a neck, a leg. Maybe survive the fall but not the current.

In the reception area, we each have to pay and place our bag on the conveyor belt. This is why we don't have ropes this time. Just our bodies. And the way that gravity will ensure our organs continue to move towards the floor even when our ribcages have stopped.

We queue for the lift. Neither of us knowing any of the

others, yet knowing what we have to do. How to get up. How to get out. How to get down.

The doors close inside the lift and it starts its ascent. The man pressing the button offers a few wisecracks and thoughtful figures. He tells the gathering that the passageways we are about to venture across are 140 feet above the Thames.

'It's not that far up, but it's a long way down,' he jokes.

Foreigners laugh at his cue.

We do not.

Domine Derige Nos is etched on parts of the magnificent construction.

Domine Derige Nos.

Lord Direct Us.

We do not need guidance from the Lord.

We know what we are doing.

The final twenty.

We are just waiting for one more.

97

Everyone hates their fucking job. Everyone.

You find some nobody cleaning streets, driving one of those pathetic, little orange road-sweeping machines and you think he's happy that he got up that morning to push your discarded crap away from the kerb? You think he told his careers advisor that this was his dream, when he was at school, not studying hard enough.

It's not just the baristas and shelf-stackers. They're not always the Nobodies.

You think teachers are happy with their shitty pay? You

think their dream of moulding the minds of tomorrow wasn't dashed within that first year when they found out that it's all about funding and results and ditching the kids who would bring your rating down rather than giving them help to raise it up. Ideology crushed.

And now these kids have grown up and they can't handle it. They expect to go into a good job, that they want, without having to try. Everything is instant. So why can't they have a job that's fun and easy with great pay? And they're too good for the menial jobs, right?

They want to get into a position where they can make a difference, make an impact. Just like the teacher that gave up on them wanted to do once. But they're not being taught to think freely.

Learn how to write an essay rather than say something.

So their hearts are in the right place. They want the impact but they haven't been given the tools to do that.

And they fail.

Failure used to be a lesson, something you learn. Now it's the reason to feel depressed and dishevelled and downtrodden. It's the reason that road sweepers and teachers and baristas are taking pills to feel better or talking to some stranger in a wooden room about their bum deal.

It's the reason the Doctor was talking to Dr Milton about her disillusionment. How she wanted to help but she feels ineffectual. And she talks about her dad and how she can't respect him because he spouts platitudes about how Jesus lived his life to a stagnating, dwindling, witless congregation. She wanted to make that same impact that the current batch of ill-educated millennials say they desire. But she works hard for it.

And she doesn't understand it anymore. Working harder and

harder for more and more sick people. More cancer. More diabetes. More heart disease. What's the point? And she's finding
herself increasingly attached to patients who end up in a metal
drawer with relatives wailing in the corridor about the unfair-
ness of it all and the Doctor feels her efforts are futile.

She tells Dr Milton all of this, and he tells her to go to
Chelsea Bridge, wrap a rope around her neck and throw herself
off.

98

And Milton is so bored of Young Levant, wasting energy on
the father that walked out on him. And sick of his agoraphobia.
And the guilt around the neglect of his canine companion,
Ergo, that he takes a couple of sessions to insidiously implant
the seed of an idea in his inferior mind that will eventually lead
him to become the Man in the Light.

Another person of choice.

The 233rd.

Rossi took two of the Nobodies. Erickson took the other.

That's all nine of them.

Artaud was responsible for none.

99

Old Levant inhales. He counts. One, two, three. And exhales.

Just as he was taught all those years ago when the blackouts
first began.

It isn't helping. He has to get out of the flat.

'Come on, boy.' The old man taps his fat thigh and Ergo comes bounding towards him. 'We're going out.' He clips the chain onto Ergo's collar, rubs his back affectionately and they leave.

This is no aimless walk with his new companion; the old man knows exactly where he is going, though he hasn't visited for many years.

You wouldn't know it was there. It's tucked away on the South Bank. Behind the National Theatre. The road is quiet. People jog along the river a hundred yards away but they don't know what's here.

There's a barrier on the left that remains open. A signpost says that the speed limit is 10MpH, and the speed bumps reinforce that. Turn right at the bottom of the road and park outside the first set of doors. Or walk, with your dog, and tie him to one of the lampposts.

London is out of sight.

The brass plaque is etched with the word ERMA, just the same as it was when Old Levant was sent here after seeing his partner electrocuted. Beneath that, four brass buzzers. Each with a name beside them.

Erickson. Told the Lovers to step up to the edge. And one of the Nobodies. The Poet, too.

Rossi. Took on two Nobodies. The Ungrateful one.

Milton. Made the Doctor jump. And Young Levant.

Artaud.

In that order.

The Old Man hits the buzzer.

'Hello, I'm looking for Dr Artaud.'

'Speaking.'

'You probably won't remember me. It has been a long while

but you helped me through a difficult time when I was working for the police.'

Artaud has helped many detectives and constables over the years. But he doesn't forget anybody.

'Your name?'

'Levant.'

The doctor buzzes him in.

100

ESCALATION

Ohio, June 1979. Steven Mark Hicks was hitchhiking his way to a concert. He was eventually picked up but decided to stop off with the driver for some drinks. Several hours of alcohol and music later, Hicks was ready to leave. They'd had a great time. The man who had offered the lift did not want Hicks to leave.

So he stopped it from happening.

He picked up a dumbbell, struck Hicks on the back of the head, then choked him with it while he lay bleeding on the floor.

You're thinking it was a stupid idea for him to go for those drinks. You were thinking it before he was killed.

The world now, we're afraid of hitchhikers and hitchhikers are afraid to get lifts.

It got worse for Hicks after he died.

The driver stood over the dead body and got excited. He dissected the young boy, who was only four days away from his nineteenth birthday, and buried him in the back garden. A few weeks later, the body was unearthed, the flesh dissolved in acid, and the bones smashed into tiny pieces with a sledgehammer. The fragments were scattered around the woods behind the driver's house.

He'd kill another sixteen boys before being caught.

This was Jeffrey Dahmer's first kill. His first. This is where it started. It got so much worse.

That's why everybody gets caught.

Some start by setting fire to insects with the sun and a magnifying glass. It may escalate to slicing the throat of a cat. Perhaps they pick up a hooker and drown her in a river.

Grabbing a hitchhiker from the side of the road and disposing of them as Dahmer did is a great way to never get caught. But if your starting point is ejaculating on a naked dead body, any escalation from that point is going to open you up for capture.

Here's some advice: don't chop off a victim's head. Don't hollow out their skull and keep it as a bowl that you use to store your red liquorice in on the coffee table. Don't be an idiot.

It's almost the end. Here is our beginning.

The People of Choice.

1 – Student.

Take two young men, nearing their twenties. Studying psychology. Thinking they know what they want to do with their lives. One of them wants a degree. The other wants to kill his roommate who wants a degree. He wants something larger.

An impact, right?

They go out and drink. Alcohol plays such a strong role in that first kill. By the time you get to the second one, you realise it never requires courage. You just need to not care.

There's a lot to discuss. Milgram and Elliot and Asch. Ego and personality. Eysenck and Cattell. A drunken, cerebral odyssey that ended back in the dorm room. More wine. A failed homosexual encounter and a late-night bath.

The morning brought hysteria from the room as the man who wanted a degree was found dead in the bathtub by the man who wanted to kill a man who wanted a degree. It looked like suicide.

It wasn't.

And it did not escalate for another 224 victims. (Listed).

It had to build at some point.

And, now, it doesn't matter if we are caught or somebody else takes the blame.

It is over.

The People of Choice have won.

That's the trick.

101

The place hasn't changed at all in thirty years. The wood. The coldness. The lack of personality. The way you know you are in a psychiatrist's office. It's not about making you feel comfortable or safe. It's about remaining critical.

'Please come and sit down, Detective.' Artaud extends an open hand into his office.

'Retired.'

'Of course.'

The old man sits on the couch that faces Dr Artaud's desk.

'I was about to leave, my appointments have finished for the day, Mr Levant. How exactly can I help you? We don't have any time booked in...' He lets it hang.

'I know. I know. I ... I just wasn't sure what to do. You see

... you helped me before. A long time ago. My partner was killed and it triggered a reaction in me. You probably don't remember.'

'Mr Levant. I remember. The shock manifested itself as blackouts, am I correct?' He knows it is correct. He wants to settle the old man. He can feel his anxiety and doesn't want him to black out on the sofa because he has a book, a cigar and a bottle of wine waiting at home.

Old Levant relaxes into the chair and explains about his nephew and the event on Chelsea Bridge and how his condition seems to have re-emerged and he can't deal with it.

'Ah. Well, firstly, I am very sorry for your loss, Mr Levant. It was a terrible incident. I would be happy to discuss this with you when we can find a time that suits both of us. I really have to leave,' he lies. 'I have retained your files, as I do with all the police personnel that I work with. Are you still contactable at the same number and address? It has been some time.'

He is.

Same flat. Same phone number. Same phone.

The old man has never been anywhere or done anything.

'And financially, are there any issues? Rossi and Erickson offer pro-bono work, but I'm sure the police would subsidise you, so that we could continue together, as this is an issue that stems from your time as a detective.'

The Old Man stumbles. 'I do have some money.' He elongates *some*, trying not to give away an idea of how much that might be.

'I am happy to talk to them for you tomorrow and then I will call to arrange something as soon as possible. How does that sound?'

The old man thanks him, sincerely. He didn't really know

what would happen. But he knows that he wants the blackouts to stop.

They talk off the record for ten minutes or so. The Old Man leaves, unties the cold dog from the post and retraces his steps back to his apartment.

Artaud returns to the lonely home that he loves. He opens a bottle of Merlot that he can tolerate, he lights a Cohiba that he adores, and he opens a copy of PG Wodehouse's *The Luck of the Bodkins*, that he is trudging his way through.

He doesn't want to read it but it is on his list of books that he feels he should read before he dies.

He also doesn't want to die.

102

Not everybody walks past.

You hear about it. Some guy climbs out to the edge of Waterloo Bridge and contemplates jumping to his death. There are people making calls or they're late for work or their coffee is getting cold too quickly, and they pass the man by.

The prospective jumper doesn't realise. He's wrapped up in himself and what he intends to do. But, then, somebody stops. And they don't really know what they are doing. They're not a trained negotiator or counsellor.

But they have been a human being for their entire life.

So they say something like, 'It's going to be okay, buddy. Everything is going to be okay.' And those simple words, that interaction is what saves him. It pops the bubble and drags him back from the edge for a moment.

It's a connection.

Maybe he says, 'Let's go for a coffee and we can talk about it.' He doesn't have to do this. He could've carried on with his own journey. He could have ignored the man on the ledge, who was shaking and stuttering towards an early end.

But it took nothing. A moment in time. A moment of kindness and compassion. It was instinct. To care. To not let somebody make the wrong decision. To take a chance.

And that wannabe jumper climbs back over the railings. They don't go for coffee because the police have arrived and they're taking him off. And he doesn't really remember what his saviour looked like or what his name was but he finds him a decade later through a social-media campaign so that he can thank him properly and tell him how his life has turned around because of that one split second that could have gone the other way entirely.

You hear about that.

Or somebody, another man, hops over the barrier at Blackfriars Bridge but, before he even has the chance for contemplation, two other men have grabbed him by his jumper and hauled him to safety. They don't try to talk him down. they don't offer the solace of a herbal tea or motivational platitude. They grab him and save him and hold him down until the police arrive and take him away.

You hear about it.

Then there's the hotel manager whose wife stepped out on him with her personal trainer. He finishes work at a stupid hour and has half a bottle of red wine before stepping over the edge of the bridge at Putney. He hits the freezing cold water and stays under, drawing water into his lungs. He floats to the surface eventually and is dragged out, to be identified by a relieved, adulterous spouse.

You don't hear about this as much.

And you don't hear about the letter he got that morning because he destroyed it before leaving for work.

You don't hear about it because there's no story there.

He's nobody.

84 – Nobody.

103

234 – WITNESS

It's difficult being so far from home. Immersing yourself in a different culture and setting is an interesting and worthwhile experience, but the simple things like being able to talk to your family become more taxing due to time differences. You're alone.

And when simple things become hard, you find that the difficult things are more unlikely to be dealt with properly.

He needed somebody to talk to. It was that simple.

Yes, there was the girl in the shorts, who was definitely teasing him towards an inevitable sexual encounter, but most of their conversations were cloaked in innuendo on account of that tension. And while the lecturers encourage you to speak to them confidentially, if required, they're not like school teachers, they're removed a step. And you're older. It doesn't sit well. It doesn't feel right.

You don't want to be the twenty-something guy who misses his mother. Your friends don't want to hear that. You're sick of waiting around for an email or a text. You're from a different country, so you're unaware of organisations like the Samaritans, who are there to talk, not just save the suicidal.

But your family has money and you receive a generous allowance that gives you the opportunities to experience all that university has to throw at you. You could use some of that money to unburden yourself. You could've paid a prostitute to listen. You don't need guidance, you just need to get it out, have somebody hear what you are saying.

Not yet.

It's not that bad.

What do you have to complain about?

Then, one late afternoon, you're on your way back to campus on the train and it stops and you wait and you look around the carriage and you gaze out of the window and nine people jump off a bridge in front of you and you freak out and you want to go home.

But you can't.

And there's screaming and filming and texting and questions and the train starts to move as though nobody has noticed anything and you're not allowed off the carriage and then you are, and some people get the hell out of there and you wish you had, too.

But you didn't.

And the police come and they ask you what you saw and they say that you have to go to the station to give an official statement and you think you're in shock because you blindly do as they ask and you go to the station and relive the event in your own words and it's recorded and things are written down and at some point in the waiting area you are given the card of a therapist with no real intention to ever use it.

But you do.

You make the choice.

He will listen. That's his job.

Also, he will massage an idea into your mind and you won't even realise. Not until you are triggered into action by seeing those four words on a page that urge you towards the next bridge.

And even though you have no issue with people who choose to go into therapy or analysis – members of your own family have done this to great success – you are different. The reaction of your peers scares you. Everybody wants an edge, to be a little crazy about something, but nobody wants the stigma of self-help.

That's the reason he told nobody about those sessions at the ERMA offices.

In a world where we show everyone pictures of the meals we are about to eat or we share videos of landmark events in our children's lives that should be just for us, where thoughts are our latest status and kindness appears to have lost its currency, it's often the things we don't say that cause most damage.

This young man should never have seen the things that he did, but keeping it secret that he was trying to come to terms with that horrific event strips him of any pity he may have deserved. Not speaking out means others will suffer. He has inadvertently perverted the course of justice. But, then, that's why he was chosen.

104

THERE IS NO RISK

There's a thing about magic tricks: Everybody thinks they want to know how you did it.

It's the same with lies. Everybody thinks they want the truth.

And crime. They want the murder to be solved and the culprit to be caught.

That's what they think.

If you've ever sat through an hour-long TV show or theatre performance by a mentalist, you'll note that it builds. It seems that there are steps throughout that are leading to that final test of an unwittingly compliant volunteer, that all the tests they have undergone have led to one final trial.

There is uncertainty from you as an audience member because part of you believes that something could go wrong; this is the human mind, after all. So complex. So random. So infinitesimally different from person to person that there is a risk it will not go as planned.

There is no risk.

The plan is foolproof.

And that thing you think you want to know, well, you don't. It would ruin it. You don't need to know everything to be satisfied.

Here's the rub. That final trial, that's the trick. That's the money shot. That's the five minutes of joy. Everything that comes before is for show. It's goddamned entertainment. Hell, it all is. But that first part is foreplay.

The trick is the way they get the participant to push a stranger off the roof of a building to save themselves. Or they stand in front of a bullet to protect somebody they don't even know. The bits before, where they're seemingly being implanted with information or they're passing things on the street that they don't see but apparently informs a decision they will make later on, that's all horse shit.

And you don't want to know that.

You could watch a video of a patient on a psychiatrist's couch. The shrink is talking in a slow monotone. And he's dropping in phrases like *nothing important* and *choose not to fear*. It could highlight words like *choice, jump* and *rope*. But just because you see it, does not make it true. This would never happen.

Of course, you have seen a hundred mind readers tell you that mind reading is not real, that it cannot be done, then they go on to seemingly read people's minds.

You say you want the truth, but the truth is often boring. The truth is usually painful.

If you were married to your wife for thirty years and she told you the truth about a dalliance that occurred ten years into your marriage that she immediately regretted and it never happened again and she made sure that she loved you even more for the next two decades, how does that truth make anything better? You don't want that.

You don't want to know why a couple with two innocent boys jump off a bridge together. You don't want to know why a successful and compassionate doctor throws everything away. Because what would that say about you? What would it say about the state of this world?

And you think you want justice. Of course. You want what is right. You want 255 people to be accounted for. You want their families to have closure, to understand that their brothers and mothers were victims. That they were murdered. They did not kill themselves.

They would never do that.

You were right.

Take Bundy. You think people wanted him in a cell each day, talking himself up, getting books written about him and for him? No. They wanted to be outside, in a mob, selling T-shirts and trinkets and chanting at the exact time they knew the executioner was going to plunge a lever or press a button that would send electricity coursing through another human's body until it ceased to work.

They cheered.

They rejoiced in the death of another person.

The murders were solved and the culprit was caught. But that wasn't what they wanted. Knowing how it was done, knowing the truth, it was never enough.

You want to know how to get people to pack it all in and kill themselves, become another member of The People of Choice? You think that will settle the curiosity?

Try this.

Moors murderer, Ian Brady, decided one day that he was not going to eat. He was imprisoned for the murder of five youngsters in the mid-sixties. Then, one day, he decided not to eat. He was going to starve himself to death. A painful and slow way to go. It made the news. It made people talk. Not of justice. Not that he should serve out his life sentence until he dies naturally, suffering a life less lived, a life in solitary. The calls were not for answers to the whereabouts of the victims that had never been found. The ones of which only he knew the location because he had buried them.

People wanted his head.

Let the fucker die. He killed kids. He can starve.

He was evil. So, if he no longer existed, it wasn't real. It's the opposite of how people view God and religion.

And this is humankind.

This is how much they want to know.

This is how they treasure the truth.

This is how dearly they crave justice.
This is why they all jump.

105

Detective Sergeant Pace is buzzed into the ERMA offices for his sixth and final session.

It's the last time he has to trudge up that stairwell and along the wood-clad corridor to Artaud's office. He stops outside the doctor's door and looks around at the other three identical doors. Milton, Rossi and Erickson are all accounted for though he has never seen anyone other than his own psychiatrist, even though Erickson is the one who apparently always works the latest.

He taps on the door four times with his knuckles.

'Come in,' says the kindly voice he recognises from inside.

And Pace pushes into the office.

'Ah, Detective, good evening.' Artaud stands up behind his desk to receive his patient. 'Our final session.' And there's something like a smile on his face, though his mouth doesn't open to show teeth and his lips are hidden behind his beard.

'This is the big one,' Pace jokes. Then he sits down, letting the weight of his torso crash into the upright portion of the chair. 'Let the healing begin.'

Artaud has come to know his patient over the five intimate hours they have spent together. Even that first session, when hardly anything was said. You can really get the measure of a person from the amount of time they can spend not saying anything. It demonstrates discipline and resolve. Pace was no walkover.

'Let me start this final hour by saying that I have already

cleared you. Any concerns your superiors may have had about your ability to function at full capacity in your role seem to be misplaced.'

'I knew that.'

'Quite. Whether you are or are not in some kind of a relationship with a former witness or defendant is inconsequential, really. It is not affecting your outlook. Though I will not be so candid in my report.' He nods as if they have some agreement.

'And this report, I guess I never get to see what you write in that? So you could be stringing me along, right? So I say something stupid in this session.'

'Is there something stupid that you have been holding back on?'

For a moment, Artaud slips back into his role as Pace's therapist.

'No. I'm just checking.'

'I will send my report, along with an invoice, to the police station. You will also receive a letter from me, Detective. I will mail it out tomorrow and it will arrive with you the following day. It's nothing important. But you should read it all the same.'

'So, what do we talk about today, if it's all settled?'

'Anything you want. It's your choice.'

The word rings through Pace's ears as he tries to focus on his therapist's eyes. Behind the older man, on the walls, Pace sees black flames creeping in from the sides. He doesn't want to but instinctively looks over his shoulder. He can't tell Artaud about what he sees. He can't say that he thinks he is being followed. He can't share his darker thoughts that bad things happen around him. And it's not just his job, he knows that. Dr Artaud would incinerate his report and rubber-stamp a new one with the words *delusional paranoia* or something.

'This is still a safe place, Detective. There's no fear of judgement in here. Less so, today.'

No fear.

Pace closes his eyes for a moment and breathes, just as Artaud taught him in week two. When he opens his eyes, the flames have disappeared.

The detective shuts his eyes once more and exhales, ready to talk. His choice. He does not fear. The report is written. What he says today is not important. He opens his eyes again and Artaud is scribbling on his yellow legal pad. He doesn't look at the time on his phone but several minutes have passed that he cannot account for. He worries.

'Breathe, detective. This is not the end. Not yet.'

Pace does as he is told.

'What were we talking about?'

'You said you had visited both bridges even though it is not your case.'

'I did?'

'Yes. Would you like some water?' The doctor moves over to a jug of water on a side cabinet and pours his patient a glass before walking it around to him. 'What is it that so interests you in the case?' He sits back behind his desk and takes the lid off his pen.

'Who isn't interested? The guys running the case are in the middle of a real shitstorm, I tell you. They've got nothing. And bodies are showing up everywhere. Membership has gone global and nobody knows where to look.'

'But you do?'

'Not really. I'll probably just show up at the next bridge, scratching my head like the rest of them.' He takes a sip of water. He has forgotten about the shadows and the flames.

'Another bridge?'

'Come on, Doctor, there's going to be another bridge. And another one after that. Until the person behind this is caught.'

'How can you be so sure?'

'This is how it works. It builds up. More people. More risk. Until somebody fucks up and blows the case wide open. Maybe they taunt the police or they go along to watch somebody die. Eventually, these psychos want to get caught. It's the only way they can stop.'

Artaud makes a note on his pad.

'Wait. What are you writing down there? I thought we were just talking.' Pace is agitated.

'Detective, you will get a chance to read my report.'

Pace leans forwards in his chair. 'How the fuck is anything I just said helping with your report?' He wants to stand up, grab the yellow pad and find the last note his doctor made.

'Please sit back, Detective Pace.' The doctor's voice is so calming. 'I merely noted that you are considering this case and that your critical thinking is in order. You can remain removed from the case. Much as I believe you remained removed from your previous case.'

He lies.

He wrote *The only way they can stop.* Then he circled *stop* three times.

Pace sits back.

Artaud starts to cough. It doesn't stop.

'Is everything okay?' Pace sits forwards. 'Maybe I should get *you* some water.'

The detective stands up and moves over to the cabinet and fills a glass. He places it down on Artaud's desk and catches a glimpse of his yellow legal pad. The doctor takes a sip, thanks Pace, and the detective returns to his seat.

'I really should quit the cigars,' Artaud half jokes. 'I'm too old for that, though.'

Pace is not resting backwards in his chair. He's seen enough. It's over. He has the all-clear. He beat the system. He just wants out.

'Look, I know we have ten minutes left, but it really is a formality, as you say, we could just end it here.'

Artaud stares at Pace and says nothing. Neither of them move. It seems the doctor is scrutinising his patient, looking into him. Eventually, he nods.

'I'll call the station tomorrow and you'll get a letter from me in a couple of days. Get yourself back on a real case.' Artaud stands up and offers his hand. Pace steps towards the desk and shakes it. It isn't until he feels the doctor's grip that he realises how frail the man is. He seems a lot bigger in his position of power.

'I've been thinking about those bridges. How do you find so many people willing to take their own life?'

'It's a condition for anything living to contemplate its own death. It's our one certainty. I think that most people at one point or another have considered what the world would be like without them.'

Pace ponders the statement then asks, 'You think there'll be another bridge?'

'I'm afraid there will be, yes.'

'I have to be there this time.'

'There is no doubt in my mind that you will be, Detective.'

With that, they part ways.

106

Dr Artaud wakes the next day with blood on his pillow. He checks his nose with his hand, then his ears, but there is nothing there. He feels his face and lips for cuts. Nothing. He has to assume he was coughing again in the night. He can smell the cigar on his fingertips.

Totally worth it.

He fixes himself an espresso from the machine in his kitchen and sits at his desk. He opens the laptop and clicks on a document that is open but minimised. And he starts typing. Four pages before he even fidgets in his seat. Somewhere in the middle, his face screws up and he hits the keys a little harder. Angry about something.

Then he reads through, prints, and places the pages on top of a pile of other printed pages lying face down on his desk. He smiles to himself, lights a cigar and slouches back into his seat, watching the smoke rise towards the ceiling. He licks one of the fillings in his mouth, loving the way the toxic fumes make it taste.

Worth it.

It's only 10:00. He has no appointments in his schedule until after noon. With the cigar finished, the doctor turns back to his work. He pulls up Detective Sergeant Pace's file and adds a few lines to the bottom of the report based on their discussion the night before. He feels fairly certain the detective was lying about his relationship but Artaud's brief was to determine his ability to function properly at work. And that was not in doubt. He hits print, folds the report, and seals it in an envelope marked for the police station.

Next he clicks on a shared ERMA file. There are files for each of the shrinks in the organisation. Artaud scrolls through the information he needs on Rossi, Erickson and Milton. He prints. He files. He shuts the laptop. That's enough admin for one day.

He makes another coffee and moves to the lounge. He opens up the Wodehouse novel and settles in for the last couple of chapters.

Artaud needs something different. He doesn't have long left. His last book should carry some weight.

He finishes the last page and sighs.

Not worth it.

And he coughs more blood into a handkerchief.

107

It's not his case.

But he wants it.

By the afternoon, Pace has received the all-clear from his superiors. They explain that it was protocol, a formality. That the stress of such a high-profile case tends to have an effect on the lead detective and with health and safety the way it is now, they had to cover their backs. They have to be more aware of mental health than ever.

Detective Sergeant Pace doesn't care what they say.

Detective Sergeant Pace does not buy their bullshit.

He wants the bridges. He wants The People of Choice. He wants back in.

But all he gets is a *welcome back*.

It's still not his case.

There were three texts on his phone when he woke up, and now she is calling.

'Hey,' he says, as though he hasn't been avoiding her.

'Hey. I've been trying to get hold of you to see how it went.' She sounds genuinely concerned. She wants to ask where the fuck he has been, hasn't he seen her messages? But she bites her tongue.

'How what went?'

'Your last session was yesterday, right?'

'Oh, that. Yes. All finished. Nothing to worry about.' Pace starts to walk away from his desk.

'Well, that's great news.'

Neither of them says anything.

Then Maeve breaks the silence. 'So...' she draws the words out '...come and see me. Tonight. After work. It's been ages. You can tell me all about it. I'll get some wine.'

Pace doesn't answer straight away. He is standing in the doorway, looking around the office, gauging the room. There's the usual bustle of activity but also a feeling of resignation, a slump.

'Tonight?' he answers, eventually.

'Unless you have other plans...'

'No. No other plans. Of course not. It's not like they're throwing big cases at me right away. I should be done by seven and I'll swing by.'

It's not exactly the response Maeve was hoping for. Swing by? Is that it? But she smiles through it.

'Great. I'll grab some food, too.'

That will stop it from being just a swing-by.

'See you then.' And he ends the call.

Detective Sergeant Pace has cases assigned to him that he is yet to complete. Boring stuff. Everyday misdemeanours. He has five hours until he's supposed to visit Maeve. His bosses have loosened the leash now they have Artaud's report; their focus is elsewhere. That's plenty of time for Pace to start looking into The People of Choice. Because Paulson is fucking it up. He's nowhere.

Pace switches his phone to silent and puts it back into his pocket. He returns to his desk, logs in to the computer and pulls up anything he can access concerning the People of Choice case.

He gets to work, waiting for Paulson to waddle his fat arse in.

Within minutes, one word has popped out of the files more than any other.

Levant.

108

Nothing important did happen today.

There is no news of another People of Choice incident from any corner of the globe. It's governmental who-can-piss-highest-up-the-wall hogwash. It's a European footballer scoring a hat-trick in the quarter finals. It's an annual televised charity tele-thon. A celebrity break-up. A reality star punch-up. Another storm on the way.

The number of followers on the People of Choice social media page has stagnated. For every person that joins, another will leave.

Some actor that made a decent film a couple of decades ago has died and everybody seems terribly upset about it, though they haven't thought about him once in the last five years. A million statuses say *RIP* like he's logged straight onto the In-ternet from whatever lies beyond this mortal realm.

People are too afraid to just think, *Oh, that's a bit sad. I remember him in that film when I was a kid.* They have to be devastated. And they have to let everybody know how overcome they feel. So they can be part of the club.

Everything is amplified.

You think your child was sweet as a singing tree in the school play? Not on social media, you don't. You are *the proudest parents ever.* (Attach humble-faced smiling emoticon.)

You're wondering what the hell is going on in parliament and how it is going to affect you? Not on social media. You're *this is a fucking shitstorm. The NHS is fucked. The trade channels are fucked. We're all fucked.*

You're feeling incredibly lost. You lack confidence. You can't stick at anything. You hate your job. Your kids are driving you mad. Not on social media. You're quoting Martin Luther King and rambling about love and positivity.

This is commonplace.

Everything is back to normal.

Apathy resumed.

And that is just where The People of Choice want you.

The last twenty letters have been sent and will be opened in the morning.

PART THREE
LEGACY

109

We wait.

We don't have to count down from three.

Or say *go*.

We just need the teacher.

We are the last People of Choice. The ones now with courage. That's what brought us here.

We paid our eight pounds to go through the turnstile. We rode in the lift to the top. We laughed at the same joke told by the same man, who presses the same buttons all day long. We squeezed up the stairs while the guard was distracted and pushed our way outside to the roof of the walkways.

And now we line up, waiting for the Teacher.

We sold you bad stocks. We took care of your kids while you pursued your career. We cooked you that meal from the specials board you liked so much, the one you told your friends about. We put you forward for that job you just interviewed for.

This is it. One solution. One certainty.

It could be the wind or the situation, but up here, it's silent. Like the world has been turned down. We are not talking. We don't have to. But everything below seems quiet. We know that people are looking at us. And they know who we are. What we are going to do. But we look out across the capital. Not down at them. They hold their breath. We breathe in, hold, one-two-three, out. And repeat.

Waiting. For the Teacher. The trigger.

Us. The People of Choice. We help run the youth club for free so your kid isn't on the street getting into trouble again.

We know your repeat prescription just by looking at your face. We pushed forward with the disciplinary hearing when you reported your supervisor for indecent behaviour. You cried on our couch when your sister passed away so suddenly.

We are still.

The teacher emerges. We don't hear her, there is no sound, but we know she is there. She walks out to the centre spot, turns her back to the growing audience, lifts her arms out to the side and lets herself fall backwards.

There's a short scream as her feet leave the platform. It's the first thing we hear. The next thing is her body hitting cement. Then another shriek. And the volume gets turned back up.

We know what we have to do.

No more waiting.

This is legacy.

110

236 – TEACHER

The year fours had been learning about fronted adverbials and they'd shown how well they could overuse them in the thirty stories she had marked the night before. She had needed the wine. Mostly, they were terrible. Often, they were worse than that. But it was another tick off the curriculum and that's what counts.

It wasn't so much about the creativity of their stories as it was the grammar and sentence construction. And that made the Teacher sad for the students she loved, who were only getting to use one side of their brains, and sadder for herself that she was helping to facilitate this manner of education.

She sits up in her bed and sighs at the view from her window. There's a pile of books on her bedside table and half a bottle of pinot grigio that helped her tick a million adverbs before she drifted away from the meaninglessness of her job into quiet, lonely slumber.

The bed is too big.

The frying pan is too wide.

She gets up, goes into the kitchen, pours herself an orange juice – no pulp – and places one slice of bread into the toaster.

And now she is on autopilot. She moves to the bathroom and gets the shower running. The landlord is useless and won't get it fixed. So, every time she wants to get clean, she has to turn it on fully, take the hose off the hook and hold it upside down while it squeaks and churns, when the water starts dribbling out, she has to wait another ten seconds before she hangs it back up. Then she has another couple of minutes for it to warm up.

That's when she gets the mail from her doormat.

One letter. White envelope. Four words.

All because she had the gumption to talk to Rossi about her disillusionment regarding her career choice. And how her boyfriend had called it off after two years, via text message.

'I got into it thinking that I was going to help shape young minds. You know? That these kids would go on to do something worthwhile in the future. Because I had helped to set the foundations. I thought that's why everybody got into teaching. A bit naive, of course.'

This is how her sessions went. There was no trouble getting her to talk. She didn't even need the therapy. She just needed to say these things out loud in order to process them herself.

'There's that thing, isn't there? Those who can't do, teach. I mean, that's derogatory. Reducing an entire occupation to one characteristic. Like everyone there has failed at something and it's the last choice. It's like, if everything in life goes wrong, you could always become a teacher.' She exhales with disgust and resignation.

Her issue was that it wasn't her fall-back. It was her first choice. It's what she wanted to do. And she feels as though she is failing at it. Failing the kids. Failing herself.

So she is failing at the thing that most people end up doing because they failed at the thing they really wanted to do. What does that say about her?

She wasn't mean or ungrateful or pessimistic or hostile. The teacher was there because she was already good but wanted to be better.

And Rossi took that from her.

The Teacher reads her note, folds it up and lights it by poking it into the toaster. It sets on fire and she places it on the dish rack, watches it burn to nothing. She spreads peanut butter on the toast when it pops up. She showers, like she always does. Stupidly, she goes to the toilet before getting in. When she flushes, it affects the water pressure in the house and the shower moans at her for another two minutes.

Then she's clean and dressed and the books are pushed into a plastic bag to take in to school. And she doesn't deserve this, at all. And her skull can protect her brain from a slap in the face, even a bottle to the head, but when you turn your back, lift your arms to the side and drop backwards off a bridge, you naturally end up turning so that your head is at the bottom. It's the first thing to hit the ground. It splits apart and spills. Your neck breaks. Your central nervous system holds its middle finger up to your face.

NOTHING IMPORTANT HAPPENED TODAY   229

Before she does any of this, she has to get the kids to work on their seven times tables.

111

237–238 – BROKER AND SALESPERSON

Chasing the sale is the same as chasing the kill.

It escalates.

And you find you're never satisfied.

You pull in your first ever million-pound deal. There's a high. Of course. Your boss is praising you. Your colleagues say 'well done' even though they're jealous. But you like that they're jealous. Because you are beating them. You are winning. You are successful.

But, then, how do you beat that high? How do you replicate that euphoria? Another million-pound deal will help, but it's not the same. You've done that. Been there.

Maybe you land a sale for two million and you wait eagerly by the printer for your purchase order so you can ring a bell in the office, so the whole team gets a drink and some pizza at lunch. Because of you. Successful you.

What's next? Five million? Ten million? It becomes stale. It's the same thing, only bigger. You find that you can't recreate that moment. Your bank balance is off the chart for someone of your age and lack of education. So you buy yourself some things.

Things.

Like *things* ever made anybody happy.

Like *things* give you a sense of fulfilment.

That's what you're missing. A full bank account is no substitute for an empty soul.

Milton could have explained this, told them that the only way they are going to register some kind of fulfilment is to try giving something back. Do something for somebody else. Altruism doesn't exist. We do things for others because it makes us feel good about ourselves. And that's totally acceptable. Because the outcome is that you feel good and you have helped someone else feel good.

And he did try to explain this to both the Broker and the Salesperson. And they, in turn, had tried. In even the smallest of ways. Donating to charity. Volunteering. It had worked to a small degree but it didn't match the sale. It helped but the gesture needed to be more.

So they kept going to Milton and he reiterated his advice. But he also informed them that they would receive a letter one day – nothing important – but they were to meet at Tower Bridge and wait for the Teacher to jump from the top. At that point, they had to ask themselves whether or not they wanted to die.

And they absorbed this information, but it was obscured. Remembered but not recalled.

Until now.

The broker slides his Zippo lighter down his leg to light it and sets fire to his activation note. He's a smoker. He started late. Mainly because everyone else at work smoked. It's a stressful environment. He still doesn't like the way it makes him feel but he looks like he belongs and that's just as important.

The Salesperson rips the page into small pieces and throws them into the waste disposal.

They're both in their suits. They both have cars they don't

need. They've both tried to fuck their way to fulfilment. And they're both on their way to the last day at the job that caused them to lose such a huge sense of their self-worth.

Later this evening they both get to die. Unfulfilled.

The Broker backs out halfway down and tries to land on his feet, snapping both femurs and dislocating his hips before his face crunches into the floor and his brain rattles around inside a broken skull.

The Salesperson embraces the fall. The ribs of her slender frame offer no protection from the impact with Earth and her lungs rupture while her heart continues to lurch forwards until it lacerates against broken bones.

Dr Milton had tried to help. He'd given them the tools to save themselves.

They thought their name at the top of the sales leader board meant they were winners.

All they are, are the two best-dressed corpses.

112

239 – AU PAIR

The problem with the Au Pair was that she ended up working for a man who, if he had been recruited into The People of Choice, would have been known as the Cliché.

He had abused his position as her employer and taken advantage of her situation. It had started with comments that flirted at the edge of decency and moved swiftly towards inappropriate touching and suggestion. By the time she was truly scared of him coming home before his wife, she found herself on her knees in the dining room doing something she didn't want to do, while the children she loved looking after were glazed over in front of the television.

Then they were fucking and he was telling her how good she was at it.

And then he was telling her that he loved her and wanted to leave his wife even though he had no intention of doing so.

But this wasn't quite the story she told Dr Erickson.

No. She told him that she had become involved with a married man. No mention of impropriety or coercion. It was any other torrid affair with an older, unavailable man. She loved London. She loved the people. She didn't want to go home yet. But she didn't know how to end things without being fired, which would mean that she would have to leave or find another job, quickly.

Or she could carry on, hoping the kids don't walk in or the wife doesn't come home early as a surprise. It's not much of a life. The pay is great but it can't go on. It's not worth it.

That's what she tells Erickson and he does the classic psychiatrist response of saying nothing because she is talking and answering herself at the same time. She needs to tell somebody who isn't going to judge her. Confession to a priest would work if it wasn't for the sentencing at the end. Though a handful of Hail Marys is a romantic stroll, kicking up fallen autumn leaves, compared to the internal haemorrhaging the Au Pair is destined for.

Three cards for Diamond Taxis pepper the doormat along with copies of the unchanged menu from the local Indian takeaway. She reads her letter, the one that tells her that nothing important happened today and she discards it piece by piece on the way to work.

She spends the day with the youngest child, on her own, playing and reading. She makes her lunch. She picks the elder two up from school, takes them back, makes them do their homework and prepares their dinner.

Their mother gets home first, which means the Au Pair doesn't have to degrade herself today, but the father manages to get home before she leaves so that he has the chance to at least grab her arse one last time.

There's no emotional goodbye for the kids, that's not allowed. All that's left is the walk to Tower Bridge, pay the eight pounds and get out on to the roof. She has no idea how many people will be there. She doesn't know any of them. All she knows is to jump on the second scream.

113

236–255

We don't want to die.

But it is very clear. Two screams.

The silence lifts over the capital. Car horns. Gasps. Boats. Cameras clicking. Engines. People. That London thrum.

This isn't a movie where the villain spends too long explaining what they have done and their motivation behind it. That's not real. Nobody is here to stop the bad guy. And we are not waiting around.

The guard that let us up here is fat and slow and doesn't get paid enough to venture out and stop us.

Nothing can stop us.

There is not even a pause between that second scream and

the next one of us to jump. Then one straight after that. And another. Until we rain down on the streets. Human hailstones. Thudding and contorting. Some of us spattering blood on by-standers, others only bleeding on the inside.

Within seconds, we have all hit the ground. Some of us die immediately. Some of us die painfully without the ability to scream out loud. If there was even a chance of surviving, the brain would be in such a state of disrepair that no information on The People of Choice could ever be gleaned.

Everybody dies.

Within seconds of the Teacher falling backwards, away from all that potential, there are another eighteen bodies that drop down all around her.

Nineteen of us in total.

There are supposed to be twenty.

It is not our job to count. We do not converse with one another. We don't have to do that. Our purpose is to stand on the edge and ask ourselves one question. Pretend we have some kind of choice.

We are the message. The spectacle.

This is the theatre of cruelty.

114

240 – FIGHTER

He wakes up at six – before the post arrives – and he's out on the streets running. He's wearing black compression tights underneath his shorts and his favourite grey hoodie that he's had for years. The latest Eminem album blasts in his headphones and blocks out the sound of the birds ringing in the new day.

The music is angry. And so is the fighter.

He is working towards his comeback. Getting himself into physical shape with forty-five minutes of cardio every morning before breakfast, strength training in the afternoon, and sparring in the evenings. He can do most of that himself; he's motivated, and his coach helps with technique and strategy for the next fight.

Dr Rossi has been helping with his mind.

Something happened in his last fight. Things were going to plan. He was scoring well and was up on points after five rounds. Then he broke.

His hands dropped. He stopped guarding his face and head. And he was crying. He didn't know why. Breaking down in front of a crowd. His opponent struck him a few times in the face but was visibly uncomfortable about hitting somebody who was clearly in the middle of a mental episode.

The Fighter told his corner not to throw in the towel, tears streaming down his face. His opponent danced around, trying not to get involved, looking over at his own team, wondering what to do.

Eventually, the referee stopped the fight. It was a loss. The first blip on an unblemished and promising record for the Fighter. More importantly, his head was screwed. Nothing to do with taking hits from other men for five years, it was, as Dr Rossi would discover, a mixture of the pressure he was putting himself under to succeed and provide for his daughter, and a debilitating fear of failure.

He set his own bar too high.

The kicker is that Rossi did his job. And he did it well. He got the Fighter's mind fit again. He made him deal with the breakdown until it became a breakthrough. That clear mind is what drives the body to achieve.

The Fighter still has the anger but he harnesses that emotion to drive him forwards. This morning it pushes him ten kilometres. And he sprints the last hundred metres.

Out of breath, he leans on the door and pants heavily, smiling because he knows he has given it everything that he has. He opens the front door, picks up the letters that were posted while he was out – the brown envelope is from Revenue and Customs, the white is from Dr Rossi.

The brown envelope details a change in the Fighter's tax code.

The white tells him that he will miss his sparring session this evening.

He places both on the kitchen counter, fixes himself a protein shake then heads to the shower as though nothing has happened.

His life is back on track. It's his turn to have his daughter on the weekend. His food for the next four days has been portioned out into plastic tubs in the fridge to ensure he has the exact macronutrients to attain the physique and weight required to fight.

The Fighter tears up the brown and the white envelopes after his shower and throws them on the stove flame.

Death and taxes.

115

241 – SHRINK

Just because you teach it or preach it, doesn't mean you know how to do it.

Sitting and listening, day in and day out, to other people venting their problems, anxieties and deepest secrets can take its toll on a person. Even a highly trained professional primed to deal with such issues.

Try spending eight hours each day with the most negative people you know. Don't say anything. Nod along to their pessimism and woe. There's an emotional osmosis that means you can't help but replicate to a certain degree.

Even a shrink, sometimes, needs a shrink.

A lot of the time, they move in similar circles so they'll throw each other a free session, which could be reciprocated at a later date. And if you happen to run a practice like ERMA, with four psychiatrists on hand, it's even easier.

You might think that planting a seed in the mind of a professional headshrinker would be more difficult than a broken boxer or a scared au pair or a sleep-deprived, drug-addled broker. Because you have to allow it to fester and create doubt. You have to massage the idea to the point where you can control that person with either fear or confidence.

You'd think someone with a degree in psychology would be wise to that. Here's the thing: if they are, Dr Erickson would listen to what they have to say and advise. No seed would be planted. They would simply be treated. Not every patient has to jump off a bridge or chew the barrel of a gun. But if they're beaten down enough by life, if the job has got to them so badly that they can't perform to the best of their ability, it's easier to take advantage. They can be recruited to a suicide cult where they never inquired about membership.

The job continued to erode the motivation of the Shrink and the seed took root. And each day that passed, he felt worse and more useless than before. The branches of doubt spread within him until the only reaction he could have to seeing the words *Nothing Important Happened Today* was to flush the note down the toilet, float through several sessions, including a couple who were both depending on alcohol to make it through the day and a morbidly obese man who was lying to himself about what he consumed, lock his filing cabinet and jump off Tower Bridge, smashing his midsection against the railing before flipping over into the Thames and drowning because he had no feeling in his body after the impact.

Easy.

Shipman never had this kind of finesse.

116

242 – DETECTIVE

He leaves the front door open when he sets off. That's it. That tiny detail leads all the way to the top of The People of Choice. Yes, you can ensure that everybody that is chosen dies. You know that you send them a letter and it will trigger a reaction to get them to a certain place at a certain time and that action will result in their death.

And you can add it to your tally.

You can catch up with Shipman and overtake him and reach

your goal and be lauded as the greatest and most prolific killer in history. But you deal with human beings. And then you forget that they are so different. That they are so complicated. That they are nuanced.

You can't account for the burnt ember of that note you sent floating across a kitchen and falling into a corner for forensics to discover and, from that, unravel an entire history of manipulation and murder. You can't imagine every outcome of how people react – from an heiress to a legal secretary. You don't have an algorithm in place that informs you of the intricacies of the Detective's daily routine that would mean he receives a note, cooks an unhealthy breakfast, doesn't shower and then leaves his home with the door left ajar.

You can plan everything. You can experiment with the human condition for decades. You can talk about how Bundy screwed up. You say how Dahmer made mistakes or Shipman got greedy or Christie was too complacent. But you never see how you will get caught, how you have fucked up.

Maybe you look at the Detective and you think he is lying about his affair. Maybe you wonder about the last case he was on, whether he would have had something to do with it. Something sinister. What if he was already seeing the widow? What if he helped her get rid of her husband? Surely not. A detective for the police. That seems too dark. Surely they wouldn't be involved in a murder. No way they would cover up something so nefarious.

Perhaps the Detective is experiencing something that is psychologically disorientating. A blackout. Lost time. You knew all along they would be back because you had treated their nephew and you knew they could be useful to you. Another kill. A patsy perhaps.

Maybe you thought you could take them both.

242 – Detective wakes up. He reads his mail. It's like he needs some kind of mathematical software to decipher which local pizza parlour has the most cost-effective offer. It's late morning. He has had a lie-in. So a pizza brunch isn't out of the question. And his head says to go local rather than one of the chains.

He reads the only letter and throws away the other menus.

Then he's on the phone asking for a large meat feast with extra cheese. Dippers. Coke. Ice-cream meal deal.

This isn't some kind of disgusting last supper. It's not a treat before dying.

Nothing important happened today.

The old man hangs up the phone. He has thirty-five minutes until his 3000-calorie breakfast arrives. And around six hours until his final blackout.

He sits in his favourite chair and switches on the news. Some white guy has gunned down a lot of people worshipping at a mosque across the other side of the world. Those on the left are quick to condemn. They call him an extremist. An Islama-phobe. A supremacist. Those on the right are saying that he acted alone. That he had mental-health issues. The broadcaster is trying its very best to be balanced and show both arguments, but it is easy to see which way they are leaning.

It means there is no mention of The People of Choice.

242 – Detective strokes Ergo's back and continues to watch. By the time he's watched some of the goals from last night and the mosque-shooting story has come back round again, his pizza has arrived.

He sets the hot food down on his lap and takes the lid off the ice-cream. He rolls the first slice of pizza and stuffs it into his mouth in one go. While he chews, he sets the tub of ice-cream down on the floor next to his feet and lets the dog lick away at it.

He naps straight after. He shits out the junk from the day before. He cleans his teeth. He sits in his private room for an hour, staring at the wall and making notes. There's another notepad in the living room with a scribble to remind him to call Dr Artaud, but he's forgotten about it. He looks at his crude drawing of Tower Bridge on the wall. Something flickers in his mind but there is a disconnect.

When he returns to the lounge for the last time, Ergo is waiting. He looks at his master. He's seen that look before. He starts barking. Somehow, he knows what's coming.

'What's wrong, boy?' the old man ask. 'What's wrong, eh?'

He trundles over to his only friend, drops down heavily onto one knee and hugs the dog around the neck, rubbing affection-ately with his hand. Ergo stops barking and accepts the old man into him. While his defences are down, the former detective, the former Old Levant, clips the lead onto Ergo's collar and wraps it around the bottom of the radiator.

He backs away, slowly.

'I'm sorry, boy. I need to go.'

Ergo doesn't bark, he tilts his head sadly to the side. Just as he did with Young Levant.

What a family.

The old detective takes his jacket off the hook, opens the door, takes one last look at the forlorn canine and walks out, leaving the door slightly open.

Anyone could walk in.

117

DELIBERATE MISTAKE

Take John Christie. A textbook serial killer.

Struggled with impotence and sought solace with prostitutes. If you wanted to look into the causes of that ineffective penis, it would undoubtedly trace back to an emasculating mother. Or a philandering father. The fact that his victims were all strangled leans things more towards the mother. It's almost boring.

Still, he followed that unwritten code that so many limp-dicked murderers do: strangle a woman of ill repute, nobody will bat an eyelid.

Christie is worth studying. But only for his mistakes.

Bodies under the floorboards. Mistake.

Burying in your own garden. Mistake.

Wrapping a victim in a blanket and leaving them in an outdoor wash house. Come on, Christie, do you want to get caught?

Here's an idea: strangle your wife in bed. Tell a different story of her whereabouts to her family, the neighbour, her friends. Sell her belongings. Collect her unemployment benefits.

Now wait.

You fucking idiot, Christie.

Find another prostitute while you're waiting for the wife thing to unravel. Gas her. Rape her. Strangle her. Rape her again. Wrap her in a blanket, stuff her in a kitchen alcove and cover up the hole with some wallpaper.

Yes, everyone has heard of him, they know he lived at 10 Rillington Place, but he wasn't a success. He killed eight people. That's it. And it's surprising he wasn't caught sooner.

But there's a certain poetry to the way in which Christie was caught. Ambling around London. Aimless. Questioned on Putney Bridge by a policeman. He had no form of identification on him. Just some coins and a goddamned newspaper clipping of the man who took the fall for two murders that Christie had committed. Jesus Christ, John, you are ridiculous.

Some serial killers are caught because they are stupid, they don't know how to get rid of a body or they don't think things through; they're impulsive. Others, like Kemper, want to be caught because it's the only way they can stop what they are doing. Or the escalation in the violence of their murders gets out of control, so there's more evidence. Whatever the reason, to be a successful serial killer, you have to become known.

You have to get caught.

But, if you follow the guidelines that have been set out, you can do this on your own terms.

Make a deliberate mistake.

After following the rules for so long, chipping away at Shipman's record for years, staying below the radar, seeking no fame, no glory, becoming the invisible cult leader, how fitting to be picked up on a London bridge by the local constabulary with no identification. A nod to Christie.

So many years, hiding away, manipulating people into choosing death. Rarely witnessing the last moments of a victim. How perfect to watch those final twenty take the leap towards eternal nothingness.

Take me.

Now wait.

118

Detective Sergeant Pace wakes up on a day where nothing important is supposed to happen.

The white envelope on the floor of his flat says exactly that.

But Detective Sergeant Pace is not at his flat this morning.

The swing-by he had planned ended up with two bottles of beer, prosecco and a light, quaffable pinot noir.

It was easier for him to stay over after that.

And it means that only nineteen people will jump off Tower Bridge later.

Maeve Beauman saved Pace's life.

He is lying on his back, staring at the ceiling. Maeve is asleep on her side next to him; her hand rests delicately on his chest. Pace turns his head to look at her face. He's not thinking how great last night was or how deep his feelings run for the woman in bed with him. His mind is on that name that kept jumping out at him during his limited investigation of The People of Choice.

Levant.

Two of them. The Man in the Light. And his uncle. Some old, retired detective, who had identified the body. He'd already been interviewed, but Pace wants a second go. Something wasn't sitting right with that part of the story.

He stares back at the ceiling. Maeve's hand moves down his body. She's awake. Pace knows she's going to try it on with him. Part of him wants to get out and get on with his working day. Head across town to the address he pulled from the system for Mr Levant. Another part wants to look up at Maeve as she works him to climax, arching her back as she slides herself back and forth. That appeals to Pace.

Pace starts to sit up. But it's half-hearted.

'Where do you think you're going?' Maeve asks, finally opening her eyes. Her hand gripping the waistband of his underwear.

'Big day. Back on the case. I need to get to work.'

Maeve leaves her hand and rolls away to look at the alarm clock on her bedside table.

'It's early. Lie back. We have some time.'

Detective Sergeant Pace does as he is told.

Then they're both downstairs in the kitchen drinking coffee and he is talking about the case that isn't even his but he can't help but investigate. And Maeve is encouraging him to pursue it – she's been fascinated by the news stories. Pace tells her that he is going to visit *this Levant character* today.

And this is how his day begins. With a hangover and a beautiful woman and sex and tenderness and a hot shower and the same clothes as the day before and black coffee and that shadow over his shoulder. Not with a hangover, cheap coffee and burning the letter that sits on the floor of his modest flat.

Detective Sergeant Pace, who told Dr Artaud that he was not seeing a woman from his previous case. Who didn't mention those black flames or the shadow or the trail of bad luck that seems to follow him. Who was cleared to return to work but has not dealt with his issues. Who could snap and be engulfed by the darkness he continues to run from.

Who should have been 255 – Detective.

119

243–248 – NOBODIES

There are six of them for the Tower Bridge finale.

The wheels of industry will not come to a grinding halt the moment their heads hit concrete. They're nobodies. Sure, they are something to somebody, but not within The People of Choice.

And that does not mean they are menial workers or unemployed or criminals or ravaged by war. There's an accountant and a software developer among them. There's a local councillor.

What they lack is the ambition and guts of the Fighter, the ideology of the Teacher, the benevolence of the Doctor, the hope of the Poet.

They're functional. They're here. They're doing something. And the world needs a ton of nobodies in order to exist and get things done. But it also won't miss them. They're replaceable.

So don't worry about the Nobodies. The six nothings that are there to make up the numbers. The ones that Rossi, Erickson and Milton infiltrated on their very first session. It was so easy for them. Six people with names and titles and families and responsibilities. All deemed to be worthless.

They get given a number.

They will get their names back in a few days once family members have identified their mangled remains. It'll be blurted out on the news for people to forget. These people have no story. They're not interesting. The public will hook on to the Fighter and his struggle and the daughter he leaves behind.

They will see the devastation of the Teacher's year-four pupils. They will speculate about the Levants and their involvement. Conspiracy theories will abound. And the Nobodies will take their rightful place in the legacy of The People of Choice. They're filler. Padding at best.

But they all count.

And how much does it really matter?

Everybody dies.

120

The door is open.

Pace taps lightly with his knuckle three times.

'Mr Levant? Mr Levant, are you there? This is the police, I'd like a word with you about your nephew. Mr Levant?'

He waits.

After leaving Maeve's house, Pace had gone straight to the office. He could have gone home and changed but he was clean enough. He just had to show his face for half the day, make it look as though he was chipping away at his caseload while, actually, pulling together details about The People of Choice.

Nobody noticed when he left in the early afternoon. He had the old man's address and that was his sole focus.

Detective Sergeant Pace pushes the door open a little further and spots what he thinks is some kind of Alsatian. It isn't barking. It doesn't seem frightened. It isn't protecting the flat. Pace thinks that a dog would only act this calm if the owner was still around. He's wary.

'Mr Levant?' he calls again, looking around the lounge. He edges inside, carefully, and looks behind the door. Nothing.

Then he spots that the dog is tied to the radiator.

'There's a good boy.'

He sidesteps his way to the back of the lounge, towards the kitchen, keeping an eye on the dog and the other end of the room. There's nobody in there, either.

Pace moves more freely, now that he knows he isn't going to get jumped from behind. He shuts the front door then checks the bathroom and the bedroom. The dog lies back down on the carpet. It doesn't make a sound.

One room left.

'What the...?'

He can see the entire room. Pace is definitely alone in this flat. Apart from the dog. It's the only tidy room in the place. There's a large table in the centre of the room, covered in papers full of notes and ideas. There's a laptop and a printer. Both of them are powered up but the laptop is password protected. Someone at the station will be technical enough to get into it.

It's the wall in front of him that stops the detective in his tracks. The Thames stretches across its length with bridges drawn in order. Pictures of the victims. String to join certain victims together. He's got more information here than has been seen on the news. He's got more than Paulson has unearthed.

Pace can't make sense of it. There's too much there. And he's worried that Levant could come back at any second. Why did he leave the door open?

One of the pieces of paper on the desk has The People of Choice's mantra printed in capital letters.

Is it him? Is he behind this? Did he kill his own nephew? That seems like such a stupid mistake to make? How would he recruit all of those people? Where the fuck is he?

Pace doesn't know what to do. He could call this in, get

Paulson down here. Then he'd have to explain why he was investigating. But he can't just leave it. Levant might be planning something else. Maybe the old man was just looking into things himself. He is displaying his findings in a psychotic way, but perhaps that's just the way he works. He's old school. An analogue guy in a digital world.

He returns to the lounge faster than he entered. The dog jumps to its feet and starts barking. Pace slows and tells the thing to be quiet. He scours around the room quickly, to see if there's anything else that might be seen as evidence of collusion with The People of Choice.

The place is a mess. It smells like dog and beer and takeaway food. There's half a tub of melted ice-cream on the carpet. Next to the landline telephone, Detective Paulson's card. Beside that is a small notepad. Written in blue ink are two words. The first is *string* and has a line through it. The second is ERMA.

Pace leaves the card and takes the pad.

121

242 – DETECTIVE

The old man is the last one to jump off Tower Bridge. It wasn't planned that way. The only stipulation regarding order was that the Teacher would lead the rest of the pack.

He hesitates.

The other eighteen jumpers were all patients of either Rossi, Erickson or Milton. 242 – Detective saw Dr Artaud.

Maybe Artaud isn't as good as the others. Maybe he's just starting out. Maybe he's not a part of it. Maybe he's being used for his police patients to give the cult some credibility. Maybe the victim thinks about his nephew before committing to his own death. Maybe he spares a thought for Ergo, being passed around from owner to owner, left alone again. Maybe a camera flash knocks him into reality and he doesn't know where he is.

Maybe you haven't been listening.

It's foolproof. You get the letter, you jump. That's it. It always works. No leader. No trail. No evidence.

Old Levant does not consider his life or what he made of himself. He doesn't reflect on how he treated his family or his friends or how he was treated by them. He doesn't reminisce about days with his partner before he was killed and he doesn't feel ill towards him for the blackouts that manifested as a result of his electrocution.

It's a 200-foot drop, but that takes a second. Nothing slows down for him. No life – good, unfulfilled or momentless – flashes through his mind in that time. There's not long enough.

It goes like this: Scream one. Scream two. Look at all the lights. Do I want to die? No. Step off the edge. Burst organs. Brain damage. Eternal blackout.

Unless Detective Sergeant Pace can figure out what has been happening. And stop it.

122

Detective Sergeant Pace left the door open, too.

Ergo was still chained to the radiator. If he got hungry, he had some melted ice-cream to lap at. He wasn't going to die.

Pace didn't call it in. He should have, of course, taken the rap for doing things his own way, working someone else's case. But his mind was focused.

ERMA. The note on that pad said ERMA.

Erickson.

Rossi.

Milton.

Artaud.

Back at the station, he searches for Levant in the records and finds that he had an exemplary career, marred only by the death of a fellow officer, which he witnessed, and treatment for the consequent blackouts he experienced after the incident.

Pace's first thought was to doubt that Levant's partner's death was an accident. Then he finds what he is looking for. The name of the doctor that had treated Levant's affliction.

Artaud.

Was he still seeing Artaud after all this time? What did the doctor know about Levant? Did he know the younger Levant?

Whatever the answers, Pace had what he needed. A link. Enough reason to go back to those offices, under the barrier, over the bumps.

He leaves the station in a rush. He doesn't tell anybody where he is going or what he is doing. He needs to speak to his doctor. To Levant's doctor.

Then he's in the car and negotiating the traffic, heading towards the ERMA offices while nineteen other people he is supposed to be meeting are making their way to Tower Bridge.

There are three missed calls from Maeve on his mobile phone that he doesn't have the time or energy to deal with right now. He sees the back of Royal Festival Hall and knows that he is close.

The barrier is open. He doesn't slow down for the speed

bumps and, when he pulls up outside the offices, he doesn't need to press one of the bells on the brass ERMA plaque, because another door has been left open for him.

123

TWO HUNDRED AND FIFTY-SIX

It could have been so many more. Decades of patients. But not everyone comes to see a therapist in secret. Not everyone is ashamed to ask for help. Those people were treated. If they ended up taking their own life somewhere down the line, it was their choice. It doesn't count towards the final number.

You can't kill everyone.

Even if you really want to.

Even if they come to you and their troubles are insignificant in your eyes. They were feeling down, but then the closure of the local boulangerie really tipped them over the edge because they don't want to support big business and the supermarkets charge so much more for the spelt ciabattas that it is criminal.

You want to kill these idiots. But you can't. Because they've told their peers that they are in analysis. It may be that they are acknowledging that they need the guidance or self-awareness. Maybe they'll get around to that story about the tactile uncle who made them sit on his lap or the way those God-fearing nuns would discipline at that Catholic school or how they find one of their parents attractive.

Maybe they do, maybe they don't. But if they're coming to you with these problems and they've let somebody else know that they're doing it, that makes it harder to kill them. Because you don't want that trail. You don't want anything to lead back to you.

You want to remain invisible.

Until the end.

Until you can kill no more.

You need to retire.

Damn, it could have been so many more. Decades of patience. Picking them off, one by one. Never getting carried away. Honing the craft. You think it's easy getting away with murder? The pleasure can eat away at you when there's nobody to share it with. Leaving no evidence, no fingerprints – physical or figurative – is the easy part. Subverting your own joy is the real pain.

But pain endures.

Take Shipman, who is now the second most prolific serial killer we've seen. He's been overtaken. Twenty-three years without detection. A strong business model. All these American hillbilly whore-killers, they've got the right idea, but there's a never-ending feed of pensioners. And, when they die, people care about it even less than they do when a prostitute is found burned in a ditch. Old people are expected to die. They're sick all the time and they need looking after and they have to be reminded to take the pills for their diabetes and arthritis and the extra pills to counteract the side-effects of these other pills they have been prescribed.

You get to a certain age and you become a drain. On your family and your carers. Your government doesn't give a shit that you paid your taxes forever or that you went to war. That doesn't mean you should be able to heat your one-bedroom palace for the whole of winter.

Your local, trusted GP gives you a little something extra for the pain and the next time you are due to wake up, you don't.

Who is going to ask questions about that? Who is going to look deeper into a ninety-three-year-old who passed away in her sleep?

It makes you wonder about Shipman. Was he a Kemper? Had he had enough? Did he want to get caught so that he could stop? Was he bored? Did he want to tell somebody? Was that greed to be included in the inheritance of one of his deceased patients a form of escalation? A cry for help?

A mistake? After all that time?

When people look back at The People of Choice, at this legacy, and they see that 224 people died before anyone had even heard of us, they won't have to ask why things escalated so dramatically and publicly, because it is all here.

It could have been so many more. But you can't account for everything. You can lay out your plan and follow your ethos and believe that you are doing the right thing in getting rid of these people, but you can't predict your own mortality.

We know the drugs don't work. We see the figures on people smoking and how it pollutes their body irreparably. We tell ourselves that the liver repairs itself, but that doesn't have to be a challenge, a target. And we know that processed meat is at the same level as cigarettes on the list of carcinogens, but we tell ourselves it's rubbish and hasn't really been proved and it's probably just warped statistics. It's Russian roulette at best.

Take obesity and heart disease and lung cancer and cirrhosis of the liver and tell them that the bacon and gin and cinnamon-flavoured vape was worth it.

Tell them you've got a plan.

That it could've been so many fucking more.

Watch them laugh in your face.

Wait. As they cloak your vital organs in fat and tar and tumours. Just as you feel you are hitting your stride.

The problem with the world isn't overpopulation. The problem is the global pandemic of apathy and entitlement. It's not caring that the world is polluted and species are being killed off. It's ruining our immediate environment, our bodies, with the crap that we are being told to eat. And it's the killing of our greatest resource, our minds.

We are so connected that we have become disconnected. We can't have a thought, we have to have an opinion. Freedom of speech has gone too fucking far when we feel the need to share everything. When we filter the image of ourselves but feel no need to filter what we say out loud, hidden behind a new status and a picture of ourselves when we were twenty pounds lighter.

And the legacy of The People of Choice will be that we high-lighted this. We held up a mirror to the hypocrites, the fakers, the online influencers.

Yes, things will get twisted and we will go down as a psycho cult. And, yes, when people discuss serial killers who have killed more than anyone else, there will be a new name at the top of the list. But someone will see what was done, that the world is still screwed. That maybe it's worse. And they'll say, 'They killed two hundred and fifty-six people.'

'It should have been so many fucking more.'

124

His office has moved.

Detective Sergeant Pace doesn't wait around like he did at Old Levant's flat. He's not cautious about being seen or dis-covered or bitten by a startled Alsatian. He wants Artaud and he wants some answers and he wants them now.

He goes in through the open door of the ERMA offices, springs up the stairs two at a time until he reaches the corridor where the four psychiatrists' offices are located. The first door on the left is where he met six times with Dr Artaud. But the name on the door says *Dr Erickson*.

The door opposite still belongs to Dr Milton and the one next to it is still Rossi.

They've swapped offices since yesterday.

Pace puts his ear closer to the door to see whether he can hear Erickson talking with a patient, but it's too quiet and he's still breathing heavily from the energetic leap up the stairs.

He walks towards Artaud's new office. Wood everywhere. It's cold. He turns his head over his shoulder. There's a shadow on the floor that looks as though it's edging towards him.

Not now.

Pace knocks politely three times on Artaud's office door. His eyes are fixed on the floor shadow.

No flames, yet.

'Dr Artaud,' Pace says at a level slightly lower than is normal. He doesn't want to disturb anyone. He just wants to talk with his therapist.

He knocks again, this time a little firmer. His voice, too.

'Dr Artaud, it's Detective Sergeant Pace. I need to talk with you.'

No answer.

He tries the handle and finds that the door is not locked. He calls the doctor's name one last time before pushing into the room to find nothing. Absolutely nothing. It's empty.

It's not empty like a transitional phase between office moves. Empty like a room that has not been used for years and years. There is nothing. No carpet. No desk. No blind over the window. No bulb attached to the wire hanging from the ceiling. The walls are grey brick. The floor is grey concrete. It isn't even being used for the storage of boxes or files or cleaning equipment.

It is abandoned. Nobody works in that office. Nobody ever has.

Opposite is Rossi's name, slid on to a holder at eye level on the door.

Pace knocks. Nothing.

He pushes straight in this time to be greeted with an identically vacated room.

Dr Rossi is grey bricks.

Dr Rossi is two centimetres of dust.

Dr Rossi is invisible.

'Fuck.'

Pace knows he is going to find the same thing in Dr Milton's office. A huge pile of nothing. Because Dr Milton is a ghost. He doesn't even knock this time. Just turns the handle, flings the door open, steps in, sees what he expects, and turns back to the last room.

He wants to kick the door down but he knows he doesn't have to. These doors have all been left unlocked on purpose. He starts to wonder whether Levant's open door was a part of this game.

Erickson's office is the last. Formerly Dr Artaud's office, only one day ago.

The detective bursts into the fourth room and everything is as it was the day before when he spoke to Dr Artaud. The same couch he had sat on. The same desk. The same books in the same order. The only thing that looks different to Pace is the name on the desk plate. Dr Erickson.

Nothing has changed in the room. Nothing at all. It's as though Artaud went home and Erickson stuck his name on the door and used his office.

Pace goes back to the door and slides Erickson's name plate out of its holder. Across the top and bottom there is a line of wear about three millimetres from the edges. This only happens from repeated use. Perhaps they just rented the one office and different shrinks used it at different times. All they had to do was swap the name badges around. Cost-effective.

To be sure, Pace checks Dr Milton's name plate and it has the same two marks on the outside where it is constantly taken from its holder on the door and placed on one of the empty rooms when Milton does not have an appointment.

He returns to what is currently Dr Erickson's office and tries some of the cupboards beneath the books but they have all been locked. Pace was hoping for some access to patients' files.

Everything has its place.

The detective moves around the other side of the desk for a different perspective on the situation. He pulls out Artaud's chair, or Erickson's chair, or whoever was last to use the room, and on the seat is the only other thing in the room that is different. A stack of paper. Freshly printed.

Pace lifts the pile of prose up, places it on the desk and sits in the seat.

He'd guess that there are easily over a hundred pages of words.

Pace flicks through the pages. Words jump out at him.

People of Choice.

Shipman.

Cult.

It could be a manifesto or an admission of guilt. A drawn-out but detailed confession of the untouchable and illusive leader.

He doesn't feel like he has the time to read it from the very beginning. Something is closing in. These doctors have made a run for it.

He stops on a short chapter with the pithy title, 'Harold Who?'.

125

HAROLD WHO?

Take the Olympic Games. Not the last one. The one before that. Maybe even the one before that. Think about the men's 100-metre race. The final. The marquee event. A quarter of the world is watching as the eight fastest humans on the planet line up for that silent, twitchy start and the nine-second roar of adrenaline that follows.

Even if it was eight years ago, you know who won that race.

Who came second?

Who also ran?

People will still talk about the short period of dominance that Maurice Greene had. They will recall Donovan Bailey and speak fondly of Frankie Fredericks. But Usain Bolt created a legacy. Not just in the world of sprinting but in the world of sport.

And his records are unlikely to be beaten for a very long time.

Go back to the Academy Awards in ninety-seven. Remember how Titanic scooped armfuls of golden trophies?

What else was up for best picture? Were you pleased with the outcome of best animated short?

You remember the performances in *As Good as It Gets* and how *Good Will Hunting* could have cleaned up on any other year. But James Cameron took $200 million and turned it into $2 billion. He got cinema-goers to sit and watch a film, not for ninety minutes, but for 195 minutes. It made huge technological advances while creating two new superstars.

It is spoken about in the same terms as *Ben Hur* and *Gone with the Wind*. It doesn't matter if it was critically acclaimed, because it created its own legend and surpassed previous records that hadn't been broken for years.

Now take The People of Choice. As a cult, they may not have as many members as The Peoples Temple but they are followed by more and more people every day. They may not go down as the largest cult ever but that's fine. Because they are not a cult. That's just what the other people call it.

The biggest cult is organised religion. We could never compete with that.

So, take me. The greatest serial killer that ever lived.

Two hundred and fifty-five people.

It's a record that's unlikely to be beaten in a long while, though I have laid out the tools for anyone who wishes to challenge.

When people talk of killers, they will remember Bundy, of course. And the brutality of the Manson Family. Even that Zodiac fraud. But when they talk of Shipman, it will be to compare him to the man who overtook him. The one in first place. The one with a murderous heritage. Who allowed himself to be captured because he had finished his work.

You will remember his name.

126

It reads like a self-help book. A manual on how to start your own fake cult so you can kill as many people as possible.

Detective Sergeant Pace doesn't know what to do.

This is not his case. But he's in it now.

If there were another three officers, they could take thirty pages each and work their way through much quicker. Maybe the book is there to delay, so that the doctors can make a run for it. The door was left wide open and the evidence Pace holds in his hands is there on purpose. Not necessarily for him to find but for somebody to find, at some point.

He decides to read the first chapter and then skim read the rest.

It starts by talking about starting a cult. How you never go into something believing it to be harmful. That a group of people with similar interests and beliefs are known as a *church*. But it is other people, those outside this possibly peaceful regime that devalue the things they do not know or under-stand. That label something that needs no label. That throw around the word *cult* like a cursed word.

Pace thinks the author sounds delusional. But the doctor he had seen six times over the last couple of months was so lucid and erudite. It couldn't be the same person.

But the front page says *written by Henri Artaud*.

Pace continues to flick and, even though he knows that nobody will be returning to the building, he keeps looking at the doorway, thinking he is seeing something or hearing move-ment.

The manual talks of those first nine people to jump from Chelsea Bridge. Later, after more rambling about other killers who turned out to be great mentors, the two young strangers from Millennium Bridge make an appearance.

Dr Artaud had been at the police station that day to report personally on the progress of two police officers undergoing therapy with him. He did not need to do that. But he needed to be around the witnesses from that train carriage. He had to hand out business cards for Rossi and Milton and Erickson.

He was recruiting.

There is an entire chapter devoted to the recruitment process.

Detective Sergeant Pace is enthralled.

Detective Sergeant Pace is wasting time.

As he reads, nineteen people have taken the lift to the top of Tower Bridge.

Detective Sergeant Pace cannot stop.

The book talks of John Christie and how he has no right to be lauded in the annuls of serial killing because he was half-witted and drowning in mistakes.

Then, a mention of twenty people. They are referred to as *the last*. Pace runs his finger beneath the words as he reads, like a little boy reading in front of his teacher at the front of class. He doesn't want to miss a thing.

It clearly states that this happened at Tower Bridge.

But it hasn't happened.

Not yet.

Detective Sergeant Pace grabs the pages and runs down the stairs two at a time and out the still open door before getting into his car. He tucks the book into the large pocket behind the passenger seat. And wheel-spins towards the speed ramps that will lead him to the place he was supposed to be jumping from today.

127

Dr Henri Artaud stands on the road that leads across Tower Bridge and he waits.

It ends here.

He is John Christie with a brain.

He is Charles Manson with a clear ideology, untouched by drugs.

He is Harold Shipman with self-awareness. And more kills.

He smiles.

He looks up at the walkways and he smiles.

Any moment now.

Dr Henri Artaud lights a cigar that could very well be his last. His lungs are too far gone and he doesn't suppose Cohibas are used as currency in jail. His insides may be drenched in black but he's not going to spend his final days with his mouth wrapped around the teat of a common cigarette. It's at this point he wishes he had a glass of wine to enjoy the show with.

At this moment, he is still behind. Only 235 kills to his name. But he has been standing here for a while, gazing down the Thames, admiring the Tower of London, and watching eight of his patients enter the bridge and pay their fee to die.

240 – Fighter. Who thought he was seeing Dr Rossi.

239 – Au Pair. Who believed she was confiding in Dr Erickson.

237 – Broker. Who complained of a life unfulfilled to Dr Milton.

There is no Rossi. No Milton. No Erickson. That wouldn't work. That wouldn't count. Artaud said that. It's in the manifesto. Keep other people out of it. Confide in nobody. It minimises the possibility of mistakes.

This is one man's vision of a better world and he is here to enjoy the finale.

Black cabs cross over the bridge and people walk from one side to the other fixed to their phone screens yet somehow avoiding walking into the person opposite. So many people have white ear plugs screwed into their ears or giant headphones that cover the ear and block out any sound from the outside world. Sure, everyone is multi-tasking but they're all so disconnected.

Artaud can empathise with the appeal of mass killings. Take out everyone on the bridge in one go. Bomb it or hide in a window and pick them off with a gun, one by one. But there's no longevity in that approach. It's a one-time deal. It's always the event that gets the headline, rather than the shooter.

He sucks on his cigar and it feels like a lifeline rather than the thing that is killing him. He looks up. He's the only one doing that, for now. Nobody even notices him. He's been invisible for so long now that he can walk among the people and remain unseen.

A double-decker bus passes by. And a police car.

You could take me now and it would make no difference.

The doctor moves towards the centre of the bridge so that he has the best view of the walkways. He brings his blood-spotted handkerchief to his mouth as he coughs. This had to happen now. It had to be this many people. Otherwise it was all for nothing.

He knows they are close. That they are up there following the ideas he manipulated into their minds. Coercively massaging the darkest of thoughts to the forefront. Playing with their fears and anxieties and using them to do his bidding.

People will speculate afterwards about hypnosis. It is not

hypnosis. It is not hypnotism. That is what they will think. It is much easier to understand something like that; it is simpler for the mind to comprehend that a person can be placed into a trance by waving a pocket watch in front of their eyes and speaking in long, whispery words. The easy conclusion is that Artaud could place somebody into a mental state where he could make them bark like a dog if he wanted. He could make them undress or impersonate Elvis.

It is possible. He could do this. It is done by hacks citing hypnotic power as the culprit, but that is the greatest lie of all.

It is not real.

Hypnosis does not exist.

It is a case of insidiously massaging a notion within the subject without actually mentioning the true details of the deed so that they arrive at the conclusion you have set out for them.

As my hand moves closer, you will feel the keys start to throb in your hand.

Artaud coughs again and then takes a large drag on his cigar. He blows out a plume of smoke and shuts his eyes like he's had an orgasm.

He doesn't have long left.

Neither do The People of No Choice that he has sent to the top of the bridge.

Now wait.

128

It is only 2.7 miles from the ERMA offices to Tower Bridge.

The fastest route is to remain on the South Bank, past the Waterloo Campus of King's College and stay on that straight road until you can turn left over Southwark Bridge. Then take a right and follow the A3211, passing Tower Hill Memorial on your way to the A100, which crosses straight over the Thames at Tower Bridge, where Artaud is standing and smoking and coughing and smiling.

It's the quickest way there and it takes twenty-one minutes. In a police car, it will be faster.

Detective Sergeant Pace still has a chance.

129

Four people emerge on top of one of the walkways that links both sides of Tower Bridge.

Artaud sees them first because he is looking up, anyway. Most of the other people on the bridge are shoegazing.

The old, dying doctor does not say a thing. He simply points towards the top of the tower. One person follows his finger and cranes their neck upwards. Then another. And another. Until people are stopping. They are pulling out their headphones but leaving on their screens, swiping to the camera setting.

Onlookers don't know what to do. Shouting up at them seems futile in this wind. And startling a person so close to the edge feels like the wrong call.

Artaud spots a man in his early thirties. The man stops and pulls his right headphone to one side and looks up as two more people step outside. He looks at his watch, rolls his eyes, places his headphone back over his ear and continues to walk.

Someone else can deal with it. That's what he is thinking.

There are six more people on the back walkway. It's difficult to see them but it means that they are all almost out. This is happening.

People are in the road now and cars have had to stop. Drivers are getting out to shout at pedestrians to *get out of the fucking way* but are halted in their tracks by the image of the people above.

They're just standing there. Not one of them looks down at the commotion and intrigue beneath them. A woman in her twenties with an oversized scarf wrapped around her neck starts to film, panning across from left to right. Her hand is shaking. Artaud wonders whether anybody would notice if he pushed her over the edge into the river.

He can hear a siren in the distance.

130

'My God, you fucking idiot, get out of the way,' Pace shouts to himself as some fuckwit in a BMW tries to pull onto the kerb but seems to care more about his wheels than he does about a policeman heading to a possible emergency.

Pace slams his horn, angrily. He shouldn't do that. But this detective often does things that he should not do.

Speeding across Southwark Bridge, he looked down the river at the majesty of Tower Bridge, so iconic. Nothing seemed out of the ordinary. He could see that the traffic was flowing, the lights were ready to come on. He could do this.

The BMW driver eventually pulls across far enough for Pace to pass. He looks over at the driver as he starts to move and the guy is texting on his phone. Detective Sergeant Pace deliberately scrapes his piece-of-shit car down the side of the idiot's perfectly polished paintwork then speeds off towards the tower.

He turns right and can see Tower Bridge. Oddly, it looks smaller the closer you get.

The traffic is backed up and immobile. Some have turned off their engines completely. Pace can see that people are not walking across the bridge but have stopped.

He gets out of his car and runs. Those eighteen steps up to Artaud's office got the detective out of breath but he is running on fear and passion, now.

By the time he arrives at the entrance to the bridge, he is so out of breath that he has to take a moment to place a hand on his knee and collect himself. He stops behind a crowd of nine people, who are all looking up. They are all somehow hugging one another.

Detective Sergeant Pace straightens up.

Detective Sergeant Pace breathes. In. One, two, three. Out.

Detective Sergeant Pace sees Dr Artaud.

131

And Artaud sees the detective.

He screws his face as if to say, *That's odd, shouldn't you be up there?* Then he smiles again. He can't stop himself. Artaud can see how much this reaction annoys Pace. He hasn't counted how many people have walked out onto the walkways so has no idea that one is missing.

Artaud spots some movement from the corner of his eye. Another person has joined the others on the front walkway. She makes her way to the centre. Everybody is facing forwards, but she turns her back to the crowd.

Dr Artaud looks Pace dead in the eyes to hold his attention then lifts up one finger as though telling him to *wait for it...*

Then a scream from somebody in the crowd.

And another as the Teacher hits the deck.

Then it rains.

The drumroll of bodies smashing into concrete and cracking onto cars causes hysteria with the waiting audience. It's like a terrorist attack, but the innocent bystanders only come to harm psychologically.

Pace sees a muscular man in his periphery fold in half as he hits the protective barrier of the bridge then slip head first down another twenty-something feet into the Thames.

But he doesn't take his eyes away from the doctor, who still has his finger pointing up, like he is pressing against Pace's lips from a distance, telling him to *shh*.

When the final body crumples and dies and panic sets into those who have viewed it, Artaud's finger changes into a full hand that turns over as though presenting his masterpiece.

He brings the other hand up, palms to the sky, offering himself to be handcuffed.

132

236–254

We are The People of Choice. But the choice was never ours.

If we don't want to die then we have to. What kind of an option is that? But if we do, if we are truly in our darkest place, if we are honest and still believe in our own worthlessness, then, and only then, can we be saved.

Then, our unknown leader will show us mercy.

He will help us through our pain.

The ones now with courage. The nerve to re-examine ourselves. To better ourselves. To talk to someone about the things we cannot say to anyone else. To trust a stranger with our secrets and emotions that we hide from the rest of the world. To break through before we break down. *And we choose not to fear.*

Yet we are judged. We are deemed unfit for this overpopulated planet. Our problems are not real. Or not real enough. We have brought this on ourselves. We are not depressed. We are spoiled. We are entitled. We are precious millennial snowflakes, only without the individuality.

This is one solution. Because he has decided it so. This is his design. Yet, *it is not the end.* It may look like the grand finale, but narcissism could never allow the Detective to be remembered as his final kill.

There are more who choose to live. Global Chinese whispers will continue to dilute and warp the message. More helpless people in the farthest reaches of the globe will take their lives in the name of our pretend cult. That is part of the ongoing legacy that we have helped create and perpetuate.

There is but one certainty. We are all dead. Crushed on the inside with a feeling of hopelessness that led us to that bridge in the first place. Then physically crushed by the weight of our organs reacting to gravity. Our hearts and lungs continuing to travel towards the ground even when our bones have stopped.

Nobody ever gets out alive.

Not even our devoted leader.

133

'You did this.'

Detective Sergeant Pace walks towards his former psychiatrist and, instead of saying, *Dr Artaud, you are under arrest on suspicion of blah blah blah*, he comes right out with exactly what is on his mind.

You did this.

'Detective Pace. I didn't expect to see you here. Well, I did. But I thought that part of your brain would be hanging off that kerb over there. It seems I underestimated that brain.'

Pace inhales. One. Two. Three. Then exhales.

'You. Did. This,' he repeats. With more venom than his first attempt.

Artaud is unflinching. There's a calmness that can only be achieved by those with nothing at all to lose.

'I programmed you to check the mail before you leave your house in the morning. So that you wouldn't miss the letter I had delivered for you.' There's a pause as the doctor plays things through in his head. He sucks down another mouthful of cigar smoke and blows it to the side of Pace's glaring face. 'So, I have to assume that I was correct and you are seeing that possibly psychotic woman. Bravo, detective. Bra-vo.'

Pace bats the cigar out of Artaud's hand then grabs him by the lapels of his jacket and pushes him towards the barrier of Tower Bridge.

'You want to push me over?'

'Who would even know? Nobody here is looking at us. Nobody here cares about anything other than the dead bodies and their own safety. Who would care? Who would come looking for you?'

'You're right. Nobody.' He still doesn't look scared at all. 'You are a man of the law, Detective. Throwing me into the Thames is not the justice that you seek.'

Pace lets go. 'You did this, Artaud. You made those people jump to their death.'

'I am quite perturbed that you have arrived so quickly. I thought I would have to wait for it to get dialled in. I'd hoped to have some time to walk among the dead. Reminisce over their tales of woe, one last time. I think the Fighter would have won his next match.'

'You killed them. I don't even know how many of them there are, yet. But you killed them.'

'There are nineteen. It was supposed to be twenty. But nineteen is still enough.'

'Say it.'

'Is that what you want? A confession? I have written it all down. You can find the details—'

'I have your book, Doctor,' Pace interrupts.

'So there you have it.'

'Say it.'

'That I killed them? Of course I did. All of them. And many more.'

That's all Pace wanted to hear. He turns Artaud around. The old man feels weak and frail but his mind is still sparking correctly. The detective places handcuffs on his suspect. He doesn't read him his Miranda rights, not yet; he tells the murdering son of a bitch, 'You're coming with me.' And he walks him along the road, away from the bridge and back to the car he left a couple of hundred yards away.

Detective Sergeant Pace does not speak. Now he is the one who listens.

'I am a person of choice. Now and always with courage. And I choose not to fear. This is the only solution. It is the end. There is but one certainty. I am the last.'

And he says it again.

'I am the last.'

134

If you ever saw the police footage of Harold Shipman being interviewed, it's odd. He's awkward. Doesn't say too much. Doesn't give anything away. You know he's psychotic, he's disgusting, what he did over that time to all those people is unthinkable. But he comes across, at times, as timid. Then he'll flip it and seem arrogant.

Dr Henri Artaud displays no such dichotomy in character.

He wants Pace to know what he did and how many people's deaths can be attributed to his name.

Artaud is strapped into the back of Pace's car, his hands still cuffed, uncomfortably, behind his back. Pace slams the door shut, not listening to his doctor.

He should have called it in. He should have waited on that bridge as the first police officer to arrive on the scene. He left the place in chaos. But he left with the man responsible. That's what matters to Detective Sergeant Pace.

They're travelling for a minute or so, back in the direction that Pace came from, and nobody speaks.

'You know it's only two hundred and fifty-four because of you?' Artaud eventually chimes in.

'What are you talking about?'

'You, Detective. You're supposed to be dead. You're supposed to be lying on the concrete of Tower Bridge with your skull smashed in. You would have taken me to two hundred and fifty-five kills. Now it's only two hundred and fifty-four.'

'Oh. Is that all?' His tone is sarcastic and you can tell he is rolling his eyes without even seeing his face.

'You cheated Death, Mr Pace. It was your time to go. You may need to keep a look over your shoulder. The shadows will be closing in.' Artaud is trying to rattle his captor. Just for fun. Just to torment him on the way back to the police station. He was his psychiatrist. He made a note of Pace's chronic paranoia the very first time they met. And Pace said hardly anything in that initial session.

'Bad luck for you, eh, Doc?'

'Don't be silly. I was there waiting for you. Not you, personally, but one of your kind. I'm done. The People of Choice will end with me.'

'Thank God for that. I'm so bored of you.' Pace gives as good as he gets.

Artaud smiles.

'There's nothing you want to know? You're waiting until you can record me before you interrogate, is that it? What about the whole *anything you say can be taken down in evidence* thing?'

'I haven't said that to you,' Pace confirms. And he hasn't. Dr Artaud has only been cuffed, he has not been formally arrested yet. 'But it seems like you are itching to tell me something. So, go ahead. I'll make a note.'

Dr Artaud has spent decades listening to other people; he is not listening to Pace, now. He doesn't have to. He continues to talk, like he is on one of his rants that can be seen in the manifesto he wrote that sits in the pocket in front of his knees.

'Look out of the window. What do you see?'

Pace looks. It's rhetorical. Artaud doesn't want a discussion, he wants to talk to somebody.

'Take a closer look. I can see eight people on this side of the road and seven of them are overweight. Five of them are probably obese. We've become lazy. Waiting around for things to happen for us rather than going out and making something happen. Everything is deliverable or downloadable. We don't even have to turn the page of a book anymore. People don't have bookcases.'

'What's your point?'

Artaud continues without acknowledging the question.

'It's easier. Things are so much easier. Yet everyone is so unhappy. Psychiatry is a booming business in the current landscape. We are needed more than funeral directors. More people are depressed than they are dying. It's ridiculous.'

Detective Sergeant Pace doesn't even need to be here for this. He's a chauffeur at best. All part of the great Artaudian plan to confess and go to prison as the greatest killer of all time. He'll probably end up being protected so he doesn't get beaten to death like Jeffery Dahmer. Or he'll be transferred to Broadmoor, where he'll spend the remainder of his days in isolation reading all the books he never got around to while he was busy duping people into offing themselves.

'We don't need these people. They are not offering anything. You soon see that getting rid of them makes no difference to anybody. They're nobodies.'

And it continues. On and on for the next twenty minutes like some kind of mobile TED talk about skimming the scum off the top of the population consommé, so that what is left is clear and pure.

Dr Artaud is so wrapped up in himself and his achievement

that he doesn't notice the car is moving away from London, that they have not arrived at the police station he has visited in the past.

And Pace continues to drive and drift in and out of the conversation. He hears the doctor mention a host of other serial killers from around the world and cults and Usain Bolt and he realises that the psycho is reiterating all the things he has written down in his future bestselling memoir.

Then he snaps back into focus when Artaud says, 'So it looks as though I will have to be number two hundred and fifty-five.'

'I'm sorry, what?'

'It has to end with me, Detective. I am the only one left from The People of Choice. It dies when I die.'

'There are tens of thousands of followers that would happily carry on your work, I'm sure. I've seen what they say.'

'Idiots. All of them. I assure you.'

'We no longer have the death penalty in this country, as I'm sure you are aware.'

'I am dying anyway. It will be on my terms.'

'The first thing they do is put you on suicide watch. It's not uncommon. See what happened to your beloved Mr Shipman.' Pace almost laughs but holds it in.

'He was a doctor,' Artaud corrects. 'And he ended up killing himself. We forget about that when we talk of how many people's lives he ended. It was one more than he is given credit for.'

'You want to die, Mr Artaud?' Pace is doing it on purpose now.

Though he skimmed through the manifesto, Detective Sergeant Pace picked out the pertinent information. He understands Artaud's ideology, no matter how warped and deluded it is.

'There are a lot more things I had hoped to achieve. So, no, of course I don't want to die.'

Detective Sergeant Pace waits a moment to respond.

Detective Sergeant Pace leaves the sentiment hanging in the air.

Detective Sergeant Pace looks in the rearview mirror until he catches Artaud's eye.

'Then I guess you have to.'

135

The news breaks quickly and videos of the incident are surfacing. No network has the audacity to show people falling to their death, instead they choose to repeatedly broadcast some footage from a bystander's phone of the Teacher appearing on the walkway where eighteen people are already standing. She turns her back, raises her arms to the side, then falls backwards, and the person taking the footage drops her phone.

You can hear the screams and the sound of a body battering against the floor.

Then eighteen more as the lens points at the sky.

There's a spike in activity on the People of Choice social media page. Geraldine from Houston, Texas, writes, 'Why are all the big events happening in the UK? All we had here was that school shooting.' There are 423 comments calling her out as an insensitive, inbred moron.

Paulson eventually arrives on the scene. He uses the word *clusterfuck* three times in the first ten minutes. He asks, 'How the hell can we keep up with this?'

The bridge is shut.

No boats are allowed to pass beneath it.

The river police are busy looking for three of the victims that ended up in the river. Just one survivor could blow the case wide open.

There are none, of course.

There is but one certainty.

Helicopters circle overhead. The sixteen bodies on the bridge are already bagged. Paulson identified one of them as Levant. It feels like a lead. He was related to the Man in the Light and now he has joined his nephew. He calls it in to get permission to force his way into the old man's home.

There's no need. The door is still open. Ready for Paulson to get it all wrong.

Ergo is hungry.

All the people that were shot and killed in that mosque have been forgotten about.

This is everything Dr Artaud hates about the world.

136

255 – LEADER

He wakes up and doesn't bother checking his mail.

He doesn't have to.

He just knows.

For he is the last person of choice. It ends with him.

He smokes his morning cigar and adds the final words to his magnum opus, his guidebook for future generations to study. Maybe it will spawn a more successful project. Perhaps it will be used as a tool by the police to further understand the psychology of the cult mentality or psychopathic serial killers. They could use it to prevent anybody from ever overtaking his record.

This ensures his legacy, he thinks.

Nothing important happens today. 255 – Leader travels to work. Over the speed bumps and under the barrier. He lets himself into the glass edifice of the ERMA offices and takes his briefcase up the stairs to his office.

The name on the door says *Dr Artaud*. The Leader places his briefcase on the floor, slides the name plate out and swaps it with Dr Erickson. He enters the office, sits at his desk, opens the top drawer, fishes around for the brass Erickson name holder and exchanges it with the one on the desk. He takes out a fresh yellow legal pad and pen and places them on the desk, ready for his first client.

A young woman in her early forties pushes the buzzer outside, asks for Dr Erickson and 255 – Leader lets her in.

He doesn't plant anything in her mind. He listens. He analyses. She needs help and he gives it to her.

Today he only has appointments as Erickson.

When he is done, he locks the files in the cupboards, places his book on the chair behind his desk and remembers to leave the door open.

Then he's at Tower Bridge and he is Artaud again. He's watching his work come to life. He's looking at Detective Sergeant Pace. He's listening to people hit the floor behind him.

And he's thrust against the barrier.

But he is the last person of choice, now. And he chooses not to fear.

Next he's in the car and the handcuffs are cutting into him but he is calm. He talks at the detective. He opens up. He doesn't have to. He wants to. And it's dark. And they're out of London.

And he tells Pace that he doesn't want to die.

The car comes to a stop.

'Where are we, Mr Pace?'

Pace takes off his seatbelt and turns around to look at the Leader. 'Here? This is Swinley Forest.' He turns back, opens the door, gets out and walks around to the back of the car. In the boot is another set of handcuffs and some tape. He takes them out and shuts the boot.

It is so black outside that Pace can't see the shadows closing in on him.

He opens the back door. 'Out you get.' He pulls at the top of the Leader's arm to urge him into the night.

'What's going on?' 255 – Leader has lost the air of arrogance and coolness he has exuded since unveiling himself on Tower Bridge.

'I'm tired of your voice. Stay still.' Detective Sergeant Pace bites off a strip of tape and pushes it down hard over the Leader's mouth. There's no way of avoiding the hair from his beard, which will have to be ripped out when the tape comes off.

With his hands still cuffed tightly behind his back, Leader is urged to walk forwards into the trees. He does not mumble beneath the tape. He doesn't drop to the floor. He cooperates and obliges the detective's commands.

They walk for twenty minutes. In a straight line. Deeper and deeper into the woods. There is no path to follow. There are leaves on the floor that are undisturbed. Nobody comes here.

Both men are silent for that twenty minutes.

Then they come to a stop.

And Pace talks.

'This will do. Now I get to do some of the talking.' He takes the spare set of handcuffs and clips one side onto 255's left wrist. 'It was at the end of our fourth session, I think. You said to me "You could Google *weird deaths* and you'd be surprised at what comes up". Well, I did that. As you know. Because you put that idea into my head.' He pulls at the cuffs to drag his ex-shrink towards one of the trees. 'One of them really stayed with me.'

He anticipates some resistance at the next part because he has to unlock the first set of handcuffs.

255 does not resist.

Pace takes his captive's hands from behind his back and places them out in front. Both arms held up either side of the tree trunk. He then fastens them back together with the cuffs he took from the boot of his car and removes his police-issued set.

'The lonely death. That's what it was called.'

Then Pace takes a folded piece of paper from his pocket. He holds it up and tells the world's most prolific serial killer that it is the mantra of The People of Choice. That he took it from the front of the manifesto that was so kindly left on the chair in the ERMA office. That the rest of the words are still in the seat pocket of the car they travelled in.

He folds the piece of paper once more so that it is small enough to be tucked into the lonely man's trouser pocket.

255 – Leader is making noise behind his tape now.

Detective Sergeant Pace does not care.

Everywhere is shadow.

'The part I don't understand is that you think so little of people. That we are disposable if we don't live up to your personal idea of decency and worthiness. Yet you trusted that I would take you back to the station for questioning. That I would let you sit in a protected cell and subject you to the British legal system. So that you could share your story and then kill yourself.'

Pace takes the key to Artaud's handcuffs, holding it between his thumb and forefinger, which are covered by the sleeve of his jacket, and he throws it just out of reach.

'You tried to kill me, Doc.'

Artaud is screaming behind his gag. He tries to kick out at the detective.

'It's over now.' He walks around to face the Leader. He wants to look him in the eyes. Artaud stops moving. He stops screaming. He adopts his usual stance as the attentive listener.

'Fuck your legacy.'

And he leaves. Walking deeper into the darkness he now has no chance of ever escaping.

Artaud will never get to finish reading his book.

137

Old Levant is the prime suspect.

Detective Sergeant Paulson arrives at the old man's flat but there is no need to break the door down. He finds a hungry dog but, more importantly, he discovers a room full of information about The People of Choice.

Diagrams of the jump sites.

Pictures of the victims.

Information on their jobs and families.

And there's the wall of death. It is understandably incriminating.

Paulson sees those images of dead strangers connected by coloured pieces of string and his conclusion is that, somehow, the retired pensioner plotted these mass suicides. That he was the mastermind behind the cult that had caused so much disruption in London and around the world.

Get yourself a number two. Somebody that you can throw under the bus when things become too heated.

It does look suspicious. Of course, Paulson will never be able to prove his theory, but it will give the police some temporary hope and the media something to chew over for a while.

For now, it's a win.

Take that, People of Choice.

138

When Pace returns to the station, Paulson is being patted on the back.

Pace doesn't join in.

'Inspector, can I get a word?'

'It's good to have you back, Pace. Nineteen people jumping off the top of Tower Bridge means all hands on deck.'

Pace fights the urge to roll his eyes.

'That's kind of what I wanted to speak to you about.'

He goes on to explain that he is grateful to have had the opportunity to speak to a professional and he is pleased that he had that time with Dr Artaud.

'It's great that he cleared me for duty, it is. And I know that there is so much going on right now with all of this bridge stuff...'

'What are you trying to say?' The inspector seems visibly

agitated. He has nineteen splattered remains to deal with and the possibility of unmasking this illusive cult leader. He doesn't have the time for this. 'Spit it out, man.'

'What I'm trying to say is that I think you were right. I need to take some time. I need to just get away for a while. Go back home to Hinton Hollow. Regroup.'

'Are you fucking kidding me? With all of this going on?'

'Especially with this going on, sir.'

The conversation goes on for longer than either man wants but it is agreed that Detective Sergeant Pace will take a short leave of absence. And with all the focus on mental health, particularly in light of the current spate of suicides, it is the outcome that was expected.

'Go,' says the inspector. 'Go home. See your family. Drink with old friends. Do what you need to do. Call me in a week and we'll take it from there. Just get out of here. We've got a heap of crap to clear up.

Pace walks out of the office. He doesn't talk to Paulson. He doesn't talk to anybody. He gets back into his car and drives straight home.

When he gets there, he steps on the envelope that would have killed him if he'd read it this morning. There's a cold beer in the fridge. Pace opens the bottle and takes a mouthful. Then he walks into the lounge, sits down on his sofa and starts to read Artaud's manifesto from the first page.

And he doesn't stop until he's finished.

The last three pages are a list of 255 victims. It has their real names and the names given to them by their killer. Pace's name is on there. Next to it are the words *255 – Detective*.

When he is finished, he goes to the front door and picks up the white envelope. He knows what will be written on the pages inside. He doesn't open it. He takes it into his kitchen, ignites the gas on the cooker and burns the envelope.

Then he does the same to every page of Artaud's book.

Blue flames ignite the truth behind The People of Choice.

Black flames surround the detective.

139

WRITE A JOURNAL

The trick to leaving behind some kind of legacy is to share your story.

Or have somebody share it for you.

Take Jesus. Take Kennedy. Take any parent who was honest with their child and lived with passion and empathy.

What would Jesus do in this situation?

What would Dad do?

Take a thirty-something law graduate who doesn't want to practise the thing she has been trained to do. Provide her with the oratory skills to hook listeners in to her ideas about what The People of Choice should be.

Now wait as meetings form. As she talks and pushes her agenda while spouting some version of the true vision. See how the group grows. Watch as it is decided that all the members should live together. Laugh as she makes the mistakes that have plagued every cult leader throughout time.

Hold tight as thirty-three members become thirty-two when one of the women in the group decides to leave after that leader sleeps with her husband. She sleeps with all the husbands. And some of the sons.

These are the stories you need.

This is legacy.

Take a lie and pass it on.

Watch on television as the police surround the complex. They are communicating with the leader. They are worried about the safety of some of the residents because they now have reason to believe it is not a peaceful religious group.

It's not a community of like-minded individuals.

Somebody just called it a compound.

One of the other people.

Look on as the net draws in. As the place is sieged. Listen to a news reporter as they say the words *People of Choice cult*. A moment has been captured. A story has been created.

It is not easy to get hold of guns in the UK so this is not another Waco. There are no bullets or fires. There is no need for tear gas. The People of Choice do not come quietly because they do not come at all.

Wait a while for the crime-scene photos to be leaked, showing those final members lying dead around the house after taking a concoction of cyanide-laced red wine. This is what people will talk about. This is what they will tell their friends.

Stick around as a dead legal graduate is credited with organising a suicide cult that was responsible for the death of sixty-two of its members. More than Heaven's Gate. More than Aileen Wournos.

Not as many as Jonestown. Or Shipman.

Or Artaud.

She is a fake leader of a fake cult.

Little work. Minimum effort. Maximum impact.

With a legacy she does not deserve. But a legacy all the same. Somebody.

This is the world that Dr Henri Artaud was fighting.

A simpler way to leave a legacy is to write a journal. Keep a diary. Leave word of how you lived your life and how others could follow after you have passed on.

Take Swinley Forest. Handcuff a doctor to a tree. Burn his journal. Kill his life's work.

Now wait. Twelve months. Check the news for a small story about a lonely man in the woods, his arms stuck on a branch above his head, his shoulder pressed into the trunk of the tree, his thighs resting on the leaf-covered detritus, the key to his handcuffs just out of reach. The public, with their seven-second attention span, have moved on. The People of Choice are no longer interesting. Who cares? They have caught the master-mind behind those atrocities.

And the note found in the dead man's pocket is inscribed with the mantra of a suicide cult. When he is examined, it will be found that he was suffering from late-stage lung cancer. He probably took his own life before the disease could consume him. That is the conclusion.

That is how it is reported.

For the few people who are still listening.

So take Dr Henri Artaud. A doctor with cancer. A smoker. That's it. Not a career criminal. Not a genius. Not a committed man. A man of ideals. Not the most prolific serial killer of modern times. Not the person who duped 255 people into taking their own lives so that he could cleanse his little corner of the world.

A doctor. With cancer.

A smoker.

A nothing.

A real nobody.

ACKNOWLEDGEMENTS

Well, I haven't managed to flush my career down the toilet again (yet), so there are a few people I should thank for that:

Karen Sullivan, whose passion and belief gives me the freedom to write the things I, actually, want to write about. Who else would say 'yes' to a book written in the third person and the collective first person, spliced between an instruction manual, where the main detective doesn't show up until the eighty-fifth page? Tireless focus and encouragement and vision.

Tom Witcomb, for saying this book was better than the last one. I needed to hear that. And for telling me that my book ideas are 'batshit crazy' but he still wants me to write them. Hopefully I can earn us some money one day, man. I mean, you've got a kid on the way.

To the Orenda team, I thank you all. West for your invaluable input and persistence, and Cole for your creativity at any hour of the day. And Liz and Anne for making sure that as much of the world as possible knows I have a new book out.

And the Orenda authors Johana and Simone, who helped me with some of the translations in this book.

Thanks to Sarah and Steve for my cover quotes on the last book and your ongoing encouragement after reading this one. I'm grateful for your support, you have better things to be doing.

To Tom Wood for being continually handsome.

Mum and Brendan, for the limitless support and endless supply of yellow labels.

To Phoebe and Coen, who I want to dedicate a book to, but I write about such horrible things, and you are the loveliest things on Earth. One day.

Forbes. I'll never unsee that *American Beauty* photo but I am grateful for your book love.

My fitness people, who work their bodies every week but now also work their minds by reading one book each year.

And to Kel, who understands the full force of an artistic meltdown. I'm sorry, these people just take so bloody long to respond to anything. I don't get it, either. I thank you for the new ritual of celebrating every step of the journey, and drinking with me on those occasions. For inspiring me to get my arse in the chair and write, and supporting me in every way possible to make sure that happens. You could make me write in the early morning.

Lastly, again, to January David. I know you are uncredited in this story, but I'm bringing you back. Don't worry. I have a plan.